# NOVEMBER'S SHADOW

# NOVEMBER'S SHADOW

## A BODOWSKI MYSTERY

BRUCE REHBURG

MP PUBLISHING

# NOVEMBER'S SHADOW

First edition published in 2014 by

MP Publishing
12 Strathallan Crescent, Douglas, Isle of Man IM2 4NR British Isles
mppublishingusa.com



Jacket designed by Alison Graihagh Crellin.

Publisher's Cataloging-in-Publication data

Rehburg, Bruce.
November's shadow : a Bodowski mystery / Bruce Rehburg.
p. cm.
ISBN 978-1-84982-309-8
1. Murder—Fiction. 2. Pedophilia—Fiction. 3. United States. Army Criminal Investigation Command—Fiction. 4. United States. Army—Foreign service—Germany—Fiction. 5. Suspense fiction. I. Title.
PS3618.E4495 N68 2014
813.6—dc23

ISBN 978-1-84982-309-8
10 9 8 7 6 5 4 3 2 1
Also available in eBook

*To Nina, an exemplar of patience.*

Much of human wisdom leads to sorrow.
More knowledge only brings more sadness.

Ecclesiastes 1:18

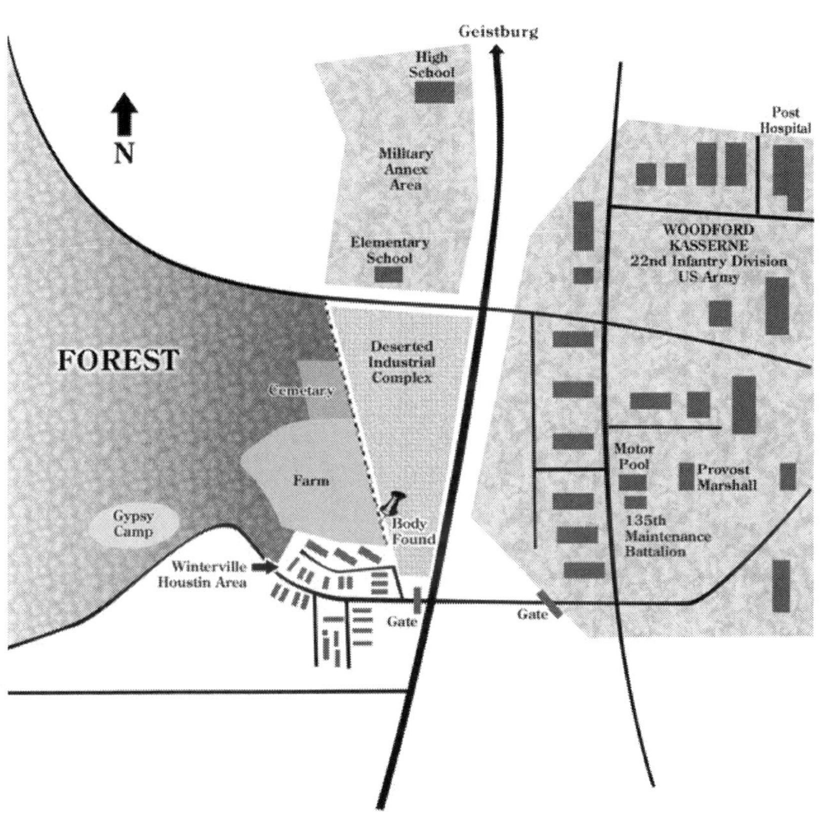

Geistburg
High School
N
Military Annex Area
Elementary School
Post Hospital
WOODFORD KASSERNE 22nd Infantry Division US Army
FOREST
Deserted Industrial Complex
Cemetary
Farm
Gypsy Camp
Body Found
Motor Pool
Provost Marshall
135th Maintenance Battalion
Winterville Houstin Area
Gate
Gate

# Prologue

Geistburg, Germany: Tuesday, November 20, 1963

The child's dark world tumbled and fell. She landed hard on her back and skull, losing consciousness. Slowly coming around, she struggled for air in the black confines of the rolled-up rug. Her throat closed on the dirty wool fibers penetrating her lungs.

Something slammed into her shoulder, rolling her over and over until the final layer of material fell away. Desperate to stop the room's wild spin, she focused on the bare incandescent bulb burning above her. Blood trickled down her throat and she coughed hard against the gag in her mouth. Her nostrils filled with the strong aroma of baked bread—so out of place that it increased her fear. Hot tears welled in her eyes.

She saw the gypsy bandolier who had stolen her from her tribe standing to her right. To her left, hovered an old woman, a *gaje*—a non-gypsy—wearing a black scarf and an apron stark with white flour. They stood so close to her middle that she crossed her hands over her herself. The gypsy leaned over her, licked his lips, and laughed. Sneering, he straightened and said something to the heavy-set *gaje*, who screeched like a witch and threw her hands into the air. The girl could not understand what either of them said, only the term *kleines Mädchen*—little girl.

The barrel-chested gypsy pushed back a strand of oily black hair and shouted a question at the hag. The girl had wet herself while imprisoned in the rug and feared this was the cause of their anger. The gypsy turned and walked into the hallway, grunting. The woman mumbled an oath as she followed, stomping out of the room.

The girl sat bolt upright and tugged at the gag cutting into the sides of her mouth, but she could not dislodge it. Sobbing, she pressed the raw flesh of her wrists against her cold, sweaty forehead. Adrenaline coursed through her body. Fingers trembling, she searched behind her neck and found the gag's knot. It was too tight to work free.

The old *gaje* appeared in the doorway, carrying a bucket and a nightgown. The girl, discovered in her minor act of defiance, hunched over in anticipation of a blow. She felt her back prickle with the sting of the woman's hard slap. She gulped air from the pain. Her tormentor pulled a small wooden stool from the corner and slammed it down next to her. The sudden movement knocked over several brötchen rolls and pretzels from one of the many cooling trays crowding the small, windowless room. Seized by the arm and forced to stand, the girl cried out through the gag—after months handcuffed to a cot, her atrophied legs could barely support her. She whimpered as she was stripped down and washed hard with a coarse sponge. The old woman forced the clean nightgown over her head and slapped her again before pushing her down onto the stool.

A short, balding man in a black apron stained with white flour handprints entered the room. The girl curled up and perched her bare heels on the stool seat. The new *gaje* wiped his thick glasses and repositioned them on his nose before looking her up and down. Turning to the old woman, he scolded her and pointed to the doorway. With a snort, the woman rushed out. The man removed his apron and hung it on a hook near the doorframe, wiped his hands on a towel as he gave the girl a smile.

She heard a toilet flush. The gypsy, buttoning his fly, walked back into the room. The little man spoke to her captor, stabbing at the man's chest with his stubby finger. Though the gypsy pretended not to hear him, shrugging and turning away, the girl knew he understood more than he let on. He leaned against the doorframe and lit a cigarette, flicking the match onto the floor. The baker untied the gag. The girl moistened her hands, running them through her wet hair and pressing them against her chaffed skin.

Laden with a glass of water and a fresh handkerchief, the old woman squeezed past the gypsy and thrust the objects into the baker's hands. He held the glass to the child's lips and spoke in a whisper as she drank, coughing between sips. Molding her hands around the half-empty glass, he gave her a reassuring smile. The baker snapped at the gypsy, who laughed before swinging his rucksack forward and throwing open the flap, retrieving a green canvas bag, whose contents the baker examined. Nodding, he fished a wad of money from his pocket and handed it to the gypsy, who leaned back and counted the bills, mouthing the numbers to himself.

Startled by a loud knock against the back door, the girl dropped the glass. It fell to the floor without breaking, the water mixing with a fine layer of baking flour. She jumped as the baker brushed against her while picking it up.

Chattering excitedly, the woman rushed down the hallway muscling past the gypsy on her way to the back door. The baker moved to the doorway and shouted another command to the woman. He repeated it to the gypsy who yawned and drifted out of sight. The baker disappeared into the hallway. Seconds later she heard the back door open followed by a hushed conversation. A man walked into the room, shaking the rain from his coat sleeves, flicking the drops away one by one with his careful fingers. He leered at her with glassy eyes. The girl's throat closed. Lips quivering, she pulled her knees tight to her chest.

# Chapter One

## A Day to Remember

**Wednesday**

The young man pedaled furiously down the narrow asphalt path and into the lifting fog of dawn. Already late for work, he stood on the pedals and weaved close to the edges of the bumpy lane that separated a complex of deserted industrial silos from a large potato farm. Nearing the end of the path, he could make out the first row of massive apartment buildings that comprised the Winterville housing area, old Wehrmacht barracks converted into living quarters for the families of American soldiers. Beyond lay Woodford Army Kaserne and his destination, the auto repair shop run by a stiff-necked American sergeant.

The bike swung from side to side as he pushed hard. Racing too close to the fence, he caught the tip of his handlebar on the chain link and tumbled to the wet pavement, his bike tumbling into the wide ditch that ran alongside the field. Brushing away the grime, the young man looked up at the gray blanket of sky and cursed God and the fence. He jumped to his feet and walked to where his bicycle had danced from sight. It rested nose down in several inches of stagnant runoff.

With one hand clutching the roots protruding from the steep embankment and the other thrown out for balance, he had just lowered himself to grab at the muddy rear wheel when something caught his eye. Twenty meters to his left, he glimpsed something, partially submerged, lying at the bottom of the ditch. Over the years, many large objects had found their way into this neglected gash in the earth, but this one stood out because of its strangeness. He wrestled the bicycle back onto the path and hopped on, coasting the short distance to the odd thing.

"*Ach, mein Gott.*"

The naked body of a little girl, her limbs twisted and her face sliced apart, lay exposed in the shallow water. He turned away from the horrific sight and vomited onto the path.

# Chapter Two

## Just Your Average Family

Charlie pressed his nose against the large rear window of the third-floor apartment that overlooked the potato farm. "Geez, Dad. You gotta see this."

"Damn it, boy. Eat your breakfast." His father, Chief Warrant Officer Henry Nowak, continued to pore over his morning copy of the *Stars and Stripes*. "You have to get ready for school."

"Wow. You never see anything ever on the path to school, ever. You gotta see this." The chubby eleven-year old attempted a whistle, but it came out only as a rush of air.

The elder Nowak lowered his paper and snapped, "What?"

"Holy smoke, you gotta see."

"Charlie, I was out early this morning getting ready for a damn inspection that didn't happen. I'd like a little peace."

Claire Nowak leaned in from the kitchen doorway. "Let your father be, Charlie. He needs to unwind. You don't have to go in today, do you, dear?"

"Yeah, but I got a few minutes before I have to head back."

"Honest, Dad. This is really something. You gotta come look."

"All right, all right."

The tall, potbellied man pushed away from the metal dining table and stood next to his son at the window. Claire dried her hands on a dishtowel and joined her small family. "What's going on?"

"Charlie's right." Staring at the scene unfolding in the distance, Nowak added, "There is something odd going on out there."

"It's the cops, Mom. See?"

"The military police, dear? Do you mean the MPs?"

"Both," Nowak answered. "The MPs and the Polizei."

From their vantage point above the brown, churned fields, the trio had an unobstructed view of the several men milling around a spot along the narrow pathway that led to Charlie's school. They recognized the MPs by their uniforms and black armbands, and inferred the presence of the German police from the gray Volkswagen with a rotating blue light idling at the head of the path.

"Do you think someone's been hurt?" Claire asked.

"Obviously. The real question is, why both the MPs and the krauts?"

"Not krauts, Germans." She motioned to her son who remained pressed to the glass.

"When I was here in forty-five, calling them krauts was about as nice as it got."

"Well, that was a long time ago." Claire glanced down at young Charlie, who bounced on the balls of his feet, his excited fingers restless against the window. "Nowadays, it's important to remember that little pitchers have big ears."

"Humph."

"Don't worry, Mom." The boy raised his head and smiled. "I call them krauts and worse all the time."

"Charlie!"

Nowak smiled and returned to watching the activity on the path. "Well, I'll be. Look there—there, where all the vehicles are."

The others peered right to see two men in white coats drawing a gurney out of the back of an ambulance. A lithe figure swathed in black emerged from the German police car and followed them down the path.

"Henry, how's Charlie going to get to school? He has to leave in a few minutes." She noticed that the boy's breakfast had gone untouched. "You didn't touch your cereal. Why do I bother?"

Charlie, fascinated by the events unfolding in the distance, did not respond.

# Chapter Three

## A Bad Scene

"For Christ's sake!" Sergeant Steve Bodowski, dressed in plainclothes, pulled his left foot out of the water. Having leapt across the bottom of the ditch, he had stumbled backward and submerged his foot to the ankle. Looking up at the big MP standing on the path, he asked, "You got a towel or something? It's colder than a witch's tit."

"No towel," answered the husky man as he looked around at the other MPs. "Nope, no towels."

"Did you radio for the camera?" He had discovered it wasn't in his kit only after arriving at the scene. Someone back at the CID office must have lifted it from his bag rather than go through the goat rope of equipment requisition—a common occurrence among the investigators. "Well?"

"Yeah. One of your guys is coming with it, I think." Broad across the shoulders and almost half a head taller than the other men loitering at the scene, the big MP leaned away from the body as he asked, "What do you think happened to her face?"

Bodowski squinted at the man's nametag. "Stark? Sergeant Stark."

"Yeah, Stark. That's right." Catching himself, he asked, "Oh, you ain't no officer, are you?"

"These are your guys, right?"

"Uh huh, from my squad."

The detective reached into his brown raincoat and produced from his suit pocket a pair of thin leather gloves. The lanky thirty-four-year-old, a shade over six feet, balanced with difficulty in the wet soil of the steep embankment. He stood on the far side of the ditch adjacent to the girl's body, almost touching her slender, twisted arms.

"Bring over the guy who reported the body, Sergeant."

"Hey, you!" The big MP caught the attention of the young man leaning against the fence. "Yeah, you. *Kommen Sie* here. *Macht schnell*, pal."

Shielding his eyes from the gruesome sight, the scrawny fellow dressed in mechanic's overalls approached the edge of the ditch.

"*Sprechen Sie* English?" Bodowski asked.

He nodded.

"Okay—I know it's pretty nasty, but I need you to look down here."

The man peeked with one eye and groaned.

"The body been moved since you first saw it?" He swept his hand over the scene. "Everything just like you found it? *Verstehen*?"

"Ya." The young man's voice cracked. "Is same."

"*Danke*."

The mechanic rushed back to the fence.

The detective turned and stared at the faceless victim. He had seen it all before, years ago and an ocean away—a depraved monster's handiwork. Experience had taught him that child predators and their special sickness would always haunt the human race. "Jesus, poor kid."

"What was that?" Stark asked. He approached the edge of the path, taking great pains to avoid looking at the body. "You need something?"

"No. It's just been a while for me. I used to do this all the time back in the world." He pointed at the body. "Hell if it ever gets any easier."

"We ought to cover her up. It ain't right leaving her there like that." Some of the other soldiers muttered agreement. The MPs on the path kept nausea at bay by standing back far enough to keep the child's remains out of sight.

Bodowski drew several deep breaths, the color returning to his cheeks as his stomach settled. Back on his game, he inspected the earth around the body, mindful to avoid contact with the translucent skin of the girl's limbs and torso.

"Who do you think killed her?" Stark asked.

Bodowski snapped, "A person. A person killed her." His kneejerk reaction to stupidity was scorn—the breastplate of psychic armor worn by many homicide detectives. To his credit, he often felt remorse after shooting a fixed target like Stark, but that never stopped him from spouting off in the first place. After a beat, he added, "I'm going to go out on a limb and say a murderer."

Stark turned away, muttering, "Goddamned CID."

"That's right, CID—criminal investigation. This is a crime. When we get finished investigating this scene, you can go back to the snack bar or directing traffic." He winced at his overreaction

Stark revved up for a fight, but stopped short. The CID was a clandestine unit. They were Army but did not wear uniforms. No one outside the base's Provost Marshal knew the standing of any of the unit's members, a necessary expedient in the pursuit of evidence within a system built upon deference to rank. Although it was common knowledge that the CID field investigators were mostly sergeants or warrant officers, one never knew when a commissioned officer might leave his warm bed on a miserable November morning and find his way into the field.

"Mallory," Stark growled, "get up the path to the school. Don't let nobody pass. Johnson, over by the entry down there. No one comes up. It's just about time for the kids to head for class."

"Too late, Sergeant." Bodowski pointed down the path, almost losing his balance in the process. "Looks like we got visitors—locals." Two German ambulance attendants, gurney in tow, came up alongside the remaining MPs. Following close behind, clad in a black leather trench coat, strode an a thin man with chiseled features and piercing blue eyes. Herr Leutnant Detektiv Hermann Kross, head lowered as he scribbled in a small notebook, stepped around the gurney and stopped next to Stark but continued writing for a moment, as if oblivious to place and company. Bodowski grunted, knowing that Kross' typical ploy to grab attention was to make a silent yet obvious entrance. The German detective glanced around, frowning at the young witness clutching the chain-link fence. When his gaze landed on Bodowski, he beamed a disingenuous smile.

"Herr Bodowski. What on earth are you doing?" Almost a mythic figure in local law enforcement, and just as roundly hated, Kross unnerved most of the Americans he encountered with his ability to speak fluent English using a proper British accent. Bodowski, eighteen months into his enlisted hitch with eleven of those served at his current station in Geistburg, knew Kross well from a series of joint taskforce robbery investigations. The angular German had solved most of the cases while snubbing the contributions of the American investigators. It left a bad taste in Bodowski's mouth. Worst yet, the young detective felt that Kross had been justified in calling some members of his team 'redundant'.

"Where I'm standing is on base, Detective." Kross grinned while setting his feet like an actor hitting his spot. "You, however, are not."

The American knew he had to draw the line to deter the angular German from laying claim to the body. Still something of an enigma even to Bodowski, experience taught him that you had to move fast to keep up with the wily Herr Leutnant.

"You got no play here, Kross."

"On the contrary, old sport, it looks as though the corpse lies in the middle of the ditch, and I don't believe that's on base." The way he emphasized *corpse* and encompassed the immediate geography with a slow sweep of his hand gave the impression that the girl's body was an object of indeterminate value over which idle men contested.

"Forget it, Kross. We control the scene." Bodowski needed the case. The daily grind of low-grade felonies interrupted by the infrequent robbery or sexual assault was the story of his hitch with Uncle Sam. At last, he had a body—a homicide. "Anyway, the guy who found her called us, not you. Better luck next time."

"Come, come, you know the law. Besides, how do you know the girl is an American?"

"I don't. Not yet." He returned to the task of inspecting the scene. Using the German's own ploy of silence, he spent the next minute poking for clues in the mud surrounding the ashen body. Wiping his forehead with the wrist of his gloved hand, he grinned at Kross. "If she's one of yours, you'll be the second to know."

Kross produced a small camera and, still clutching his pencil and notebook, paced along the edge of the ditch snapping photographs of the body. Bodowski, alerted by the click of the camera, glanced at Kross and then in the direction of the pathway.

"What? No photos of your own?" Kross asked dryly.

"It'll be here any minute," Bodowski snapped.

"But of course."

"You'd better go, Kross. We've got it in hand. You go tell your boss we'll keep you up-to-date."

"Perhaps I can be of assistance at the present time," Kross insisted.

Bodowski was having none of it. "Hey there, Sergeant. How about you see to it that our good friend and ally gets safely back to his car?"

"Sir?" Stark addressed Kross and gestured toward the head of the path in a pretense of civility. The CID was one thing, but the Polizei were outsiders.

The German shot the big MP a withering stare. Stark stared back for a moment but soon broke off, turning his head. Kross grinned at his victory. "Very well." He faced the ambulance attendants, and in contrast to his English, which he spoke in a lilting, almost effeminate manner, issued a few commands in deep, guttural German. The attendants rushed the gurney down the path.

Kross watched for a moment before packing the camera into its case. “So it goes. I’ll take this opportunity to question the young man who discovered this awful business while memories are still intact.”

“Hey, wait a minute.” Bodowski looked up at Stark from the ditch. “I’m not finished with him yet. I might have a few more questions.”

“I got to hand him over,” Stark pleaded, “I ain’t got no choice, you know. He’s a local. The Polizei got jurisdiction on their own people.”

“Damn it, Kross. You’re going to keep him here, right?”

“Don’t worry, old sport. If I discover anything of interest, you’ll be the second to know.” Kross signaled to the young man, who grabbed his bike and followed the detective. Without looking back, Herr Leutnant added, “I’ll share the photos with you.”

“Shit.”

Bodowski resumed his inspection of the ground surrounding the body. Noting the only impressions in the soft ground were his, he climbed to the top of the ditch and stepped onto the potato field. The dull pain in his right hamstring reminded him of the injury he had received years before, during one of his early homicide investigations.

The stench of manure, faint in the ditch, hit full force once he stood on the dark brown earth of the field. He imagined invisible waves of the obnoxious odor streaming into the air. Scanning the scene, he detected a small section of rusty chain link lying inside the plowed furrow nearest him. Careful to note that no footprints led to the castoff remnant, he observed that the loose earth around it had been disturbed much like the depression dug out by a long jumper in a sand pit. Looking back to the path side of the ditch opposite the body, he saw that the bank was smooth on the surface—an indication that someone had obliterated any tracks left in the mud. The killer had carried the body down the path.

"You got something there, Detective?" Stark asked.

"Yeah." He walked back toward the ditch, stopping at the edge just above the body. "I need someone to go to my car and get a few of the large brown bags out of the trunk." Reaching into his pocket, he produced a set of keys attached to a large nail clipper.

"Here, catch."

Stark caught them with one hand.

"I also need the temperature gauge from the glove box. You understand, Sergeant?"

"Sure. Bauer! You heard him. Take these and go get that stuff."

The young man accepted the keys and ran down the path toward the vehicles.

Turning to the detective, Stark asked, "Can't we cover up her face?"

Bodowski shook his head. He climbed into the ditch and perched alongside the body, one foot below the other to support his weight in the wet soil of the steep embankment. He stood there doing nothing, hoping in vain for the arrival of a camera. He glanced at Stark, who milled about avoiding his gaze. In minutes, Private Bauer returned with several large evidence bags and the desired gauge.

"Go ahead and set the gizmo on the path and give me the reading."

Handing Stark the bags and the keys, Bauer did as instructed. "It says nine. It ain't nine degrees out here."

"It's in centigrade." Bodowski wrote the number in his small spiral notebook. Doing the math in his head, he added, "That's about forty-eight degrees to you and me."

The MPs looked at each other and shrugged.

"Oh yeah, Detective?" Bauer asked. "I forgot to tell you that the kraut guy wanted me to remind you that he'd get you a copy of the pictures he took. He said he didn't want you to wait out here all day and get wet. That guy's a real prick, if you don't mind me saying so."

"You don't know the half of it."

"Damn, a body. Holy Christ, just look at her." The voice of Warrant Officer Stan Melcher, a fellow CID investigator, took Bodowski by surprise.

"I didn't see you come up the path." He coughed into his shirtsleeve.

"Oh my God." Leaning over the edge, the short young man pursed his lips. "Jesus Almighty."

"You got a camera."

Melcher held up a Leica with his right hand and jiggled the small Polaroid camera that hung off his left wrist.

"Good. Mel, get some angles on the body, then come on down here and try not to step on either bank directly opposite of the girl." He had a way of making a request sound like an order.

"Well, I don't have a lot of practice shooting bodies, but I'll give it a go."

"You ain't seen one before, neither?" Stark asked.

"Nope. Well, bodies, yeah, but five years in and this is my first homicide."

"Don't it make you sick? Seeing her there with her face all cut up?"

Melcher crouched by the edge of the path and took a photograph of the body using the Leica and a second one with the Polaroid.

"You know, I imagined I would be sick too." Changing positions, he snapped two more images. "Maybe if I think about it long enough you'll get to see my breakfast." Making light of it did not work for long. "Uh oh."

"You okay?" Stark asked.

"Hey, let him do his job," Bodowski shouted. "We still have a lot to do."

Captivated by the proceedings but leery of the body, Private Bauer squatted and asked Bodowski, "You look at everything out here, sir? Everything?"

"Sure." He continued to write. "But I usually wait until a medical examiner shows and we get ready to move the body." Putting away his notebook, he climbed to the top of the ditch on the field side and commanded, "Throw me the bags. They're heavy enough."

Stark threw the bags so hard they sailed over the detective's head. Walking over to collect the errantly tossed items, it struck him that the killer may have doubled up on his bets to delay rigor by dumping the body into the shallow, cold water.

"C'mon. Hurry up and get down in the ditch. We're going to need some close shots before I check out the body."

"Listen to him, would you?" Melcher smiled, and Bauer held onto his arm while he descended the near side of the ditch. "I outrank the guy, but there he is calling the shots."

Letting go of his wrist, the MP leaned over and asked, "Beg pardon, sir, but why do you let him do that?"

"Because he's the homicide dick—our only one. Besides, he gets cranky when folks don't listen to him." The familiar click of the camera cut through the cold, soggy air. Four photographs in various stages of development protruded from the Polaroid. "Damn, it's too cold out here. Hey, come here." Melcher handed Bauer the wet snapshots. "You and your giant pal there, shake these babies until they develop."

"What?"

"Slowly, you know, like a pelican taking off." He burped and made a face as a trace of bile moved up his throat.

Bauer shoved two of the photographs at Stark, who accepted them as one might two pieces of radioactive material. The MPs began waving in a sorry imitation of a large bird in flight.

"Oh, Jesus." Holding the cameras above his head, Melcher vomited into the ditch away from the body. Stark, still waving the photographs, spun and vomited onto the fence. Bauer convulsed.

Bodowski recognized the signs of contagion at work. "Turn around. You hear me? Turn around."

Bauer obeyed the order. He managed to control his retching.

Melcher was not so fortunate. "Oh damn it, not again." He dry heaved and took short, rapid breaths in hopes of forestalling another episode.

"No shame in it, boys," Bodowski offered. "I couldn't stop doing it until after six months of looking at bodies on the job. You empty yet? I need you over here."

"Just wish I hadn't eaten that bear claw on the way over here." Stuffing the Leica into his coat pocket, Melcher scaled the far side of the ditch and wiped his mouth with a handkerchief. "There aren't any footprints beside your clodhoppers? Didn't it rain last night? No way you wouldn't leave footprints."

Bodowski pointed at the rusty chain-link fragment and the disturbed soil. "Get a close-up of this piece of junk before I bag it, and this part of the ground too. With all this rust and no large surfaces, I don't see how we can get prints. Body got dumped from the path. Whoever did it tossed this crap over here after using it to smooth out where he stepped in the ditch."

"Just like an Indian scout—a homicidal Indian scout." Melcher waited for a reaction to his lame offering, but his partner ignored him. Shrugging, he pulled the Leica from his coat and took photographs as instructed.

Bodowski rubbed the palm of his left hand with the thumb of his right, a tic that overtook him when he was deep in concentration. Farther up the path in the direction of the school, he could see the MP Stark had sent up there kicking at the ground in boredom.

"It's about a klick or so to the American elementary school from here, Mel. You have to walk past a walled cemetery."

"You know the area?"

"Yeah. I worked a case last year where a couple of GIs got tanked and started busting up headstones." Distracted by Melcher wiping his forehead, he asked, "You sure you're all right?"

"Yeah. The ralphing made me sweat. Go figure."

"Anyway, if I remember right, the entry to the school gets gated pretty late at night and doesn't open until five."

"Oh-five-hundred?"

"Yeah, oh-five-hundred." He shook his head and continued, "I don't see how our guy could come from that direction."

"Could be more than one guy." Melcher set down the camera and fished a stick of gum out of his shirt pocket.

"Wouldn't matter—too far and too heavy a load." Bodowski looked in the opposite direction. "No, he came up the path from the housing area."

"I'm going to get a canvass started," Melcher said. "We got MPs coming out of our ears and more arriving every minute." He folded the gum into his mouth and watched as Stark shoved Bauer and shouted an obscenity. "On second thought, I'm going to try to get investigators to handle it."

Bodowski squatted and pulled off a glove. Rubbing some wet soil between his fingers, he said, "See if you can't get some guys to drag the ditch for several meters in both directions."

"Can do. Oh, and I got a lot of shots of the body and the ground. When are you going to check her out?"

"I can't wait forever on the examiner. Let's go." He stood and wiped the soil from his fingers. "Stay close with the camera. We may need some more photos."

Retrieving the Polaroid, Melcher followed his partner to the ditch.

Lowering himself down the steep embankment, Bodowski straddled the body. "Christ. Look at me. I've only been out here for a little while and I'm already muddy as hell." His partner took a shot of him holding up a pant leg.

Stark, still waving the photographs, caught Melcher's attention by clearing his throat. "Sir? Do we just keep standing here?"

"Yeah, we might need something."

"Mel, how about getting everybody to be quiet for a minute?"

"Sure, man." He signaled to the MPs who backed away and leaned against the fence.

Bodowski stared at the young victim. "Look how thin she is." He thought about the position of the body and how the unnatural twisting of the limbs suggested a drop of several feet. Given the lack of blood at the scene, he reckoned the killer had sliced her postmortem, but only an autopsy could establish that. Detecting no cuts aside from the terrible violation of her face, he examined all of the body exposed above the water line. He found neither open wounds nor blood but did note reddened areas on the wrist, throat, and pubis. Reaching for her right wrist, he stopped.

"You got closeups on all this, right?"

"No sweat."

Bodowski extracted the arm from the muddy embankment and flexed it. Lack of rigor mortis made him consider the impact of the cold, wet conditions. He examined the fingernails of the right hand. They were dirty, but it looked like mud and nothing else.

"Are you going to move her? Aren't we going to wait for the examiner for that?"

With great effort, Bodowski maneuvered to stand just behind her head. "Screw it. Who knows when he's going to get here." When he touched the left ear, her jaw fell open, causing him to recoil as he flashed upon a long-forgotten memory. Recovering swiftly, he inspected the inside of the mouth. The general state of her dental health looked poor—multiple cavities, but no fillings. He figured her age to be around ten. Both eyes showed burst capillaries—a telltale sign of oxygen deprivation. He broke off the examination and wrote down his findings.

"What have you got, man?"

"Probably asphyxiation. You can tell by the eyes."

"What about the face?"

"After the fact, I figure. Maybe he wanted to hide her identity—don't know yet."

"Shit, you have to give me a second." Melcher took a few deep breaths, each time emitting a humming sound. "Okay, I'm back with you."

Noting the bruising around her groin, Bodowski blurted, "I'm going to get this asshole. I'm going to get him."

"Fuckin' A. And I want to be there when it happens."

Examining the path side of the ditch just above the body, Bodowski noticed two jagged root fragments halfway up the embankment, about two feet apart. The roots protruded through the spot where someone had raked over the soil with the piece of chain-link fence.

"We have to get a shot of this."

Melcher leaned over and took a photograph of the snags. "Hey, did you see Kross, man? I saw him when I was coming in. He's talking to some young kraut in his car down there."

"Yeah. We had words."

"I'll bet he wants this scene." Melcher glanced toward the head of the path and the growing number of vehicles. "You know he's going to ask the Provost Marshal to turn over the case. He'll say it's on their ground."

"Let him try. We command the scene and Palls hates his guts."

Still, Bodowski chewed his lip.

# Chapter Four

## Those Who Live in Fear

Marc mashed the remains of old homework while rummaging through the papers in his rucksack. The sixth-grader threw the bag to the floor and yelled, "Shit."

"Jesus, Marc. Be quiet." Tony, his older brother, ran up behind him and spoke in a distressed whisper. "You want him to wake up?" He pointed at the closed door to their sister's room. "You want him to come out of there?"

"I'm sorry, Tony. I can't find my book report." Tears welled in Marc's eyes.

"Look, I'll help you find it." He took Marc by the hand, mindful to avoid the fresh bruises on his wrist, and led him down the hallway to their room. Shutting the door from the inside and locking it, he patted his younger brother on the shoulder. "Okay—we're not leaving here without it."

Warmth surged through the little boy's chest, as it always did when his older brother paid attention to him. Marc dried his eyes with his shirtsleeves and offered a weak smile. Together, they searched the small mountain range of dirty clothes that occupied the center of the room. They looked through the closets packed with old clothes and the broken remains of long-forgotten toys, and inspected the paper dinner plates strewn about the room, some still holding the dried remnants of recent meals.

Marc stood up with several half-torn sheets of lined notebook paper that had found their way behind the radiator. "Look, look. I found it."

"See? You big baby." Tony smiled with the crooked grin he reserved only for Marc. "C'mon, let's get going."

Quietly unlocking the door, the boys left the room and pulled on their coats. Down the hall and into the living room, Tony glanced over to see his mother sitting bolt upright on the sofa, arms crossed over her tattered house robe, staring at the large radio console that dominated the center of the room.

"Mom?" Tony whispered. Marc hurried out the front door of the apartment without looking at her, but Tony persisted. Something in him would not settle. "Mom. We're going now." She did not acknowledge him. He sighed and walked out to join his brother.

Dozens of children, running, laughing, and shouting, emerged from the stairwells of the Winterville apartments. The two boys ran to catch up with their chums.

Just before they reached the pack, Marc slowed down and yanked on his brother's sleeve. "Do you think we'll ever see Tammy again?"

Tony, who had been hailing one of his friends, stopped and scowled down at his brother. "Don't."

Cheeks reddening, Marc lowered his head. A silence passed between them as the laughter and conversation of the other children filled the air. Tony watched his little brother mope along, shuffling his feet. Swallowing the truth about his sister, he switched gears, slugging Marc on the arm.

"C'mon, you little turd. You got a big day ahead of you."

The boys joined with a few friends and soon arrived at the path that led to the elementary school. A large group of youngsters had already gathered there. Tony and Marc managed to squeeze through to the front rank of children, and they watched in amusement as an MP attempted to herd the growing mob in another direction. The frustrated GI shouted commands, but the kids failed to move, uncertain of where to go. The crowd buzzed with conversation until a single voice rang out. "Hey, look! It's the Gestapo." A number of the children laughed.

Detektiv Kross had unfolded his leather-clad frame from the confines of his gray Volkswagen. Striding toward the passenger side of the car to release the young witness, the lean figure paused a moment to beam at the crowd. The laughter ceased. Even children living in the insular world created by the U.S. Army in Germany recognized a dangerous adult.

"Get a move on, kids," The MP shouted. "You can't go this way. We gotta keep it clear. Now git!"

Nowak's sedan pulled up to a stop sign next to the crowd of children. Charlie got on his knees on the passenger's seat to see around his father. Claire had demanded that Henry drive their son to school.

"Dad, what do you think is going on over there?" The car stopped at the street crossing closest to the path.

"I don't know, Charlie." Nowak did not look at the crowd of milling youngsters.

"Hey, Dad, there's Marc. Let's give him a ride, okay?"

"All right," Nowak snorted. "Hurry it up."

Charlie threw open the passenger's side door and crossed in front of the aging vehicle. Waving his hands, he shouted, "Marc. Hey, Marc! Come with us."

Marc and Tony had just reached the rear of the pack, about to begin the long trek to school around the old industrial compound, and they noticed Charlie at once. Marc tugged on his brother's sleeve.

"Sure, Marc. Why not."

Charlie jumped into the front seat of the old sedan while the brothers piled into the back.

"Thanks for the ride, sir," Tony said.

"No problem, kid," Nowak sniffed.

Moments later, the sullen warrant officer and his passengers found themselves behind a long line of vehicles waiting to exit the housing area. For the past twenty hours, the MPs had been conducting a readiness drill for all American-owned vehicles leaving the complex. Not scheduled to end until noon, the exercise required the MPs to inspect every vehicle. Everyone was subject to the invasive searches, including the higher-ranking officers who lived in an enclave at the far end of the housing area. The two younger boys speculated about both the traffic snarl and the police business at the blockaded path.

Several minutes passed with just a few car lengths gained. As the boys' lively chatter built to a fever pitch, Nowak roared, "Shut up, goddamnit!" Charlie's cheeks burned with embarrassment over his father's outburst.

An awkward silence, broken only by Nowak's occasional muttered expletive, invaded the car as they awaited their turn at inspection. Ten minutes passed before they reached the inspection point marked by a single sawhorse. Two soldiers staffed the exercise, one to inspect the vehicles and the other to control traffic. An MP carrying a flashlight stepped up to their car and tapped on the window.

"What?" Nowak shouted through the glass.

"Roll down the window, sir."

"Why?"

"Sir, please get out of the vehicle and open your trunk. This is a readiness drill."

"I've already been through it once today."

"Sorry, sir. You got to do it every time you go through."

"Sure, fine, whatever the hell you need." Nowak slammed the column shifter into park and threw the car door open, almost striking the MP. Marching to the rear of the vehicle, he unlocked the trunk and stood back to allow the soldier access.

"Tony?" Marc asked.

"What's up, little brother?"

"What's a readiness drill?"

"They want to make sure we got enough food and water and stuff in our cars to last about five days if the Russians attack."

"Wow," Charlie said. "Do you think that'll happen?"

"Yeah, sure. I don't know. All I know is that all dependents are supposed to hightail it for France or Switzerland if the Russians come rolling over the border."

"What about our dads?"

"They have to go off to stop the reds. They'll probably be toast."

"Do you think our dads would be heroes in the war?" Charlie asked.

Marc and Tony did not answer.

The inspection completed, Nowak got back into the car with a huff and slammed the door. His scowl advised the boys to spend the remainder of the short ride in silence.

Arriving at the elementary school, Marc and Charlie tumbled out of the vehicle and ran to class. The high school was still a kilometer away.

"You can walk the rest, right, kid?" Nowak demanded.

"Yes, sir." Tony got out and Nowak drove away without waiting for the rear door to close.

# Chapter Five

## Dark Passage

Rain spattered the windshield of Bodowski's sedan as the MP waved him through the inspection point. With the body on its way to the morgue at the base hospital, and what little physical evidence there was in hand, he maneuvered through the crowded cobblestone streets that led to Woodford Kaserne.

His thoughts drifted back to his days as a newly minted detective for the Tacoma, Washington, police. The youngest detective in the department's history, he had worked on one of the most notorious murders in the city's casebook—another terrible crime, still vivid in his mind, involving the brutal death of a little girl. He couldn't help smiling at the memory of Jack Cranston, his foul-mouthed, chain-smoking partner, who plowed through every regulation to make an arrest.

Bodowski slammed on the brakes, stalling the olive-drab sedan as several German children crossed against the light in a crowded intersection. He picked up the radio and called the duty desk. While restarting the car, he checked in on any recent missing person reports, either on post or with the Polizei. There were none. He drove through the front gate of the Kaserne and pulled into the gravel parking lot of the old stone building that housed both the Provost Marshal and the MP Battalion HQ. Sitting behind the wheel with the motor running, the wipers whisking away the cold, dense rain, he considered the odd location of the crime scene—the body left in the open for anyone to find. Why there? Why go to the trouble of carting the body down the path?

Knuckles banging on the driver's side window startled him out of his thoughts. Hunching under his poncho against the cold November rain, an MP shouted to penetrate the barrier of the glass.

"Where you been? The major wants you in there on the double."

"Okay, I'm headed in."

He watched as the soldier retreated inside the massive building that in years past had been the headquarters for the 18th Waffen SS, but instead of following at once he hesitated inside the car, deciding to wait a moment and further consider the morning's events before jumping into the maelstrom of questions that awaited him in Major Palls' office. Palls, the assistant Provost Marshal, was directly responsible for law enforcement on base, performing all the heavy lifting for his boss. Word from the scene had traveled fast. Colonel Fulbright, the Provost Marshal for the 22nd Infantry Division, would be wringing his hands over the implications of a child murdered on his watch. Bodowski had not met the colonel, and he had little solid information with which to form an opinion of the man, other than the nickname he'd been given in the MP barracks and CID office: CYA—short for "Cover Your Ass."

Preeminent among Major Palls' self-appointed tasks was the filtering of every scrap of information prior to it reaching the colonel. Bodowski sighed and thought the better of stalling. He turned up his collar and stepped out into the rain.

# Chapter Six

Tacoma, Washington: Tuesday, November 6, 1956

"C'mon, Polack. We got a good lead." Cranston slapped Bodowski on the shoulder as he sat at his desk in Homicide, typing out his day log. "Ain't time to get your snoot full yet."

For their first three months as city detectives, newcomers to the squad found themselves paired with the aging bigot. Now, it was Bodowski's turn.

"The law-abiding citizens of Tacoma need your invaluable experience. Ha ha. Didn't you hear me, Polack?"

"What do you mean, a good lead?"

"Got word from one of my snitches on the docks about a couple of real candidates." With a burning cigarette dangling from his lips, Cranston pulled on his suit coat, which caught on his shoulder holster. "You just going to sit there playing pretend detective, or do you want to learn how to be the murder police? It's your chance to crack some skulls. Ain't you excited?"

Bodowski, newly promoted from walking a beat, stood and pulled on his raincoat. He towered over the squat man who continued to wrestle with his coat.

"So where are we headed?"

"You thirsty? This could be just your spot."

The two made their way downstairs to the station parking lot and got into Cranston's unmarked cruiser.

"It's going to be a miserable fucking night. Jesus, six o'clock and it's already pitch black. I hate the fucking Northwest." Cranston's habit when driving was to fill every spare moment with the sound of his voice. Nothing of import fell from his tar-stained lips as he alternately spoke and took drags off an ever-present cigarette. Now and then, he would interrupt his monologue to ask a question.

"How come you don't smoke, pal?" Cranston let go of the steering wheel long enough to flick the long gray ash of his cigarette out the wing window.

"I do. I breathe your goddamned smoke every second I ride with you." Bodowski looked up from his notebook and jerked his chin at Cranston's wing window. "You think keeping that little thing open is going to help? Forget it. It's like sitting in a toxic cloud." Having survived a childhood of poverty and violence, Bodowski had defended his dockside turf as a uniformed cop for six years, trading on his ability to read a man quickly. He pegged Cranston as one who gave it rough and respected only those who handed it back in kind.

"Ha ha. That's fucking rich, Polack." Cranston picked up where he'd left off, spewing a steady ration of profanity and lurid imagery. The young detective ignored the verbal bait. He leaned back and took the opportunity to sift through the day's events.

The morning had been difficult. The partners caught a case that took them to a rundown city park, where a couple walking their dog in the early morning drizzle had discovered the naked body of a young girl. Bodowski's years on the beat had exposed him to several kinds of bodies: the bum that just looked asleep, as if you could shake him out of it; the stevedore who walked off the pier following a night of binge drinking, who looked more like he'd died in someone's refrigerator after the long hours in the cold saltwater. To Bodowski, they were just lifeless forms, husks that had held the souls of the dregs—nothing to lose sleep over. This, however, was a new ballgame.

The child had been raped and strangled. The bastard who left the body to rot in the open had gouged out her eyes. The medical examiner believed that the monstrous act had been committed postmortem, but he would not be certain until after the autopsy. Bodowski had convinced himself he could handle whatever the new job threw at him, but one glimpse of the horror mask that had once been the child's face overwhelmed the new detective, forcing him to vomit until he had nothing left to give. Beyond the initial shock, what gnawed at him was the feeling that maybe he was not cut out for detective work. Back on the beat, life seemed simpler.

"Hey there." The senior detective punched him on the arm. "You listening to me?"

"What?"

"I asked if you know this place we're heading to?"

"Bell's Tavern?" He flipped through his notebook. "No, don't know it. I worked down on the waterway, not up around the piers. You know that."

"Well, I been there plenty of times. It's a good place to make some headway on this dirty business. You know, every nob from the mayor's office down to the PTA will be howling for a scalp on this one, and you and me is on the hook." Cranston rolled down his window and spat out onto the wet pavement. He wiped his mouth on his sleeve. "Look, until I get word back on a missing child report or something solid from the coroner, I'm going to work the usual suspects. It pays off more often than you might think."

"The usual suspects?"

"Here's what you don't get, Polack—the trash off those ships? Well, whatever they can't eat or drink, they steal or screw. These guys are a regular fucking crime wave. I know it wasn't like that down on the waterway—that's just the Coast Guard and Canadian logging ships. Down where we're going, it's a bottomless bucket of deep-water scum just steps ahead of the jailer."

Within minutes, gravel crunched beneath the tires as Cranston muscled the car into a tight parking spot between two ramshackle pickup trucks.

"Looks like some locals going to be mixed in with the foreign trash in Bell's tonight."

"Jesus. From the looks of this lot, the place has got to be packed."

Cranston grinned. "What's wrong, Polack, afraid you and me can't handle it?"

"For Christ's sake, that's not what I was getting at. Would you give me a—"

"Car Twenty-Three, come in," crackled the female voice over the radio.

The detective grunted at his young partner, then answered the call. "Car Twenty-Three, over."

"Only two cargo ships at Schuster, over."

Cranston opened his door and stepped out, stretching the microphone cable to the limit. Looking over the tops of the vehicles toward the dimly lighted pier, he responded, "Yeah, I can just make them both out, over."

Bodowski emerged to join him.

"The Cable Ship *Americus* out of New Orleans and the *Tuan Jim* from Djakarta," said the voice. "I think that's Indonesia, over."

"Thanks, babe. Twenty-Three out." He tossed the receiver onto the driver's seat and shut the door. "I asked Dispatch to look up the current port assignments before we took off. Judging by where them ship's come from, it'll be a real fine brown stew in Bell's. You ready, kid?"

"An old bastard like you is going to stir up trouble whether it's called for or not." Bodowski jerked his snub-nosed revolver and popped open the cylinder to check the rounds, flipped it shut with his thumb. "Okay—ready to end my career before it starts."

"Ha ha, love that cracking wise. But you ain't going to puke like you did this morning if someone gets a nose bleed or something, are you, Polack?"

"Let's get to it."

The detectives made their way through a minefield of empty bottles and broken glass to get to the entrance. Once inside, loud music and a thick cloud of cigarette smoke assaulted their senses. Characters of every stripe huddled over packed tables, nursing beers and downing shots. Rockabilly blared from the jukebox. The detectives navigated to the bar past laughing sailors jamming pool tables and in between harried barmaids toting overloaded trays full of watered-down drinks. No one looked directly at them, only in sidelong glances. Bodowski surveyed the motley crowd. He kept his head on a swivel, knowing that the best defense in this situation was to predict from which direction trouble would come. Cranston wedged himself between two men seated on stools and hailed the bartender, a thin, oily-haired man wearing grimy motorcycle denims. From his position guarding his partner's back, Bodowski saw the skinny man's face change from friendly to flat upon recognizing Cranston. Too noisy to talk, the senior detective signaled with a wag of his crooked finger. Cranston had a way of maximizing the disrespect inherent in that simple gesture.

"What do you want, Cranston?" the bartender shouted. He stepped back and checked side to side as though preparing to run. From where he stood, Bodowski could just pick out the shouted conversation over the din.

"Got to talk to you, pal."

"So, talk."

"Not like this—too damn loud."

"Jesus—can't leave—got all these customers."

"Come outside."

"What?"

"Leave someone to watch things."

"No. Too busy."

"What'd you say to me?"

"Okay. Okay. I don't want no trouble." He gestured to his bar-back, who nodded.

The three squeezed through the crowd and out the back door. Standing in the misting rain next to the garbage cans and stacks of empty bottle crates, Cranston wasted no time.

"You got a lot of niggers and Chinamen in there. One of them, maybe more, fucked up a little girl—probably did it late last night. Who you got for me?"

"What the hell? Are you kidding me? How am I supposed to know about shit like that?"

The feigned indignation made Bodowski smile.

"Assholes get a little in their snoot and they brag about anything. C'mon, who's talking?"

The skinny man waited a beat before answering. "No one."

"What?" Cranston moved closer, almost touching noses, and gestured to his right ear. "See this? Best lie detector in the whole world." The detective gave the bartender a moment to squirm. "Want to ditch that lie so I don't get pissed off?"

"Maybe I heard something."

"Maybe I'll give you a goddamned beating right here."

The man stiffened. "Two guys—off the *Americus*, I think—been in drinking since noon today. They was also in last night for a while—did some bragging today before it got too loud. I could hear them."

"Uh huh."

"Well, I didn't catch all of it, but it sounded like they got some real young tail last night."

"How young?"

"I dunno. Young to one ain't young to another."

"Out-fucking-standing! Words to live by." Cranston laughed and grabbed a hunk of filthy denim. "When we finish here, I'll have that tattooed on my forehead." He jerked the bartender toward the back door and said, "You're going to point them out to me."

"I got regular customers." Providing some resistance, he added, "Regular customers, you know. What are they going to think if I start squealing?"

Cranston jerked the bartender again. "All I know is that this arm I got ahold of is going to go in there and point out the two bastards. The rest of your miserable ass can stay out here for all I care."

Bodowski analyzed the older detective's moves the way a budding athlete might a professional fullback. Aside from the racist talk, he liked the way Cranston worked the bartender.

Cranston threw the door open and pushed the man inside the back hallway. Flustered, the bartender twisted around and declared, "They're Creoles off the *Americus*—Creoles. Just so as you know I wouldn't serve no spooks."

Bodowski coughed to suppress laughing at the man's idiotic comment.

In the main room of the tavern again, the detectives and the bartender stood against the wall near the jukebox. Cranston shouted into the man's ear. The bartender pointed his chin toward two men waiting their turn at the pool table. Cranston motioned with his head and Bodowski fell in behind him as they picked their way through the boisterous throng, heading straight for two young Creoles standing near the middle of the room. Clad in deck clothes and leaning against into their pool cues with both hands, they shared a shouted joke, then laughed aloud, the sound lost in the roar. Cranston pushed his way between them and the edge of the pool table. The two men, startled by his sudden appearance, stood upright. Bodowski could see the joy drain from their faces as Cranston opened one side of his suit coat to display his badge, then opened the other to reveal his weapon. He jerked his head to get them moving in the direction of the back door. The taller of the two stood his ground and glared at Cranston. The shorter man noted Bodowski and seized his companion's shoulder. Cranston motioned again, and this time they complied, turning and moving toward the door. Before they had taken three steps, Bodowski confronted them and pulled at the pool cues in their hands. The shorter man let go, but the taller one held onto his stick and glowered down at the young detective.

"Let go," Bodowski shouted. He tugged at the cue again. He decided to wait a few seconds and then deliver the command for a second time. If that didn't work, he knew that they would be in a bad spot. He prepared to throw an elbow shiver if he could not budge the tall Creole on the next attempt. It was the surest way both to immobilize the larger man and to create fighting space.

The shorter man hit his friend on the arm. The big man sneered but let go of the stick. Bodowski still had a bad feeling about the whole scene and never took his eyes off either of the men as they sidled through the crowd and out the back door. Once outside, he backed up several feet and placed himself to box the Creoles between the wall and the garbage cans. As a precaution, he reached into his waistband and rested his hand on the rubber-coated metal sap he carried. Back on the waterway beat, a gun was seldom necessary, but often fists were not enough. He still held both pool cues in this other hand.

A single light bulb in a wire cage hung above the rear door, illuminating the fog of light rain as it drifted down and enveloped the four men.

"You two out of Loosiana? From Narlans?" Cranston laughed at his own mockery of a Creole accent.

"What you want with us?" asked the shorter man. His larger companion stood rigid.

"Let's start off with a name, pal."

"We don't want no trouble. What this all about? We don't do nothing wrong."

"I asked for names, asshole. You got some ID?"

"Oh mister policeman, you don't have to call us that. I is Jerome Patnay and this my brother, Daniel. We just sailors, no? We ain't got no wallets on us. We just in working clothes and it be stupid we go in a bar with a wallet. Keeps our drinking money in the pocket and the wallet back safe on the ship."

"You two have a little fun last night?"

"Sure, plenty of fun. We gets real drunk and shoot pool all night. Don't have no duty while the ship's in port."

The tall Creole identified as Daniel continued to glower in silence, his fists balled up tight. Bodowski's muscles tensed as he readied himself for action.

"I mean some special fun. You boys get yourselves some trim last night—a little tang?" With that, Cranston smelled his index finger.

"Oh no, mister policeman," Jerome grinned, "we don't have that kind of bread. Just money for some booze."

"You boys go on a little trip last night? Go exploring?"

"No, we here till real late, then bunk out on the ship. Come back here at noon—get shit-faced all over again."

Bodowski broke in, "We can check with the taxi companies. We're going to find out if you were here all night." He threw the pool cues behind him.

"Oh, last night. You mean last night?" Jerome redirected his answers to the younger detective. "Last night maybe we take a little ride. Boy, I so drunk I don't remember. How about you, Daniel? You remember?"

The taller man vibrated with tension. Bodowski squeezed the handle of his sap.

"My brother don't remember, neither."

"You two monkeys get laid? Took a little taxi ride and found some trim? Get your dicks wet?"

Jerome looked at Cranston. "Ha ha. Sure, maybe, hell if I know. I so damn in my cups, I don't remember shit."

"You and your mute pal are pretty confused. Maybe we'll take this little party down to the station and have a nice talk there."

Cranston reached out to grab Jerome by the arm, but Daniel intercepted him. Shoving his brother aside, the large Creole pushed the older detective against the wall, knocking the wind out of him. A bolt of adrenaline shot through Bodowski as he pulled the sap from his waistband and leapt toward the men. With one hand on Cranston's throat, Daniel threw out an arm to ward off the coming attack; Bodowski blocked the move and brought the sap down hard on the back of the large man's skull, sending him reeling into the trashcans. From behind, Jerome kicked Bodowski on the thigh and jumped onto the detective's back, wrapping a forearm around his neck. With his assailant off the ground, he spun and launched himself backward into the brick wall of the tavern. Jerome let go and crumpled to the wet pavement. At the same moment, Daniel recovered sufficiently to rush Cranston. The older detective had enough left in him to deliver a kick to the large Creole's groin, smashing one of his testicles. The big man screamed and dropped to the ground, writhing in pain.

"Jesus." Cranston doubled over as he sought to recover his breath. Pulling the handcuffs from the back of his waistband, he looked sidelong at his young partner, who had already turned the semiconscious Jerome over onto his stomach. "Good move. I owe you one."

"Okay, I'll collect on that right now." He gathered the man's wrists and slapped on the cuffs. Standing up, he rubbed his leg and grimaced. "Never call me Polack again." His heart raced, his hands shook from the adrenaline, and a knot formed in his hamstring. He'd never felt so exhilarated.

# Chapter Seven

## The Hardest Ass of All

The aging stone building with the redbrick façade had escaped destruction during a dozen raids by the Army Air Force only to become the headquarters of the base Provost Marshal. Bodowski did not like the place. To him, it felt more like a mausoleum than an office building. Ducking in from the rain, he slogged down the hall past the desk sergeant's station.

"Bodowski. Major Palls wants to see you, pronto." The Duty NCO banged a pencil against his desk.

Without turning, he answered, "Yeah, I got it."

"Hey, you ain't going no place until you check in with Major Palls."

The detective pivoted and began walking in the opposite direction.

"Damn, you actually think you was going straight up to CID?" The burly man laughed.

Bodowski glared as he walked past.

"Get used to it, pal." His tone changed and he asked, "Hey, is she one of ours?"

The detective did not answer. His mind was on the anticipated barrage of questions. The major, nearing the end of his three-year assignment, sought to avoid rotation out of Germany by moving into the Provost Marshal's slot. He'd made no secret of his desire to secure a promotion for the colonel in exchange for a recommendation as his replacement.

Bodowski wondered why the little bastard would want to spend another three years on site. He had been around the Army long enough to know the best career path lay in changing duty stations.

He drew a deep breath before entering the small anteroom that guarded Palls' office. Cluttered with filing cabinets and piles of manila folders containing case files, the room stank of ink and mildew. Seated behind the lone metal desk in the room, Palls' secretary, a rude, overbearing woman whose manner matched that of her boss, looked up at him and inquired, "Is she one of ours?"

He pointed toward the inner office door. "The major in?"

"Yes. And you'd better get on it." Lowering her head to peer over the black-rimmed spectacles that perched on the end of her nose, she added, "I hear the colonel's sitting on some pins with this one."

Bodowski knocked once on the inner office door, but the tenor voice of Major Palls rang out before he could announce his arrival.

"Get in here."

Bodowski stepped into the inner sanctum and closed the door behind him. Jammed to the gunnels with case files stacked high on folding tables and cabinets, the major's office was a continuation of the smaller anteroom. Seated behind a massive gray metal desk that took up a third of the room, the small-framed Palls, head shaved to a close crew cut and sporting a pencil-thin moustache, looked like a child impersonating an Army officer on Halloween. The detective quashed a slight comical impulse.

"Is she one of ours?" Palls stared hard at the young sergeant as he stood at attention.

"I don't know, but it's not likely."

"Based on what?"

"Not sure at the moment—just a feeling. Like I said, I don't know."

"What do you mean you don't know?"

"There's no report on a missing child yet, and we couldn't find any identifying evidence."

"Sir!" Palls, despite stature and voice, knew damn well who was in charge. "You're not in Seattle anymore."

"Yes. I'm sorry, sir." He paused and added, "Tacoma."

"Did you canvass the housing area?"

"Melcher and a lot of MPs are on that right now, sir."

"No idea?"

"Not yet, Major."

"What else is cooking on this?"

"I called ahead to get the ladies upstairs working to match up anything they can with existing reports. Cross-reference with family violence and so on."

"At ease." The small man got up and walked around the desk to face the detective. Looking up at Bodowski, he asked, "What are the chances the fucking limey faggot is right?"

Upon hearing the question, Bodowski figured Kross had contacted the Provost Marshal's office while still at the crime scene and was doing everything he could to get his foot in the door.

"Beg pardon, sir?"

"Don't give me that. You know who I'm talking about."

"Oh. Well, Major, he's German, not British. He just sounds British."

"Yeah, I know he's a kraut, Sergeant." The diminutive officer returned to his chair and sat. "But he's a faggot, right?"

"I don't know, sir."

"You don't know much, do you?"

"No, sir, I guess not." Although skating on thin ice, Bodowski could not restrain himself. After his first few meetings with the major, he had caught on that the little tyrant was more mouth than action.

"Do I need to put someone else on this? Maybe someone with more experience?"

"Sir, you got plenty of investigators. But I'm the only one ever worked a homicide."

"Could any of the other dicks be helpful in all this?"

"Sure. Melcher's okay. But it's best you tell him I'm lead on the case."

"No problem, I guess—as long as he doesn't mind taking shit from a subordinate. Fuck him. He's a limp dick anyway."

"I'll handle that, sir."

Palls lit a cigarette. "You know, we're getting ahead of ourselves. Maybe she's not one of ours. That's the first line of business. And, even if she's not, then we still have to figure out if one of our guys did it." He reclined in the large office chair, blowing smoke toward the ceiling. "Hell, we could argue that the body wasn't found on base. Maybe, if the cards fall just right, this will drop off our table and into their fucking laps. A kraut kid murdered by some kraut asshole."

"I'm going to do my damn best to find out where we stand, sir."

"That's right. That's the spirit." Palls leaned forward, bracing his elbows on the desk. "But you're going to have to coordinate with that dickhead Kross. I already cleared it with Geistburg's Chief of Detectives or whatever the fuck name they call him this week. Those guys have a fetish for reorganization."

"Sir, what did you mean before, when you asked about Kross being right?"

"You know, that she's not ours."

"He never said that to me—just that he believed that she was found off base, meaning it was his catch."

"Kross says the girl's a local. He says he can prove it. But he's fed us bullshit in the past just to get his way. Anyway, I arranged for you to coordinate with him—get to the bottom of this fast. A little girl, all cut up and lying naked in a ditch? That's bad fucking news. The colonel's shorts are in a wad and they're going to stay that way until we can clear this up. So you have to coordinate with Kross. We can use their resources. You guys help each other. Got it?"

"Yes, sir. I take it the colonel wants to keep up on the progress of the case."

"Of course—with something like this. I can hardly wait to head over to his office and blow off thirty minutes while listening to him whine about not making general because of this shit. As for you? Get your ass downtown and get on board with the krauts. Where's the girl now?"

"We got the body in the morgue over at the base hospital."

"We'd better hold off on the autopsy until we can establish jurisdiction. I'll call the med chief and take care of it."

"Anything else, sir?"

"Yeah. Don't screw this up."

# Chapter Eight

## Drunk and Disorderly

Monica LeMarc quivered in response to the muffled curses emanating from her daughter's room. A chill ran through her body. Nothing much on earth could rouse her from her listless state, except for him. She stood up and crossed to the front door. From this vantage point, leaning against the cold sheet metal, she could see down the hallway—see the door open—see him coming for her. Tony and Marc were off to school, out of harm's way for the moment. She could get the hell out of there, run out into the hallway, away from him and to safety with another family. They all knew about him—what he was like. They would welcome her, harbor her against the bastard's cruelty.

The door at the end of the hallway burst open and slammed against the wall, breaking the spring-loaded doorstop. Sergeant Cramer LeMarc, still drunk and reeking of urine and stale whiskey, stumbled into the hallway and landed against the opposing wall. Holding himself up with one arm, the stout man, wearing soaked boxers and a filthy undershirt, rubbed his face. Monica tightened her grip on the door handle and involuntarily emitted a squeaking noise as fear throttled her windpipe. He looked at her sideways as though she did not merit the effort of turning his head.

"Hey, baby. Long time no see." The words dripped with menace.

"Are you hungry, Cramer?" It caught in her throat. "Maybe

I could make you something to eat." The tremor in her own voice reinforced her fear.

"Fuck that! I know what I need." He reached into the opening of his underwear.

"Please, I could make you something to—"

"Get the fuck over here!" The entire apartment shook as if in an earthquake. He stood erect, facing her. "Get over here now, you bitch!" Spittle flew, his face turning crimson. He balled his large hands and thrust them forward, then brought them back to his chest in a pantomime of grabbing her by the lapels and dragging her toward him.

She let go of the door handle and drifted down the hallway, powerless to stop. She imagined an entire world that could not help her—not her neighbors, not her children, not the police. As she neared him, a thin smile of satisfaction grew across his reddened face.

# Chapter Nine

## A Kross to Bear

"No trouble getting here, I trust." Kross sat down, his head turned away as though some pressing business existed for him outside the tall, narrow windows of the German Polizei station.

"No sweat." The young detective took off his raincoat and draped it over his arm.

Kross continued to stare out the window. "Herr Bodowski, I received word from your Major Palls that we will take possession of the body. He stopped your medical examiner from performing an autopsy in the nick of time. I understand he was completing a preliminary examination when he got the call. Our people will do a proper job of it." He looked at Bodowski and smiled. "Of course, I'll share everything of note with you."

"Gee, thanks, Kross." Bodowski sat down across the small wooden desk from the smug German. He worried Kross would stay ahead of him, always interfering. He wondered what had prompted Palls to relinquish control of the body, apparently without a fight. "Okay, what do you want?"

"Come now, I can want something and still be civil, Herr Bodowski."

"Look, Kross—why always so formal with the 'Herr Bodowski'? You've known me for almost a year."

"Why would I address you any differently and with less deference than I do these fine specimens?" Waving his hand, he included the half-dozen German detectives milling about the squad room.

"Jesus, man. They're all standing right here."

"Observe." Catching the eye of one of the younger detectives, Kross asked, "Well, how's it to you, you half-brained twit?"

The police officer stopped what he was doing and asked, "*Was haben Sie fragen*, Herr Leutnant?"

Laughing, Kross rejoined, "*Nichts. Es macht nichts.*" Looking to Bodowski, who was shaking his head, he said, "An occupying force has lived among us since he was a boy, and yet he understands only a few words of their language." Kross leaned back in his swivel chair and sighed. "I'm easily bored."

"Let's get back to it, Kross. You want the body and anything we may have uncovered, don't you?"

The German leaned forward and turned his palms upward. "Look, good fellow. I believe she is not an American dependent. Therefore, we should obtain the report, the body, and all evidence recovered during your man's preliminary examination. Let us hope your people have not bungled this business."

"What makes you think she's not a dependent?"

"No missing person's report from your command."

"Jesus, it's only been a few hours."

"Of course, other pertinent information has come to my attention."

"So tell me."

"I'm sorry, old sport, but it's part of an ongoing investigation, the sensitive details of which I cannot presently—"

"Are you kidding? You're copping the body and evidence from us based on something you can't let us in on?"

Kross blinked but his expression did not change.

"C'mon, that's not going to fly. Maybe if you guys got to the body first—well, then that would be a different matter."

"We'll see, old sport. The autopsy evidence should help us to identify where she is from."

"You don't think you can figure out her nationality from an autopsy, do you?"

Kross folded his arms and smiled. He picked some imaginary lint from his sleeve before asking, "What do you think of this fellow, Palls?"

"Quite a detour there. You're asking me to talk out of school about a superior officer? And one who could ruin me at the drop of a hat?" Bodowski tapped on the desk like it was a snare drum.

"He is, oh, what is it that you Yanks say? Oh, yes—'a piece of work'?" Kross selected a cigarette from his silver case, squeezed it into a red holder, and lit it with an American Zippo lighter.

"He's an experienced cop." Bodowski was grudging in the compliment. It was a safe thing to say.

Kross blew a smoke ring lassoing the American's face.

"Hmm. Yes. Say, how would you characterize Colonel Fulbright? Something of an amateur politician—a bit feckless, don't you think?"

Annoyed, Bodowski waved away the smoke.

"Oh, my apologies. Does that bother you, Herr Bodowski?"

"I get enough with my own people blowing smoke in my face."

"Well, at least mine is not going up your arse."

He knew Kross was manipulating him, and he had been around the man long enough to know when to stop talking and head out.

"Gotta go." Bodowski stood up and moved toward the door. "I hear there's a new examiner at our morgue, but I'll try to wrestle some findings from the prelim—today if I can, tomorrow at the latest. You can probably count on the body staying put until I get with Palls again."

Kross rose halfway from his chair but thought the better of it. He sat down and leaned back. Smiling, he flicked the Zippo lighter several times. Kross liked to show it off. Adorned with the insignia of the American Army's 26th Infantry Regiment, a unit that suffered huge losses in the humiliating Allied defeat at the Kasserine Pass, it was a reminder that although the Germans lost the war, they often prevailed in a single battle.

"Tomorrow, then, Herr Bodowski." Pausing, Koss added, "At the latest."

Grudgingly, Bodowski remembered Palls had sent him downtown with orders to cooperate. "I was told to come over here to get a handle on how we'll pool resources to solve this one." He stepped back toward the desk. "Let's go into that."

"There's seems to have been some confusion. I'm not prepared to commit any resources until we have a clearer view of jurisdiction."

Bodowski turned and walked out. "Waste of goddamned time," he mumbled.

Kross put his feet up on his wastebasket and stared out the window. An ironic beam grew across his face as he watched the raindrops spatter against the glass.

# Chapter Ten

London, England: Friday, August 11, 1944

"Your change, Mr. Putnam. Mr. Putnam?"

Kross smiled at the clerk, who held several coins in his outstretched hand. "Oh, dear. Please forgive me, I was lost in reverie." Accepting the silver and copper pieces embossed with the profiles of British monarchs, he picked up his cup of tea and carried it to his customary table next to the large picture window that looked out on a quiet street in the heart of London's West End. He was the lone customer in the shop.

"Mr. Richardson late today, sir?"

"Afraid so. His work keeps him very busy." Kross, hidden behind thick, black-rimmed glasses and wearing a lightweight gray linen suit, picked up a cloth napkin and fanned himself.

"It's hot, Mr. Putnam."

"'Tis."

A British soldier smoking a pipe, together with a young woman sporting an air raid warden's armband, passed in front of the shop. Kross smiled at the incongruous image of a beautiful girl in a summer dress clinging to a gas mask slung over her shoulder.

"Last year and '42, now those were hot summers. I don't think it's so bad this year, Mr. Putnam. I hope it's not a strain on your poor, weak heart. Oh, there he is now."

Richardson, a sturdy fellow dressed in a green warden's outfit, doffed his hat as he entered the small sweet shop and placed a portable chess box on the table in front of Kross. He waved to the clerk and sat down.

"Sorry, Leslie," he said to Kross, "but damn Jerry won't defeat himself. He's making us do all the work." The three men laughed. Opening the hinged box, the two removed the chess pieces, turned the box over and set the men up for play.

"You gentlemen certainly are dedicated to the game."

Kross beamed. "Hardly miss a day."

The two played for about half an hour. Richardson hunched over the table, his chin in his hands. Kross, as the proper Mr. Putnam, sat ramrod straight and moved his pieces with distant authority.

"Checkmate." Kross grinned as he seized the opposing king. Out of view of the clerk, he deftly exchanged it with an identical piece secreted in his coat pocket. Kross always played black, and he always won. Richardson, actually Gerhardt Kunz of Frankfurt am Main, wondered how he would fare against Kross in a real game.

"Well, sorry, old boy. At least your game is improving."

"Not to worry." Kunz smiled as he packed up the set. "You're teaching me a great deal. Besides, we all need a break, what?"

"I'm glad you feel that way." Kross dropped the last piece into the box.

Clasping the box shut, Kunz stood and grabbed his hat.

"Oh, I almost forgot, Leslie."

"What's that?"

"Won't be able to make it tomorrow."

"Pity."

"Sunday, then?"

"Sunday it is."

Kunz nodded to the clerk but saw he was busy drying glasses. He walked out and disappeared down the empty street. Kross stretched luxuriously and squeezed a cigarette into his holder.

"Time for me to brave the heat."

"You watch your ticker there, sir."

He smiled at the clerk and stepped into the late afternoon sun.

Kross arrived at his flat and dropped the hollow chess piece onto the small table in his kitchenette. He set about making dinner, ignoring the operating procedure that demanded he decode and inspect the message contents prior to re-encoding for transmission that same evening. For the past several months, Kunz passed along information that, in Kross' estimation, seemed not worth the effort, details surrounding the replacement of mid-level field commanders or the occasional discussion of war production quotas. Resentful, the angular German took out his displeasure on the station-monitoring teams in Hanover by forcing them to wait for his transmission until the final minutes of his assigned window of time.

After dinner, he cleared away the dishes and sat at the table reading the evening newspaper. Bored, he set it aside and turned off the light. He lit a cigarette and stared out the window at the apartment building across the narrow courtyard. Lights burned in several flats but, as time passed, only a single apartment stuck out in the darkness. Like his, it was on the first floor. He knew about the occupant from his research prior to taking up permanent assignment: a woman in her late fifties left crippled and mute by the shrapnel from a V-1 rocket. Smashing out his cigarette, he turned on the light, forgetting to draw the window shade. He retrieved the codebook from a hollow panel space in the wall and decoded the day's message, only to discover that he held the operations data for a bombing raid scheduled for the next morning at an industrial complex on the outskirts of Munich.

A sense of urgency gripped him as he realized the station-monitoring window for his frequency would close in the next few minutes. He encoded the message and hurried into the bedroom to retrieve the radio transmitter from behind a panel in the closet just as the ceiling light died with a loud pop. He could see, but not well enough to work the transmitter mechanisms. Racing back into the tiny kitchenette, he searched in vain for his flashlight. Frustrated, he grabbed a spare light bulb from the pantry and ran into the bedroom. He stepped up on an empty steamer trunk and removed the opaque glass covering the single bulb, threw it onto his bed, and began unscrewing the spent bulb. The ancient ceramic fixture came apart under the pressure and fell in a shower to the floor.

"*Schiese*!"

Catching himself—sounds of sufficient volume made it through the plaster and lath—he ran into the living room and unplugged the lone floor lamp. Stymied by the lack of a working electrical outlet in the bedroom, he dropped the lamp on the bed and considered his next move. Pulling the panel in the closet, he lifted the cumbersome radio transmitter and carried it into the kitchenette.

Several minutes later, he had tapped out the vital message. He draped a spare tablecloth over the radio and lit a cigarette, glanced at his watch and smiled. Then something caught his eye. He turned off the light and looked out the window. An instant later, the light in the flat across the courtyard went out.

"*Gottverdammt*!" She had seen him. In his rush to transmit the message, he had forgotten to close the curtains.

Kross raced across the courtyard to her apartment. He knocked hard and then cooed, "My dear, please come to the door. It's very important. It's war business." Hearing nothing, he persisted on a different tack: "It's not what you think. I can explain what you saw."

The German knew that sounded asinine, and decided to try the door. Though locked, it gave under firm pressure. From the rear of the apartment, he heard a window open. He rushed toward the bedroom, grabbing a heavy brass lamp and stripping it of its shade. He shouldered the thick door open, forcing the half-dressed woman to stumble backward on her crutches. The German spy saw the terror in her eyes but did not hesitate. He brought the lamp base down on the crown of her skull for all he was worth, producing a loud crack. Her arms flew from the crutches. A fountain of bright red blood gushed from her head as she collapsed to the floor. Kross swung the lamp away, casting blood across the room. He had never before killed someone with his own hands. Seized by an odd curiosity, he examined the streaks of blood that had showered the walls and ceiling. He watched, detached, as the dark blood flowed from the woman's head onto the worn planking of the floor. Her eyes stayed open, staring at nothing. Kross dropped the lamp and walked back toward the apartment door. For a moment, he stood dumbly among the old furniture in her little room. Shaking himself out of it, he paced the length of the small apartment several times before settling upon a plan. He gathered all the flammable liquids he could find from the woman's pantry, and then, dousing her body and the surrounding area, he put them to the match.

An hour later, he sat by the large window of his own flat and watched as a local fire brigade worked to contain the flames in the building across the courtyard. An earnest young man had come by a few minutes earlier and urged him to leave for his own safety. Instead, Kross had come back to the vantage point of the window to witness the results of his handiwork. He retired for the evening once the firemen established control over the blaze and the apartment was nothing but embers.

After a night of florid dreams, none of which touched upon the strange calculus of duty-bound murder, he awoke and walked into his small bathroom to gaze at the figure in the mirror. His reflection smiled back at him, pleased at the facility he had displayed by keeping his head when the whole business was about to go awry. He retrieved his brush and soap and began his morning routine.

# Chapter Eleven

## A Soldier in the Rain

Warrant Officer Nowak got out of his car and threw a raincoat over his shoulders to fend off the pouring rain. Startled by a car horn, he ran across the cobblestone street. The vehicle tore past, its fender passing within inches of his haunch. Close calls like that were always unnerving, but all the more so when he was downtown, away from his duty station on one of his unscheduled breaks.

He stood outside the entrance to the little bakery shop and fastened the raincoat over his fatigue uniform, making certain to cover his nametag. Previously, he had taken the precaution of wearing civilian clothes when visiting the shop, but he grew bolder and decided that simply covering up identifying patches would suffice. After all, it was obvious he was an American soldier, just one of thousands stationed at several posts in the area. Surely that afforded him an acceptable level of anonymity.

The little bell attached to the door made a tinkling noise as he entered the shop. The aroma of fresh baked bread greeted him as he stood on the doormat and waited for the shop owner to acknowledge his presence. The owner, a small round man with a balding pate who stared at his customers through wire-rimmed glasses, served a young girl standing at the counter. He noticed Nowak out of the corner of his eye. Transaction completed, the child, not more than eight years of age, traded pleasantries with the baker and then excused herself to Nowak as she pushed past him to leave. He took advantage of the awkward movement to pat her on the head, his fingers reveling in the fine silk of her blond hair.

"*Guten Tag, mein Herr.*" She beamed up at him.

Lips trembling, he returned the smile. She left the shop eating a frosted pastry, blissfully unaware of her brush with depravity.

"Cute, isn't she?" The owner smiled at Nowak, who glanced around the shop. "Don't worry. We're alone." His English, a byproduct of working for German intelligence during the war, was excellent.

The officer stepped up to the old wooden counter and pursed his lips. "Okay, Utz, you got them?"

"Back so soon? I just saw you."

"C'mon, damn it."

The small man backed away, nodding and holding up a finger to indicate he should wait. Nowak, already on edge just being in the store, surveyed the street through the large picture window. A minute passed before Herr Utz emerged from the back room with a green canvas bag, which he held up with both hands as though presenting a crown on a pillow. Nowak reached for the bag, but the little man pulled it away to his side.

"You cannot believe how much this cost me."

"Give them to me. I paid you good money," Nowak shot back.

"Not enough. I didn't know it was going to be this expensive. And you still owe me for that special treat."

"What the hell is this?" Nowak banged his fist on the counter, rattling the jars filled with biscotti and breadsticks. "You told me how much it would cost. You get your cut too. I know that. Goddamnit, we had a deal."

The hotter Nowak got, the calmer Utz became, his voice quiet but determined.

"Two hundred Marks more."

"Two hundred extra Marks?! That's double." Catching himself, Nowak mustered a semblance of control and continued through his teeth, "I ought to just take it. What are you going to do? Call the Polizei?"

"No, but I assure you that this will be our last business together if you try something foolish. Besides," the baker paused and leaned forward, "I would call someone else."

Nowak cursed himself for flying off the handle. He stepped back from the counter and took a moment to cool off by poking at the wrapped pastry on the shelves. He broke the silence with a more conciliatory tone.

"Explain to me why it costs so damn much."

"This is what you Americans call 'upping the ante.'" Utz continued to hold the bag off to his side as though he were about to run away with it. Imagining the contents, Nowak could barely contain himself. He had to have them. However, he also knew he had to keep a grip on himself.

"That's more than fifty bucks, all told. That's a lot. I already gave you two hundred Marks, plus the money I gave you yesterday—for the other business. That cost me a bundle." Stammering, he continued, "I don't have that much left on me, and it'll take a while to get it." Like an addict, he would try every approach and entertain any debasement to get his fix. "Is there something else I could do, maybe?"

"Just the money."

Nowak reeled under the weight of his addiction. "How about just some, huh? Just something for my money and I'll get the rest soon. You know I'm good for it."

"All right." Utz pretended to make a sacrifice, knowing Nowak would be back for the remaining items. "I will give you one, for now."

"One? C'mon, at least three."

"One. Only one. That is all you get until you bring me the additional two hundred Marks. And, of course, until we settle the other issue."

Working to control himself, Nowak spun away from Utz. He blew some air through his lips before turning back to face the little man. "Okay. Yeah." Nowak clacked his teeth as he held out his hand.

The shop owner smiled and pulled a length of white butcher

paper from a roll he kept under the counter. He removed a single eight-by-ten photograph from the canvas bag and rolled it up in the waxy paper. Crimping the top, he handed it to Nowak. The soldier stuffed it under his raincoat and turned to walk out.

"Wait, you forgot," said Utz.

"What?"

"Here." The shop owner held out a large, doughy pretzel.

"For Christ's sake." Nowak spun around and snatched the pretzel from Utz's hand. He stepped toward the door and stopped. Without looking back, he said, "If this photo is any good, I'll be back with the rest of the money."

Neither man had any doubts about Nowak's return.

Sitting in his car, motor running and wipers on, Nowak tore open the butcher paper and placed the photograph face down on his lap. Hands trembling, he checked in all directions before taking a deep breath and turning it over. His eyes widened at the grainy image of a little girl, naked, bound flat on her stomach to a bench. The look of terror on her face would have sickened and angered another man. Nowak, overcome with excitement, unbuttoned his fly.

# Chapter Twelve

## The Doctor in Spite of Himself

"Hey. You're Bodowski. You're the CID guy they said was coming over, right?" The tall, curly-haired man in a stained lab coat slapped the sleeping detective on the knee with a manila file. Getting no response, he swatted him again, this time with more purpose. "Hey!"

Bodowski, slumped on a bench outside the morgue in the basement of the main post hospital, struggled to pull himself upright. He blinked to brush away the mental cobwebs. "Sorry. Yeah, I'm Bodowski." He stood up and rubbed his forehead with the palm of his hand.

"Little shy on sleep, are we?"

The sergeant noted a pair of captain's bars on the man's collar underneath the lab coat.

"Yes, sir." He suppressed a yawn. "Got up early—big morning."

"Well, as they say, follow me. By the way, I'm Larson. And you can forget about calling me sir. How about 'Doc'? I like the sound of that." The pathologist lit a cigarette and beckoned the detective with the file. They walked past several bodies on gurneys, each covered by a white sheet. The doctor began a lopsided conversation. "Haven't seen you down here before. Hell, I haven't seen anybody here on a case for the MPs, ever. You're with the MPs, right?"

Bodowski opened his mouth to answer but was cut off.

"Damn, what am I thinking? Of course you're with the MPs. I mean, who the hell else would a CID guy be with? I like the fact you're wearing civilian clothes. Makes it seem like everything you're doing is more important somehow. This is probably the first murder that wasn't a soldier or his wife. Boy, was she murdered. Poor kid. Just a little girl. That isn't right. You know, it was me who brought her back this morning. Oh, but you were talking with some other people, so you don't remember. I got the body ready and all. I signaled you before we took it, but you just waved me off. You yelled at me about something to do with the autopsy. I didn't quite get it. Don't you remember me?"

The detective began to reply but got cut off again.

"Maybe the guy who worked here before me did some murdered kids. Well, not the murders, but the autopsies. You know what I mean. I've been here three months, three long months. Ha ha. You can tell I'm really enjoying this posting." Larson took a long drag off the cigarette to quiet himself. His fingers twitched. Swinging open the large stainless-steel doors of the morgue, the doctor exhaled a stream of smoke and announced, "*Entre vous.*"

"Thanks, Doc."

Bodowski did not know what to think about Larson, but he knew he hated morgues. His first visit to one, occasioned years ago by the death of a drunken stevedore, had left him shaken. The bodies, like so many hunks of meat, awaited their turn at the knife. It gave him the willies. Still, from then on, it was all business. And the accompanying odors, at first repellent, became just part of the deal. Now, years later and a long time since he'd been in a morgue, it made his skin crawl all over again.

"Smoke?"

"No thanks, sir—I mean Doc. I gave up the habit a while back."

"Yeah, I guess you know we're not supposed to smoke in here anyway, but sometimes I forget. Nah, that's a lie. I just don't give a shit. Ha ha." With that, Larson smashed out the butt on the concrete floor and kicked it to the wall.

The body of the little girl lay on the dissection table in the middle of the room. Her torso had turned a light shade of blue. Without a face, she looked more like a naked store mannequin than a human being. A pulse of sadness hit Bodowski as he stood over her.

Larson stopped behind him, checking the file. "This Palls fellow—what's his rank? Major Palls, yeah. He told me to put a hold on the cut job. That's what we call them down here, cut jobs. Well, it's a good thing he called when he did. I already did a prelim and had scalpel in hand, ready to go. I thought you wanted it, but I guess your boss didn't. What's a guy to do? Just human, after all. Ha. He says I should give the Germans what I have and let them take the body. Boy, just think of the paperwork. He must have called them to come get her by now—you think? Anyway, I almost started the cut job thinking it was okay, but man, he was pissed when he called."

"Doc?" He gave Larson a leading look.

"Oh. I figured out a bunch even with just the few things I checked on so far." Larson stuck a cigarette into the side of his mouth and walked around the body. "Check this out." He held up her left hand as if he were a puppeteer. "See these calluses? What little girl has calluses like these?" He grabbed the other hand to show Bodowski and managed to drag his sleeve through the sticky residue that clung to her body. "More calluses. And," holding up a finger to indicate he'd found something important, he stepped to the foot of the table and performed a grandiloquent sweep with both arms. "Voila! These puppies are as hard as rocks—lots of calluses on both soles."

"She was mostly barefoot? Doesn't sound like a dependent or a local."

"Wait. There's more." Larson lit his cigarette and hummed as he stepped to the head of the dissection table. Cupping the dead girl's temples with both hands, he said, "This pale look—ashen, really—you can see it on the pieces of her face that are left. You know, every dead person's got this problem. Ha ha. But if you look close under all the cuts and slices, she's really dark-complexioned—or was in life, that is." He smiled and tapped his lower lip.

"She's a negro?" Bodowski was surprised.

"No, no. Nowhere near that dark. More like a Spaniard or something."

"How old do you figure she is? I thought ten."

"You know you can usually tell by the teeth? Well, I think I got it down to nine or ten. Not bad shootin', huh, Tex?" He blew away imaginary smoke from his index finger.

"Where the hell is she from?" Bodowski asked himself.

"I guess that's your department. Or maybe it's up to our German friends now. You might be right, you know. Maybe she's not one of ours." Larson patted her temples.

The detective retrieved his notebook and jotted down the findings. He looked up at the doctor, half expecting him to continue his verbal onslaught. Greeted instead by an inquisitive stare, he took the cue and asked, "What about sexual assault?"

Larson let out a quick laugh as though he had been holding his breath. "Thought you'd never ask." He stepped to the foot of the table and threw apart the child's legs.

Bodowski felt a flash of anger over the disrespectful treatment of the body but kept it in check.

Larson pointed at her groin, "See there? Right there. There wasn't any semen, but there sure was a hell of a lot of water."

"Water?"

"I think someone stuffed a garden hose, or something like it, up her vagina and let loose. Water up there everywhere."

"Cleared everything out?"

"Yeah, would have done permanent damage if wasn't for the fact it was done postmortem." As if to punctuate the reality of her demise, Larson drew a finger across his throat. "Oh, and another thing—this was one experienced kid."

"What do you mean?"

"This little girl has all kinds of vaginal and anal scars and some recent tearing, mostly healed. This poor kid's been handled in a rough manner for a long time."

"What? Like a prostitute or something?"

"I dunno. Her being so young and all, I'd say more like a sex slave."

Writing in his notebook, Bodowski asked, "Cause of death? Suffocation?"

"Well..." Larson sucked in around the cigarette and blew the smoke toward the ceiling before continuing, "I haven't really nailed that yet. The agent of death is some form of asphyxiation. I can't quite figure out how, but I'm working on it, at least until the Germans get here. I wish I could cut her open."

"The marks on her wrists. Cuffs? Ropes?"

"Handcuffs, definitely."

"How about her face? Got any idea what was used?"

"Small blade. Yeah, a small blade like a pen knife."

"Thanks, Doc. Give the duty desk over at the Provost Marshal's a call if you find out anything else. Tell them to contact me." Bodowski marched out of the morgue and down the hall.

Larson ran after him as far as the doorway and shouted, "Should I call the German authorities? They're probably on their way, already. Right? I don't know what to do."

"No, don't worry. I'm sure Major Palls has got it covered." Bodowski, halfway around the corner, waved him off.

"Okay, then I'll just keep working on this until they get here, but no cutting so I don't get in Dutch." Larson stepped into the morgue. Snapping his fingers, he ran back into the hallway and shouted after the detective, "And thanks for calling me Doc!"

# Chapter Thirteen

## Working Without a Clue

"Hey, there you are." Melcher smiled as his partner stepped out of the unmarked sedan. The nondescript radio car joined the half-dozen green military police vehicles still crowding the entryway to the path. "I got the call you were coming back to the scene." He dug into his shirt pocket and produced an unfiltered cigarette.

"That shit'll kill you. You could at least switch to filters."

"Thanks for the advice, Dad." Melcher lit the cigarette with a match. Watching the flame consume the paper stem until it neared his fingers, he remarked, "Not a breath of wind. I'll never get used to this place. Either it's a gale or nothing. You'll notice that the rain has stopped, but it'll start up again by the time I stop talking."

Bodowski walked to the head of the path. He watched from a distance as the lone guard talked with the two MPs in fishing waders who were scouring the bottom of the ditch in both directions.

"Anything yet, Mel?"

"Not so far, at least not in the ditch and not much anywhere else, either." He blew smoke through his nose.

"I'm glad to see you recovered from seeing the body."

"I'm feeling a little better." Hesitating, he added, "I'm trying to keep it in perspective. Truth is, I just don't think about the kid, at least not in some personal way. It helps."

"They trained you well at CID school."

Melcher smiled at the mild dig. He knew Bodowski had trouble getting close. If you were going to be around him, you just had to take him as he came. Holding the cigarette between his fingertips, he pointed at the men in the ditch. "Check out what they're wearing."

"Where the hell did they get the fishing waders?"

"Sergeant major."

"Who? Walters?"

"Yeah. I knew he was a big-time angler. I called him and voila, he brought them right down."

"That's the second time I've heard that word in the last hour."

"What word?"

"Voila. Larson, the new pathologist over at the base hospital, used it. Crazy sonofabitch."

"What's his story?"

"Dropped on his head as a kid. Hell if I know. He came up with a few gems, though."

"What? He do the autopsy this fast? How's that possible?"

"No autopsy. Palls put the kibosh on that. We have to hand her over to the krauts."

"Get the hell out of town! What's that about? How are we supposed to conduct a decent investigation without control of the body?"

"Take it easy. We still have plenty to work with. The doc—Larson—he did a prelim, and he's going to keep working on it until the krauts pick up the body. Like I said, he came up with some pretty good stuff."

Melcher flicked his cigarette into the ditch. "I'm all ears."

"First off, he figured out she has a dark complexion." He shivered against the cold and squinted toward the sky as a light rain fell.

"I don't get it. She's colored? Man, she looked mighty pale to me. I mean, what you could see of her face. Damn. Her body looked almost white."

"Death and blood loss has a funny way of making you look a little drawn." Pulling up his collar, Bodowski hunched forward and frowned. "Doc thinks she had a swarthy complexion in life, like a Spaniard or someone like that."

"What's that tell you?"

"Dependents are going to be like their parents. We've got a lot of white bread." He pointed toward the large apartment buildings with his chin. "Especially here—mostly officers. That means palefaces."

"She'll stand out." Melcher seemed encouraged. "We can zero in on the non-whites."

"Maybe Kross is right. Maybe she's not one of ours. Of course, the doc could be full of shit. This whole dark-complexion business could be nothing." Bodowski ground his teeth, reminded of the prospect of losing control of the case.

"What else did this Larson fellow come up with?"

"Calluses. All over her hands and feet."

"A farm girl? Something like that?"

"I don't know." He looked at the three large apartment buildings facing the potato farm. "Too early to tell what that really means." He good-naturedly shoved his pal as Melcher popped another cigarette into his mouth and struck a match. "You were going to light that thing right in my face. You know you're personally keeping the tobacco industry afloat, don't you?"

Recovering, Melcher laughed and lit his cigarette. "I'm just doing my bit to keep both American tobacco companies and my lungs in the black." He took a long drag. "I'm going to have to arrest you for striking a superior officer."

Bodowski struggled to keep a straight face. "I'll give you the officer part."

"I get the feeling you're enjoying yourself. You finally have a murder to solve. Well, at least until they take it away from you."

The rain stopped. Bodowski lowered his collar. "Enjoy is the wrong word. It's more complicated than that."

"Sort of like you?"

"This was the last, worst day of that little girl's life. I feel that in my bones. But it's the kind of day I live for. I don't think I can explain it."

"Enough said. Maybe when I get a few of these under my belt I'll really start to understand."

"I'll tell you one thing. Even if we can keep a grip on this case, assholes like Palls and Kross will still make life miserable."

"Business as usual."

Bodowski squatted and pulled at the dead autumn weeds. "The girl was abused. Heavily. Sexually. Just like I thought."

"You get this from the doc?"

"Yeah." He stood and brushed his hands clean. "Doesn't have a bearing on whether she's foreign, local, or whatever. And we don't have a clue who could have done the deed. Could be some sick bastard, a male family member, or maybe someone else. I don't know."

"How are we going to play this?"

"How far along are you on the canvass?"

"I still got an agent and a half-dozen guys from Battalion on it. I was able to use all Provost Marshal Investigators—better than those MP jocks. Anyway, we've been hitting the apartments hard. We started with the buildings here and fanned out."

"So what have you got?"

Melcher retrieved his notebook and flipped through several pages. "There's only been one check-in by the crew so far." He raised an eyebrow and cleared his throat. "Of course, no one saw shit. But we got something. We're looking at two men out late last night. One's got an alibi—so says his wife—and the other I can't get anything on yet. I called the info over to the ladies back at the office. They'll try to match them up with any reports." He closed the notebook and put it away. "They said you already called and told them to get working on any incidents involving family violence. Maybe they'll have some luck cross-referencing." Struck by a thought, he nudged Bodowski's shoulder. "Hey. What'd you get off the piece of chain link?"

"I got it to Buckingham, but he doesn't think he'll be able to lift any prints. If the killer has two brain cells to rub together, he'll have worn gloves. Oh, yeah—there's something I want to check out." He walked toward the near corner of the closest apartment building.

"Whoa. I've got to wait here until the guys on canvass finish. They're expecting me to be here."

"Just take a minute. C'mon."

"All right." Catching up, Melcher asked, "You want to fill me in?"

Bodowski pointed and hurried his pace. "See there?"

"What?"

"The hose on the reel. See? Right there on the corner of the building?"

"I see it. So what?"

Reaching the apartment building, the detective picked up the hose mouth hanging from the coiled spool and rubbed a finger around the inside of the metal fitting. "Dry as a bone."

"What do you expect? Not a lot of watering going on for the past few months. I'm surprised these things are still out." He surveyed the sky. "Regular freezes will be coming any day now. Why the big interest in garden hoses?"

"Doc Larson said she'd been hosed out." He slapped the hose end against his palm.

"Christ."

"Yeah." He stared at his friend while banging the metal fitting against the concrete wall of the building.

"What are you thinking? You want to check all the hoses?"

He dropped the hose end and folded his arms. "I think once your canvass team finishes, you should send them back out to check every external hose they can find in the housing area, including at the houses of the field-grade officers—everybody."

"Got it. I'll have them check for recent use, like you just did."

"Tell them not to handle the fittings on the outside. Maybe we can get a print."

"This is not my first rodeo, sport. You don't have to tell me how it's done."

Bodowski smiled. "Sorry, pal. I didn't mean anything by it. I just get a head of steam up, you know."

Melcher smiled and slapped him on the arm. "Uppity enlisted men. Work a few dozen murders to my none, and you think you can tell me what to do."

"Actually, it was more than that."

"You kept count?"

Interrupted by shouts from the guard, the two men walked back toward the ditch.

"Look, Mel. He's signaling us. He wants us to come over to the ditch."

They hurried up the path.

The guard pointed to one of the MPs standing below them and addressed Melcher. "Sir, I think we found something." Wearing a pair of blue dishwashing gloves, the MP held up a small metallic object in his cupped hands.

"What is that?" asked Melcher.

"It's a jackknife, sir. I know it's hard to tell with all that mud on it. See? The blade's out."

"Put that in a bag and hand it up here," Bodowski ordered.

The guard handed over one of the small evidence bags lying on the asphalt path, and the MP slipped the muddy object into the wax-lined bag, then passed it up to Melcher. Both detectives peered into the open bag.

"I think it's a Boy Scout knife," Bodowski said. "Check out the etched design on the handle. No way we'll get prints."

"What do you want to do, man? Take it to the examiner or the lab?"

"In this case," he took the bag and sealed it, "I'll skip the lab and get it to the doc. I don't know how long before the body disappears into the kraut system. Maybe he can take a stab at matching up the cuts with the blade."

"I'm going to let that one slide." Melcher smiled.

"What? What did I say?"

Another MP approached from the path entryway.

"Hey, that's my replacement," the guard said. "I'll run that right over for you, sir. The medical examiner at the hospital? What's his name?"

"Larson—Captain Larson. But call him Doc. Make sure to tell him it's for me, Bodowski." He read the guard's nametag. "Slidell." He nodded. "We're looking for a match with the cuts, got it?"

"Right on it, sir." He took the bag and saluted Bodowski. Melcher clumsily returned the gesture. The young man angled to face the warrant officer and finished the salute, then took off on the run.

"Make sure to tell him which case it's for," Bodowski called after him.

"Jesus, man. How many bodies does he have down there?"

After a few words with the MPs, the two detectives walked down the path toward the entryway.

"Snappy salute back there, pal."

"You know, I need a better class of friends." Melcher tossed the lit cigarette into the ditch and fished another from his shirt pocket.

# Chapter Fourteen

## Casting a Pall

Bodowski flipped his notebook shut and stuck it into his overcoat pocket, wrapping up his summary of the case so far. Palls leaned forward in his chair, almost smiling.

"Good work. Excellent to hear she may not be a dependent. Still, doesn't mean one of our guys didn't do the deed. I'd hate to think it's a soldier. I want you to know that." The major coughed and reached into the small wooden box on his desk to retrieve a cigarette. The little man placed it between his lips and struck the lighter three times. "Hosed her out, huh? That's a sick fuck. Tell me again—you mentioned a knife?"

"We found it in the ditch. But like I told you, sir, I don't think we'll get prints." He wondered why they were going back over this.

"Shit. My mind was drifting when you read it off to me before. Give it to me again."

He pulled out the notebook and thumbed through a few pages.

"Boy scout knife—silver, bad surface for prints—blade out—no apparent blood—possibly used to carve face—gave to Slidell to take to Doc Larson. That's about it. I won't know until later."

"You figure it's an important piece of evidence?"

"Maybe. But I don't see how I'll match it to anyone. There's no serial number, no unique identifying marks. Still, you never know."

"You didn't embarrass yourself on that joint taskforce with the krauts last year, so we're going to replay that." Palls banged the lighter on the desk. "Piece of crap." He threw it to the side and grabbed a match. "Only this time it's murder." He leaned back in his chair, his small frame swallowed by the plush leather.

"I'm not playing second fiddle to Kross, right?" It was less a question than a demand.

"No way." Palls blew a jet of smoke toward the ceiling. "Don't sweat it. You follow your own leads, but keep Kross up on what's happening." Palls grunted. "That's the new way—cooperation and all. You and the faggot should have a good time. This is right up your respective alleys."

"Why did you turn the body over?" He forgot himself, asking the question as though Palls were a suspect. The major's eye twitched, but he went on.

"Kross read me in on some factors about an ongoing investigation. He convinced me they should take the body. Don't sweat it. You'll get to see the krauts' autopsy report. Hell, they'll do a better job than our guy anyway."

"Kross mentioned something about that investigation to me too." Bodowski eased back on his tone. "What can you fill me in on, sir?"

"This one's on the hush. Sorry, pal. It's way above your rank." Palls sneered and flicked the ash from his cigarette.

"Anything else, sir?"

"Yeah. I hope you caught my drift about it probably not being one of our people and, oh yeah, just one more thing." Palls produced a file from his top drawer. Leafing through the folder, he said, "Something I should have a done a while back."

"What's that, sir?"

"Given you a closer look."

It was his personnel file in the major's hands.

Palls added unnecessary emphasis as he read, "'Reached settlement resulting in termination from Tacoma Police Department on July 15, 1961.'" He looked up. "'Reached settlement'? To be fired?"

"I was represented by the union." Standing with his hands behind his back, Bodowski shifted his feet and made a fist with his right hand, digging his fingernails into his palm.

Palls continued. "'Subject to alcohol abuse.' Yadda, yadda, 'excessive absences,' so on and—ah—here we go. 'Dereliction of duty by reason of intoxication resulting in lost opportunity for prosecution.'" Palls threw the folder onto the desk. Loose papers skated across the surface. "Jesus, that's a mouthful just to say that you were a drunken fuck-up."

"I don't get it, sir." Bodowski's lip curled. "Now that you know this, why do want me working this case—or any case, for that matter?"

"Yeah. You don't get it, do you?" Palls crossed around his desk to confront the larger man. "I had you checked out. I probably should have done it before the taskforce business last year, but I never got around to it. You blew your chance at home, so you went to the only place that would still have a lush as a cop. Uncle Sam." Palls smiled, hesitated. "But you cleaned up. Like I said, I checked up on you." He returned to his chair. "You did okay last year, and all the other dicks say they trust you enough." He leaned back. "I'm going to stick with you for now. But if you even come within a mile of a drink—"

"It's not going to happen." Grim-faced, Bodowski stared a hole through the officer's forehead.

Palls leaned forward and smiled. "That's the spirit. Now get out there and make sure it wasn't some sick GI with poor impulse control. We need to leave the krauts holding the bag." He opened a folder and began leafing through it. "After all, the old man needs his star."

# Chapter Fifteen

## Akron, Ohio: Wednesday, September 4, 1946

"Listen up, guys. Pipsqueak here wants to become a Zeto." The tall fellow wearing a varsity athlete's sweater aimed a finger at the boy and laughed. "You want to tell me why I should give you a second look, shorty?"

Randolph Palls stood at the front of a group of young men gathered in the courtyard of the Zeta Omega fraternity house. He explored the inside of his cheeks with his tongue in hopes of conjuring up a little moisture.

"I'll do what it takes to become a Zeto." The squeak in his voice made him sound younger than his seventeen years. "I got what it takes. You'll see."

"Got what it takes? Why don't you run on home to Mama, little boy? We've got some men, some veterans here. Let's see a show of hands." A number of the men, all in their early twenties, raised a hand. However, V-J Day, just a year past, had yet to deliver the expected supply of young candidates.

Palls could not have known it then, but, short of a complete meltdown, he could rely on becoming a freshman Zeto.

He stepped forward and shouted his response. "Just try me. Tell me what I have to do and I'll do it, damn it!" He surprised both himself and the young man with his vehement delivery.

"Well, I'll be. The midget's got spunk. Sure, kid. We'll see what you got besides that whistle you call a voice." The young man smirked and motioned toward the door with his chin. "Go on inside and tell them you can sign up for the rush. We'll see how long it takes you to wash out."

As the weeks passed, the pledges lived on tenterhooks, waiting for the ritualistic hazing of the freshman to begin in earnest. The older frat boys considered the paddling and other physical punishments necessary character-building experiences, whereas the several pledges who had seen action in the war looked upon them as asinine and sophomoric. But no one quit. The lure of social acceptance was too high.

The diminutive Palls often found himself singled out for special treatment, yet he managed to impress his tormentors by stoically absorbing every new indignity. Asked after each bout of humiliation why he wanted to be a member of their house, Palls responded, "Because I want to be a Zeto." What went unsaid was that he cared nothing for the promise of brotherhood and fraternity. He had targeted Zeta Omega as the fraternity most likely to provide him with the social and business contacts he'd need after college.

The hazing, like most shared trials, brought the pledges closer together. But Palls' acerbic manner and manipulative personality eroded the few passing friendships he developed. A single incident that occurred on the final day of hazing spoke volumes.

"You're not going to make it, Randy."

"What?" Palls, like the other twenty-three pledges wearing only a baby bonnet and a cloth diaper, stood in line waiting his turn for the paddle for the seventh time that day.

"You heard me," said the upperclassman as he rolled up his sleeve. "It's a sure thing that the council will vote you out tonight."

"What did I do wrong?" Palls' voice whistled higher than usual. "Tell me what I have to do to make this right."

The young man pulled Palls aside and spoke in a confidential manner. "You need to show us your mettle—what you really got between your legs."

Palls did not understand.

"C'mon, Randy—you know what I mean. You got to show us you're a real man by giving up something special, something important to you. You show us that, and I know that talk about you getting the boot will go away." The young man laughed and shoved Palls back into line.

The upperclassmen arranged for a party to take place that evening in the main hall of the fraternity, which pledges could attend provided they brought a date—a final challenge for the harried freshmen. Palls thought of Janet Barnhof, a young woman who shared a dissecting table with him in their freshman biology class. Although not yet well acquainted, having spent most of his time next to her staring at her breasts, he thought she would make an excellent date. Later that day, he ran into her outside the university library.

"Hi, Janet, would you like to go to my fraternity party, I mean a party at my fraternity, tonight?" Anticipating rejection, he frowned.

The petite redhead smiled, though perhaps less at him than at the thought of the host of upperclassmen sure to attend the party. "I'd be delighted, Randy."

Taken aback by her positive response, Palls tripped over his reply. "Okay—that's good, you know. Great. You know where the house is, right?"

"Just down the street from my sorority. What time does the party start?"

"Eight." Waiting a beat, he asked, "Maybe I should come and pick you up, huh?"

"Maybe you should."

A new sensation, something akin to a sense of well-being, lingered in his chest as he watched her walk away, though it faded upon recalling the upperclassman's threat delivered.

Later that evening, the fraternity jumped with music, dancing, and the shouted conversations of young men and women. Though banned on fraternity row, drinking was rampant, and this night proved no exception as the partygoers ran through a case of whiskey.

Despite the cloud lingering over Palls, he sought to enjoy himself. Janet's presence made it easy for him to set his troubles aside until his tormentor, smashed to the gills, came up behind Palls as he sat next to his date and whispered into his ear.

"I haven't seen anything from you. Time is ticking away." He straightened and guffawed, swinging a finger back and forth like a metronome.

Palls fell silent, then excused himself and left the room. Returning, he asked Janet to join him in the kitchen. She stood and followed him through the swinging doors, laughing and stumbling as she went.

"You've got to sober up before you go home, Janet. I fixed you a remedy. This'll sober you up in no time."

"Okie dokie." She accepted the full glass and downed it in several swallows.

"Professor Weyland puts me to sleep."

"He's a real snoozer."

"I don't think biology is for me."

"I'm just taking it as my science—" She steadied herself against the wall. "Gosh, I'm getting tipsy."

Fifteen minutes of stilted conversation passed before the straight whiskey had its full effect. Throwing Janet's arm over his neck, Palls supported her as they ascended the wide stairs to the second floor. He banged on the door of the senior lounge several times, but it was lost in the laughter and music emanating from the smoke-filled room. Palls' nemesis staggered up the stairs at a broken run and came up behind the little man and his human burden.

"Hey, frosh. What do you think you're doing there? That's the senior lounge."

"Look." He raised Janet's arm off his shoulder and held her from behind. She hummed along to the music, resting in his arms like a ragdoll. "I brought you guys a little something—just like you asked."

"What the fuck? Are you crazy, Palls?"

"No, wait. You don't understand. She likes to do it all the time with guys. She told me." Searching for a way to make his point, he blurted out, "She said sometimes she does it for money."

"A pro, huh? Funny, she looks just like a co-ed." The upperclassman blinked through his drunkenness as though that would help clarify matters.

"Yeah, a pro. That's right."

The older boy took the girl and, with some difficulty, hoisted her over his shoulder. She grabbed the seat of the young man's pants and laughed.

Palls left the party and climbed the stairs to the large room on the third floor that contained the freshman bunks. Sitting alone, listening to the muffled party noise seeping through layers of flooring, he wondered whether his offering would be sufficient to turn the tide in his favor. He considered the implications of what he had done. Although attracted to Janet, he decided she was a necessary sacrifice to achieve his goal. Sleep eluded him that night, but not the next.

Janet never returned to biology class.

After graduation, Palls joined the Army. He met a mousy young woman at a mixer on post during his first assignment. Plain and meek, she feared spinsterhood more than the prospect of a loveless marriage. For Palls, it was a mechanical process. Like Janet, the sensation he had felt while standing on the university's library steps had vanished forever.

# Chapter Sixteen

## Ladies in Waiting

"There you are, you little bugger."

Hunched over her desk in the third-floor offices of the CID, Nancy Burrows selected a file from one of the bulging stacks of manila folders and pored over it. A red-haired beauty with soft blue eyes and delicate features who her friends called "a pistol," she had become a civil servant following her divorce from a philandering young officer, and still attracted her share of attention from the male agents.

A hand on her arm surprised her. "What?"

Fresh from his ordeal with Palls, Bodowski smiled and asked, "You find anything for me?" Moving his hand to the back of her neck, he leaned over to see which file she was inspecting. "Great system you got there."

She lifted her shoulders to shake off his advance. Her friend and coworker, Mavis Nelson, gave a disapproving shake of her head.

"See, Mr. Workplace Lothario?" Nancy grinned adjusted her collar. "You upset Mavis. No one likes to see the ladies getting pawed."

Bodowski threw his hands up in mock surrender.

Mavis, the married mother of a grown daughter, piped in, "It's not about him being fresh, honey. It's about you becoming stale."

Two passing CID agents sent them curious glances as Bodowski and the female clerks laughed. It was a good moment for the detective, who still felt bruised after his meeting with Palls. Back on point, he revealed to Nancy and Mavis what he had learned from the medical examiner, the mood in the room instantly sobering.

Surprised by the victim's odd condition, Nancy asked, "What sort of little girl has heavily callused hands and feet? Sounds rural, like a wild child."

"They say that poor girl's been hurt. You know, down there." Mavis motioned toward her groin.

The three looked at one another but said nothing. Nancy broke the silence by offering Bodowski a folder filled with recent complaints involving children.

"This is pretty meager, Steve. Melcher and the boys on canvass have called in two possibles—at least, they weren't tucked in during the wee hours this morning. We don't have a lot else to go on, so we'll just have to establish alibis on these two."

He scanned the file. "You're right. There's not much to go on here."

"Yeah, but look here on one of the night owls. This man's wife said he was out for several hours last night getting ready for an inspection that never happened." She pointed to the report on top. "Six months ago, a corporal over at the one-three-five Maintenance Battalion—same unit as our guy—was accused by this same man of possessing child pornography. It only came to light because the soldier took a swing at the accusing officer."

"All charges were dropped and the corporal rotated home last month. It says that in the margin notation. So what?"

"Here, look. Right here." She flipped over the page and tapped on the paper. "Read it and tell me that doesn't grab your attention."

"Damn. Three months later, the same officer accuses yet another soldier of possessing child pornography. It goes on to say he recommended to his battalion CO that the man in question be processed for theft and an undesirable discharge based on 'moral turpitude.'" Bodowski lifted his head. "What are the chances?"

"I don't know—a kiddie porn ring at the one-three-five? Or maybe something else, but to be honest, I'm not sure what."

"It says Martinson caught both cases—which is no help. He rotated back to the States two weeks ago. Hell, it's not much. Still, we'll need to get the officer's alibi for last night." He held the folder against his side and rubbed the palm of his hand. "I mean, some kind of who-knows connection to dirty kiddie pictures is a long way from a body in a ditch." He sighed and tossed the folder back onto the pile crowding the young woman's desk. "Palls wants to see the Army in the clear on this business. He'll get pretty hot if he thinks I'm turning over too many odd rocks looking for a suspect in a crime he's trying to dump."

Mavis jumped in. "Are you going to let a little thing like Palls get in your way? Did you and CYA have a blood-brother ceremony over breakfast this morning?"

"C'mon, I need something more substantial."

"Okay, how about this?" Nancy offered. "This is our other missing man for the night." She picked up a different folder, flipped several pages, and stuck it under his nose.

Bodowski read for a moment and laughed. "You see this black tape running down the page? You know what this means. Why bother handing this to me?"

"What about black tape? Fill me in," Mavis demanded.

Nancy beat him to the punch. "The rule got established before you transferred in. Black tape means you don't check them out. Either Palls or some other bigwig personally excluded this individual from further investigation."

"They can do that?"

"Not officially. But that won't make a lot of difference to Steve or any of the other agents if they find themselves in a headlock with the Provost Marshal because they ignored the tape."

"I still don't get it. Who the heck is so high and mighty he gets a free pass?"

"LeMarc. Specifically, Master Sergeant Cramer LeMarc," Bodowski said while thumbing through several pages of reports.

"No less than seven calls by neighbors to the MPs over the last year. Let's see, mostly noise—'sounds of screaming heard,' and, here's a good one: 'Caller says she witnessed subject, LeMarc, dragging wife out onto the second-floor landing. Swearing heard and wife beaten.'" He laughed after reading the report.

"What's so amusing about that?" Mavis asked. "It sounds awful."

Nancy jumped in for Bodowski, who continued to read to himself. "I think Dick Tracy here finds it amusing that the witness seemed to think the swearing was the most offensive part. Or maybe because this hero's got feet of clay."

Mavis turned up her palms. "A hero, Nancy? What are you talking about?"

"This guy, LeMarc? He won the Medal of Honor in Korea. One of the few who lived to tell about it and, even rarer, still on active duty. He's the post commander's pet. They sober him up and trot him out whenever the general wants to impress someone. That's what gives with the black tape. Untouchable."

Bodowski smiled. "Now I see why you flagged this one, gorgeous. Right here on the personnel excerpt—'Registered dependents, Anthony, Marc and Tamera.' The girl's birth date is listed as May 28, 1953."

"She's ten," Mavis piped.

Bodowski continued, "'9034 request for stateside rotation of dependent LeMarc, Tamera on file—9034A Incomplete.'" Lost in thought, he tapped on the folder. "Leave it to you to come up with this, Nancy."

"What?" asked Mavis. "Would one of you please tell me? I know I don't have a lot of experience with this kind of business. I swear, it's like you two are on your own private wavelength."

"What young Miss Burrows here figured out is that this girl, LeMarc's daughter, was scheduled for travel back to the States, but no record of her actual departure exists."

"Because of the incomplete form?"

"You've got to understand that a 9034A is serious business," Nancy said.

"Don't military forms go missing all the time?"

"Sure, Mavis," she said, "but there are forms and then there are *forms*."

"The beautiful lady is right on the money again," Bodowski said. "There's only two ways out of Germany for dependents: either a ship out of Bremerhaven or a plane from Rhein-Main up near Frankfurt. The folks at both places are as serious as a heart attack about matching 9034s with 9034As. Otherwise, there'd be a lot of troops pulling travel scams."

"So, maybe they decided at the last minute not to send the girl, that's all."

"I don't know about that, Mavis," Nancy said. "You go through the paperwork hoops it takes to arrange a move to the States and then nothing happens? Believe me, there's something fishy about this."

Bodowski nodded. "This report says, 'Complainant heard children screaming from subject's apartment—girl ran into stairwell.' Dated October 15. Okay, that's a little over a month ago, and the 9034 transport deadline is dated as of November 18—just the other day. Looking to move her out in a hurry." He scanned several pages. "No mention of the girl in the two succeeding reports." Leafing through the paperwork, he walked over to his own desk and sat with a thump. His swivel chair squeaked in protest. "Nancy, get the dental records on this girl. And please place a call to this woman, Paisley Blaine—the wife's sister. There's a phone number on the back page of the 9034. She's listed as the responsible party to receive the kid stateside."

"Thinking about checking out LeMarc?" Nancy asked.

"Why not. Nothing to lose but my stripes."

"Wait a minute," said Mavis. "What about the black tape?"

"I'll figure something out. You know, I saw this guy once at a brigade function. It looked like someone had dressed up a bulldog and pinned medals to its chest."

"Hey, cowboy." Nancy clapped her hands in anticipation. "Don't forget that first one we were looking at. There's no black tape on him. He's a freebie."

He looked at the topmost report. "Chief Warrant Officer Henry Nowak. Probably nothing there, but I'll give it a shot." He got up to leave. "Only a couple of hours and you flesh out these leads. You're quite the investigator, Nancy. You ought to be out in the field with us."

Straightening a pile of folders, she replied, "What? And get these new shoes dirty?"

As he reached the door, Bodowski asked, "Everything else garden variety?"

"Just a typical year's worth of spankings gone bad on a busy Army base. Watch out you don't get tangled up in that black tape."

He smacked the folder with his hand. "Never happen."

Watching the interplay, the older woman wondered how long the two had been sleeping together.

# Chapter Seventeen

## Out of the Mouths of Babes

"I think that's the spot."

"Where they found the kid?"

"Uh-huh. See?" Young Charlie Nowak stood at the edge of the ditch and pointed at the other side. The MPs had released the site an hour earlier. "It was a girl. I heard that at first recess. See, there's a bunch of footprints and stuff from all the MPs climbing around. Anyways, I saw it from my window. It's a long way from here, but I could still see everything this morning."

"You saw the kid? That's creepy." Marc LeMarc tucked his hands into his armpits and hunched his shoulders.

"No, I couldn't see her—but who cares? Let's jump over there and look at things just like they do in detective flicks."

Several children on their way home navigated around the two boys.

"This is stupid. You're going to get in trouble."

"Maybe with my mom a little, if I get my shoes dirty."

"What about your dad?"

"Nah. He doesn't give a damn what I do."

"All I know is, if my dad finds out I did something, I get the hell beat outta me."

"Okay, scaredy-cat." Charlie held up an arm, stopping two girls about to walk in front of him. He took a deep breath and rushed to the edge of the path. Yelling "Geronimo," he launched himself into the air, legs churning, and landed face first in the filthy rivulet at the bottom of the ditch. The two girls let out a little scream, and a few older boys coming along behind them stopped to laugh.

"Are you okay?" Marc shouted.

"Oh shit, shit!" His front soaked, Charlie staggered to his feet in the ankle-high water and scrambled up the path side of the ditch. He fumbled for purchase on the last foothold, and Marc grabbed his friend's forearm, tugging hard. Charlie flopped onto the path spraying muddy water onto two senior high boys.

"Dumb fucking fatass. Watch what you're doing!" The older boys stopped and brushed at their pants. "I ought to kick your stupid ass for this."

Marc stood frozen with fear. Charlie, dazed and lying on his stomach, could do no more than look up at the angry boys with a blank expression.

Tony LeMarc had witnessed the misadventure from some ways back and pushed past several children to reach his younger brother.

"Okay, everybody. Let's take it easy."

"You take it easy. These fucking idiots got me wet."

"Hey, what's wrong with you? There's girls here." Tony pushed Marc aside and stepped between the older boys and Charlie. "Let's just all go, all right? They're just kids."

"You getting in my face?"

After a beat, Tony answered, "Yeah, I guess so."

"Well let's see it."

"No problem." Marc's older brother moved to stand nose to nose with the belligerent young man. A moment of silent male posturing passed before the other boy's friend spoke.

"C'mon, Cal, we need to get to your place. This ain't worth it."

Cal smirked and backed away, mouthing a few choice parting words as the pair turned away.

"You all right, Marc?" Tony asked, shaking his younger brother's shoulder. Marc's lips quivered as he lowered his head to hide eyes filled with tears. Tony turned and helped Charlie to his feet. Recovering a bit, the young Nowak's face turned red.

"Look at me. I went swimming." He glanced around, hoping his self-deprecating humor would somehow make the whole affair seem less humiliating.

"You going to be okay?" Tony asked Marc. "I got to run ahead and meet somebody."

Marc wiped his tears on his sleeve and nodded.

"You're sure?" Marc nodded again. "Okay." Turning to go, Tony told Charlie, "Jesus, try to keep out of trouble, will you?" and then turned and ran down the path.

Marc picked up Charlie's books, and the two began the trek homeward, slowed to a crawl by their embarrassment and the discomfort of Charlie's wet clothes. For a few minutes they walked in silence, enduring the occasional taunts of their passing classmates, until they were the last two on the path and Marc found the will to open his mouth once more.

"Tony's the best brother a guy could have."

"I wish I had a big brother," Charlie mumbled.

"I miss my sister," Marc said.

"I met her once. Tammy, right?"

"Tamera, but she likes Tammy."

"Where is she? I never see her."

"Don't know." Marc sighed.

"Don't know? She doesn't live at home anymore?"

"Nah. I went with Mrs. Carter across the hall to go shopping at the PX a couple days ago. You know, my mom doesn't go there anymore. Anyway, when we got back, Tammy was gone. My mom told me she'd moved away. Then my dad came home and started to act real crazy. I didn't know what was wrong with him, besides the usual."

"Wow."

"Yeah. And Tony sassed him about something, and my dad almost killed him. You should see his stomach. It's all bruised up."

"I don't get it. She's just a kid. Why would she go away? Was she in trouble or retarded or something?"

"I don't want to talk about this anymore, Charlie."

"Why not?"

The boy shivered. "Just don't ask, okay? Every time I ask someone at home, I get into big trouble."

"Okay." They neared Charlie's apartment building. "Hey, you want to hang out over at my place for a while?"

"Sure." Marc had no desire to rush home.

"You know, I used to have a sister," Charlie mumbled.

"Yeah?"

"I don't remember her much. Her name was Susan, and she died when I was just a little kid."

"Gee, that's too bad."

"Yeah. My mom told me she was only five years old."

"How'd she die?"

"I don't remember exactly, but it was some kind of accident where she got twisted up or something and couldn't breathe."

# Chapter Eighteen

## Autopsy, Anyone?

Bodowski drove the short distance from the Provost Marshal's office to the base hospital. A heavy downpour began as he pulled into the parking lot. He sat in his car and watched as shallow rapids developed in the drainage depression of the lot. Gripping the steering wheel, he rested his chin on his hands and thought about the case. Something about the condition of the body was nagging him, but he could not put his finger on it. Despite misgivings about the eccentric pathologist, he thought a closer examination might help. The rain lessened and the runoff drained. He broke from his car and ran to the stairwell leading to the basement.

Upon entering the morgue, he noticed the young girl's body was no longer on the main dissecting table in the middle of the lab. He stood at the empty table tapping on the steel surface. He noticed Captain Larson scribbling away at his desk in the far corner of the cavernous room.

"Hey, Doc?"

"Huh?" Surprised, Larson stood up as if caught in a mischievous undertaking. Recognizing Bodowski, he smiled and shouted, "Hey yourself. I'm glad you came back." He trotted across the lab to greet his visitor.

"I had a few more questions." He waved at the dissecting table. "Where's the girl?"

"Germans came and got her. Major Palls called me just a minute after you left and told me to wrap up everything and get it ready for the Polizei. Man, they got here lickety-split. Wow, I said to myself, everything's happening at lightning speed. What's the deal, Detective?" Larson lit an unfiltered cigarette.

Bodowski, too, wondered at the extreme urgency displayed by both Palls and the Germans.

"Oh, yeah." Larson exhaled a billow of smoke and picked some tobacco from the tip of his tongue. "You should have seen who came by to get her. I don't just mean the usual troglodytes in white coats. No. Some member of the master race growling orders at them. Talked down to me like I was an idiot."

"Let me guess. Gestapo impersonator, looks a little like me but not as handsome?"

"Ha ha. You bet. He was waving a release order signed by Major Palls. The son of a bitch was straight out of central casting—black leather everything. He looked like one of those old posters for Hilter's SS, and he spoke English so well I thought he was going to start correcting my grammar—British accent, too. I felt like I was in a movie." Larson ran a hand through his thinning hair and shrugged. "So what brings you back, Detective? Agent? What do they call you guys anyway?"

"Bodowski will do." Searching the room, he said, "To be honest, I'm not sure what brought me back. I just knew I had to have another look at the body. Did you learn any more before the krauts grabbed her?" He glanced at the empty dissecting table. "Did you get a chance to match up any cut marks with the Boy Scout knife?"

"What knife?"

"Didn't an MP, a guy named Slidell—didn't he get a knife to you? I sent him over."

"No."

"You been here the whole time, Doc?"

"Yeah, I haven't gone anywhere since you were here last time."

"I'll be damned." He knew the MP understood the urgency of getting the knife to Larson.

"They took most everything else, but I still got the carbons to my report. You want me to get them for you?" Before Bodowski could answer, Larson ran to his desk, snatched the folder, and returned, dragging on his cigarette. Bodowski thought of a steam engine as he watched little puffs of smoke trail behind the doctor.

Larson opened the folder and presented it to the detective with a crooked grin. "Got the exact cause of death." Tapping on the page, he continued, "Got it right here. The Germans didn't even ask. They just kiped the body. They took my preliminary findings and ran. I asked if they wanted my final write-up of the preliminary examination, but Mr. High-and-Mighty just told me to send it along whenever I got the paperwork completed. He was in a big hurry to get the body—but not so much for the report. Don't that beat all?"

Bodowski answered while reading. "The Germans want to perform the autopsy in this case." Peering up, he detected a faint look of disappointment on Larson's face. "It's not that they wouldn't trust your findings. It's just the krauts' way of doing things." Referring to the report, he asked, "A Ping-Pong ball? You sure about that?"

"Two Ping-Pong balls, to be exact. Oops, I guess I only wrote down one. Oh, well." The pathologist produced a small evidence bag from his lab coat pocket. "They're right here, or what's left of them. I 'forgot' to give them to the Germans."

"She suffocated to death on two Ping-Pong balls? That's hard to swallow, Doc."

Larson suppressed nervous laughter at the unintended pun. "One ball. She needed just one to choke to death. Two—that's how you know it's murder. I figure an older child like her could down a single Ping-Pong ball and get it caught in her throat somehow, but two? That defies imagination."

"Well, Doc, chopping up her face—post mortem, right?"

Larson nodded.

"That's also a good indicator of murder."

"You're a card, Bodowski." He blew smoke out the side of his mouth and smiled.

"In any case, good work, Doc. Thank you."

He grinned. "At your service, Agent." He dropped his cigarette and smashed it out with his foot.

Bodowski reached over and extracted the evidence bag from the doctor's hand. "Got to be going, Doc. Do me a favor and don't say anything to the krauts about this. If they read your prelim, they'll figure it out for themselves. Anything else you want to tell me?"

"Sure, lots. Of course, it's all in there, in the carbons. Also, I got another set of carbons in case I need to refer to anything. Think I'll need to do anything else on this? I got plenty of time. You'd figure I'd be busy. I mean, I may be the only pathologist for the whole division, but people don't die every day—at least not ones needing an autopsy." He sighed.

"I would say I'll try to send some business your way, but that just seems like the wrong sentiment, Doc."

"Toodleloo," Larson called out as the detective stepped into the hallway.

Once outside, Bodowski looked up into the falling rain and wondered if the sun would ever make an appearance. From his vehicle, he radioed the CID office and requested someone get Battalion to track down Slidell.

# Chapter Nineteen

## Sifting for Nuggets

"You keep blowing that smoke at me and there'll be another body to go along with the one we found."

"Sorry, man." Melcher swiveled his head and blew a stream of smoke away from the driver's side window, open so he and Bodowski could talk through it. A light rain popped against the back of his raincoat. He kept the cigarette at his side, cupping his hand to protect it from the weather. "Who the hell kills somebody with Ping-Pong balls anyway?

Tapping on the steering wheel, Bodowski looked down the path to the spot where they had found the body. "That MP, Slidell? He didn't show with the knife."

"What?"

"Doc Larson said he never saw the man."

"Are you tracking him?"

"I called it in to the head shed."

Melcher took a short drag off his cigarette and exhaled toward the gray clouds blanketing the sky. "That lazy jackass is probably yukking it up at the snack bar. If I see him, I'm going to kick his ass into his shoulder blades."

"It's my fault." Bodowski banged on the steering wheel. "I should have delivered it myself, or had one of the investigators do it." He adjusted the rearview mirror. "I need to stop thinking I'm still with the Tacoma PD with a decent chain of evidence."

"Here we go again. 'When I was a detective with the real police—'"

"Okay, okay. Look, I wanted to mention that both those guys you fed us are worth a look. I'm headed over to talk to LeMarc's wife as soon as we break this up. Have you spoken to her?"

"No, one of the other investigators took her statement. This is the drunk sergeant, right?"

"You've heard of him. He's a Medal of Honor winner."

"Oh, yeah. Sure. The general's champion show dog, pride of the muckety-mucks." Melcher coughed and smashed out his cigarette.

The rain was picking up. Bodowski shook his head. "The water's coming in through the window. Get in the car."

Melcher obliged, running around the radio car and jumping into the passenger seat. "Damn, man. I hate this place."

"This walkway is used all day, Mel. Right up until dark."

"Yeah." He warmed his hands on the heater vent. "It gets used at night, too, when the German workers from the Kaserne head home." Melcher gave him a look. "I can tell something's rumbling around in your noggin. So give already."

"I'm just thinking about the hoses. Get anything on that?"

"No. I had them checked out like you said. The hoses on the big apartment buildings hadn't been used in a while." He made a circular motion with his finger. "Wet on the outside from the rain but dry inside."

"What about the field-grade officers?"

"Most of those hoses have already been removed."

"Okay."

"C'mon, man. What are you thinking?"

"The person who dumped the body knows this area—knows how the path is used." Bodowski twisted almost sideways and stretched his arm behind Melcher. "She was killed here, in the housing area."

"What makes you so sure? Access to the dump site?"

"More than that." Leaning over, Bodowski pressed, "Who in their right mind is going to chance discovery by driving a body into the housing area during a readiness drill?"

"They only check vehicles going out, not in."

"Right. If the suspect knows that, it goes a long way toward proving it's a GI, or at least someone familiar with procedure."

"Yeah, I get that. That's good. We checked the perimeter while you were off having fun with Palls and the doc. No way could someone hump that dead weight all this way from across the highway. Besides, the guy would be exposed that whole time. You know, the killer probably didn't have much time, else he would've dumped the body somewhere else. No, wait. Maybe he wanted us to find her. Or, no, that doesn't make sense."

"At this point, I don't know what to think, either." Bodowski straightened in his seat and placed his hands on the wheel. "Except that I'm pretty sure the girl was killed here."

"Palls all spun up over this?"

"Like you wouldn't believe." The detective pulled a handkerchief and blew his nose. "Little fucker's bent out of shape."

"Did he give you the colonel-must-get-his-star speech?"

"Ever know him to open his mouth *without* adding that somewhere in the conversation?"

"What I don't get about Palls is his trying to stay in Germany for another tour." Melcher produced a cigarette from his shirt pocket and waved it around. "All this time, I thought Palls would jump through a hoop of fire if it got him moved up the ladder. Staying here isn't much of a promotion."

Bodowski glared at him. "Do you want me to shoot you?"

"What? Oh." Melcher put the cigarette back into his pocket. "It's a habit."

"Well, wanting to stay a while longer on station isn't all that unusual. Look at Mavis, for example. She's trying to extend for at least a year."

"Hey, genius—it's because here, she's one of the few single gals swimming around in a sea of unmarried guys."

Bodowski ignored him, refocusing on the rain. "The canvass is just about done, right? Once it's over, how about you snoop around the MPs who manned the checkpoint on the readiness drill? And maybe step up the search for our guy, Slidell, and the missing knife."

"Consider it done, Kemosabe. What are you up to?"

"I'm going to interview LeMarc's wife, if she's still at home."

"So what's got you so interested in this LeMarc character? All our leads are weak."

"History of violence—lots of complaints. A wise homicide dick once told me that the best tell for a murder suspect was a history of violence." He smiled and added, "Of course, there are some exceptions to that."

"Then why not talk to LeMarc straight out? I wouldn't go round about."

"Well, you know me. I have to work from the outside in. I want to see what others have to say before I tip my hand to the one I'm looking at."

"You want me to talk to the other one on the list? Shit. I can't remember his name." Melcher retrieved his notebook, but Bodowski waved him off.

"No, not now. We can take our time on that one. Some business about kiddie porn, but he's the complainant. It's probably nothing. I looked at the yellow sheets, and there weren't any tickets on him. We need to concentrate on this LeMarc character until we can work up some other suspects."

"What about the krauts?"

"I'm not going to deal with them. I don't give a damn what Palls wants."

"You need some help with LeMarc?" Melcher slipped the notebook back into his suit coat pocket.

"No, I'll take care of it." He stared out the front window of the car.

"Now what?"

"There's some confusion with travel forms and LeMarc's daughter. I think I'll approach this in a different way, in case the wife hasn't heard yet about what happened out here."

"How?"

"I'll pretend to be a clerk or something—hell, anything but

a cop. I want to get straight information."

"You pulled that kind of shit all the time during the taskforce last year—pretending to be somebody else. I have to admit, you got a lot of good info, but it's way out of procedure. You get caught pretending not to be CID, it could mean your badge. Melcher straightened. Hey, wait a minute. LeMarc's got the Medal of Honor, right? I can't believe Palls or Colonel Fulbright or some other tight-ass hasn't slapped some black tape on his file."

"They have."

"And you're still going to look into him?" Laughing, Melcher said, "Jesus. You won't just lose your shield. You'll be at the bottom of a mountain of shit. I would like to officially withdraw my offer to help in the LeMarc interview."

"Courageous stand on your part."

"Hey, don't be an asshole. I like my Army career."

The two men sat for a moment.

"You're off tomorrow, aren't you, Mel?"

"It ain't exactly off. I have to testify on that robbery case down at I Corps. No way I can wrangle out of a court appearance. Don't worry, I'll see you bright and early on Friday."

"What about finding Slidell?"

"Like I said, don't worry. I've got it handled. I was planning to slough it off to some working stiffs anyhow."

"I appreciate you letting me take the lead on this."

"You'll just owe me a gigantic favor. Of course, with you cutting through the black tape, you'll probably need a few favors of your own."

# Chapter Twenty

## Blood from a Stone

"What do you want?" Monica LeMarc peered over the chain on the apartment door.

"Mrs. LeMarc?" Bodowski asked. "I just have a few questions—just some Army business."

A musty odor wafted into the hallway. The woman looked haggard, beaten down.

"A few questions, that's all." He flipped his ID open and shut. "Master sergeant at home?"

"You're not supposed to be here. You're not supposed to question him." She checked behind her. "I don't want any trouble."

"Oh, I don't see how this would cause trouble. It's only an administrative matter—just paperwork. Army bureaucracy and all."

"Not some complaint? Not about the noise? You're an MP, aren't you? Why aren't you wearing a uniform?"

"Do I look like an MP?" He opened his arms as if modeling a suit, careful not to expose his shoulder holster.

"He's not at home. He went to be in some parade. I don't know when he'll get back. You should call his CO."

He sensed she was about to shut the door. "Maybe you can help me out." Trying his best to sound innocuous, he added, "I don't need your husband. You can help me clear up this little paperwork matter. What do you say?"

She chewed on her lip for a moment. "All right, go ahead."

"It's kind of a list." Bodowski laughed. "I've got no choice here but to get these questions answered." Bending forward, he spoke in confidence, "My hind end's on the line if I don't get this paperwork snafu fixed. Can I come in for just a minute?" He straightened. "If you want, I could get a lady from our office to come down, if me being alone here with you is a problem."

Mrs. LeMarc closed the door and unhooked the chain. Clutching the worn house robe close to her neck, she opened the door halfway and motioned for him to enter. Grinning, he squeezed through the door.

There was trash everywhere. Dirty dishes covered the stained furniture, and several ashtrays overflowed with old butts. The place stunk of rot. A large radio console sitting in the middle of the living room struck him as odd. Leaving the apartment door open, she positioned herself to block access to the hallway leading to the bedrooms.

"What do you want?"

"Just need to verify—let's see." He moved toward her while thumbing through the reports in the folder Nancy had given him. "Ah, yes. I need to verify completion of a 9034A." Standing only a few feet from the battered woman, he observed the nicks and scars on her face and the bruises running down her neck.

"What's a ninety, what?" She eyed him.

"9034A, ma'am." Holding his smile, his eyes darted between her and the folder. He stole a few glances down the hallway. To his left, he observed a single photograph in a metal frame sitting on a windowsill. It showed the LeMarcs holding their three children in a close embrace. The little girl had pigtails.

"What is that? Is that an official form of some kind?" She wrung her hands and then hid them behind her.

Bodowski recognized the signs of someone who lived in fear of a violent partner. Too often, both in his personal life and as a detective, he had dealt with chronically abused women. Feigning a coughing attack, the detective held up a hand. He strained between fits to ask her for water.

"Well, okay. You stay right there."

She drifted into the kitchen. The instant she rounded the corner, he walked down the hall, coughing as he went. To the left sat an empty room, save for a broken table tennis setup with several Ping-Pong balls scattered over the floor. The room across the hall contained bunk beds surrounded by a sea of paper and fetid organic trash. He moved toward the rooms at the end of the hallway. The open door to his left revealed another bedroom, painted pink—he assumed it was the girl's room. Large, soaking stains covered the bare mattress on the single bed. The stench of urine helped motivate another phony coughing attack. He ran back toward the living room just in time for Mrs. LeMarc to catch him coming out of the hallway.

"Get out. Get out of my house!"

"Okay, okay, I'm going." Moving backward toward the front door, he added, "But I still need to settle the issue of the 9034A."

"What were you doing down there? I'm going to call the MPs." Mrs. LeMarc clutched at her house robe and shook the glass of water at him, spilling it onto the bare wooden floor.

"I'm so sorry." He backed up to the open apartment door. "I was just looking for the bathroom. I'm sorry. I wasn't snooping." Managing to tighten his throat, he choked out, "Darn dust allergies. You're sure I can't use your bathroom? I'll just drink from the tap."

She hesitated, then offered him the glass.

He took it and gulped a mouthful. "Oh, thank you. Thank you so much. Sometimes I get a cough and I think my darn head's about to come off."

Mrs. LeMarc took the glass and pressed it to her chest. Vacantly, she asked, "You'll stay there, right? You won't go back down there?"

"Oh gosh, no. I'm so sorry." He opened the folder. "I should have asked before roaming around looking for the bathroom. So anyway, maybe you can help me clear up this business?"

"What business?" The woman shuffled to the sofa and sat upright on the edge, staring at the radio.

The sudden change in her manner convinced him she would be of little help unraveling the mystery of the missing paperwork. Still, he had to give it a shot. Checking his report, he said, "You filled out a form 9034 so Tamera could go back to the States. Well, the 9034A didn't get stamped. Where did she leave from? Rhein-Main or Bremerhaven?"

Still staring at the radio, she answered, "Tammy."

"Pardon?"

"She likes Tammy."

"Okay, sure. Did Tammy leave on a plane or a boat?" Her bathrobe fell open, exposing the telltale green and yellow discolorations of bruises on the mend. "You know when your husband will be home?"

"What?" She did not move.

"Home. When will he get home?"

"I don't know." She spoke in a monotone and continued to stare at the radio. "I never know."

"He didn't come home until this morning, did he? He stayed out all night, right?"

"Yes. All night." Her voice trailed off as if in a trance.

"When did he get home this morning? Do you remember?"

In a sudden turnabout of behavior, she stood and faced him with narrowed eyes. "You're not a clerk. Why are you asking me these questions? Someone came around today and asked me about Cramer. Are you a policeman?"

"Yes, ma'am. I—"

"Get out." She covered her breasts with both arms and pointed at the door with her chin. "Get out. Do you hear me?"

Backing out in haste, he shut the door. Pausing on the second-floor landing, he wrote down everything he could remember. He underlined *Ping-Pong balls*. An older, heavyset German woman, her woolen dress protected by a thick blue apron, trudged up the stairs. The white, knee-length stockings did little to hide the network of large veins bulging from her calves.

"*Guten Tag*." He shoved the notebook into his coat pocket.

"Ya," the woman puffed. She stopped in front of LeMarc's apartment and dug through her large canvas purse, producing a key.

"*Entschuldigen Sie mich. Sprechen Sie* English?"

"Ya sir, of course."

"You're going in there, ma'am?"

"Ya, I speak with Frau LeMarc." Her expression left no doubt she did not want to pursue the conversation.

Undeterred, he produced his badge. The old woman startled and dropped the key onto the concrete landing. Both of them went to retrieve it, neither taking their eyes off the other. The woman radiated foreboding. Bodowski understood. The ordinary German citizen still remembered the Gestapo. He got to the key first, hesitating only a moment before dropping it into her hand.

"I just want to ask, how is it that you know Mrs. LeMarc?"

Clearing her throat, she responded, "I clean for her."

"Oh." He laughed a little and added, "Beg your pardon, ma'am, but I don't think so."

"No, not anymore. I have clean for her before, ya. Now that monster drives me away. *Alkoholiker*!" She dry spat on the landing.

"He try to hurt you? Did he hit you?"

Trembling, she had trouble getting the key into the lock. "I go now, okay?"

"How do you know he's not in there right now?"

"No, he is not. The auto is not in the parking lot." After considerable effort, she connected with the door lock.

"What's your name?"

"Frau Mueller."

"First name?"

"Anna." Exasperated, she pleaded, "May I go now? My *Freund*, Frau LeMarc, she needs me."

"One more question. When's the last time you saw Tammy?"

Giving the detective a quizzical look, she answered, "Oh, the *kleines Mädchen*? I don't know." She shrugged, adding,

"Maybe last week."

"Okay, ma'am. Thanks."

She rushed into the apartment, closing the door behind her. The sound of the deadbolt echoed through the hallway. Bodowski retrieved his notebook and wrote her name in the section titled *LeMarc*, adding, *Cleaning lady might know more—don't push too hard.*

# Chapter Twenty-One

## Tacoma, Washington: Thursday, August 22, 1940

Young Steve Bodowski squinted at the hot August sun while waiting for the slow-moving train to reach the crossing. Sweat poured in rivulets along his thin, bare arms and onto his fingers, lubricating the handlebar grips of his bicycle. Worn down from hauling groceries since dawn, he regretted not taking the other way home from work.

He felt the deep vibration in his stomach as the steel monster rumbled toward him, dragging dozens of empty boxcars through the nearly deserted Tacoma waterfront. Despite his exhaustion, something about the train excited him. A vague notion of freedom swirled through his mind as he imagined the black locomotive racing across the open plains of the West in the dark of night, howling at the moon and stars.

He shouted greetings to the engineer sitting in the behemoth's darkened eye socket as it lumbered past the paint-blistered crossing gates. The unshaven man turned and waved at the eleven-year-old boy. He bent an ear to demonstrate the futility of yelling against the roar of the engine. The boy didn't know why he had shouted at the man. He only knew it was something everybody did.

A few minutes passed before the red caboose had cleared the crossing, prompting a man in greasy overalls and a torn undershirt to emerge from the gatehouse on the other side of the tracks. Grunting, he raised both gates by pushing on their concrete counterweights.

Steve wiped his hands on his thin cotton shirt and walked the bicycle across the tracks. Once past the second gate, he jumped on the bike and pedaled along the waterfront, bucking over potholes as he rode past towering grain silos and rusting steel warehouses. The twin blows of a dockworkers' strike and the Great Depression had left the port in a state of unnatural quiet. A few freighters lay moored at the piers, their cargoes rotting as the seawater ate away at the hulls. Steve imagined he was passing by a graveyard, and that the handful of strikers camped out in front of the fenced dockyards were mourners.

Turning onto McCarver Street, the tired boy began the long, slow climb home. Standing on the pedals got him only so far. He dismounted and pushed his old bike up the last five blocks—the steepest leg of the journey. Still huffing from the ordeal, he coasted along North 26th until he reached his house, a small clapboard two-story originally painted marine blue. Neglect and weather had left the saddest house on the block a dirty gray. As he passed through the sprung gate of the picket fence, he squinted to recall the way the house had looked when he was small enough to sit in his sleepers by the picture window and watch the neighborhood children head off to school.

"Steve? Are you out there? I thought I heard you."

The sound of his mother's voice made his chest feel warm. "Yeah, Mom. I got a big surprise." Despite his exhausting labor and the long trip home, a second wind had come along to fill his sails. Setting his bicycle against the dingy white latticework, he ran up the porch and threw open the torn screen door. The crooked thing squealed on its hinges as it slammed against the frame.

"Honey, please be careful. You're going to bust that door."

Mimi Bodowski, thin and raven-haired with pale green eyes that lit up at the sight of her only son, hunched over her ironing board in the tiny living room. Cluttered with hand-me-down furniture, the family gathering place had become unrecognizable beneath piles of clean laundry. One side of the room was dedicated to tall mounds of wrinkled clothes, each strata of ownership separated by a large piece of butcher paper with an attached ticket. Tightly bound cubes of ironed clothes crowded the side of the room closest to the front door.

Steve rushed in and faced his mother across the ironing board. She moved the iron aside and bent over, pecking him on the lips. Steve adored his mother but wondered if it was time to stop kissing her so much. He never saw his friends kiss their mothers. Of course, he was always standing there with them at the time.

"What's the big surprise?" she asked.

"I got a dollar tip from a customer." He pulled the wrinkled bill from his front pants pocket and placed it on the ironing board. Beaming, he added, "What do you think of that?"

A smile grew on his mother's drawn face. "My goodness," she announced, "that's wonderful." She smoothed out the crumpled bill, sprinkled a little water on it and picked up the iron.

"What are you doing, Mom?"

With a few deft strokes, she flattened the bill. Holding it up, she said, "There—fresh from the mint." They laughed. Her countenance changed. "Who gave you this?" She set the bill down.

"Some rich guy, honest."

"I believe you." She coaxed him with her eyes.

"Mr. Sheldraw let me keep it."

"So, you showed it to your boss?"

"He told me if I got any big tips that he wanted to know about it." The young man slid the bill over the surface of the ironing board as if it were a paper toboggan. "You know he said that to me, before."

"How come he let you keep it?" She turned, exposing a large bruise on her neck, and grabbed another piece of laundry. He could not remember a time when his mother did not carry a mark.

"He always lets me keep my tips. He just wants to know who the nobs are."

"Why did this man give you so much money? What did he want?"

"Nothing, Mom. I never been there before. He had a big house and his maid answered the door. She paid me for the groceries and started to give me a nickel tip, but the man came to the door. He was an English guy all dressed up with a funny tie and everything. He talked just like Ronald Coleman."

"Okay, slow down."

"He looked at me and gave me a big smile and fished a buck out of his pocket and handed it to me."

"That's it?"

"Honest Injun." He crossed his heart. "Oh—he said something like I must be a 'street urchin.' Yeah, that's what he said." The young boy had sensed the term might be an insult, but he took the money anyway.

Mimi's face reddened. She looked away from her son and pretended to sort through some laundry. "I'll put the dollar away for you someplace safe." She folded the dollar and slipped it into her brassiere.

"Pop won't take my dollar, will he? You don't have to hide it from him." He said it even though he knew better.

"He takes everything else." She spun and blurted out, "Everything!" Grimacing, she steadied herself on the ironing board.

"Are you okay, Mom?" Steve worried about the latest injury to her head. Her thick black hair concealed a knot on the crown of her skull.

"I'm sorry I said that, Steve."

"It's okay." His mother's pain made him anxious. "Is there anything I can do for you, Mom?"

"No, I—"

"Mimi." June Blanchard, neighbor and friend, cut her off mid-sentence. She had opened the screen door and was leaning into the entryway. "I got a call."

"A call?"

"Yeah." The middle-aged woman looked at the boy and hesitated.

"Go ahead," Mimi said. "He sees and hears everything anyway."

"Donald called and said your man's over at the Lucky Shamrock. Forgive me, dear, but I've got to get back." She left.

"Oh no." Mimi covered her mouth. She had forgotten it was payday at the shoe store where her husband worked. His stop at the dilapidated Irish tavern meant falling another week behind on the bills. Untying her apron, she bent over to face her son. "Go upstairs and look after your little sister. I'll be back as soon as I can." She unplugged the iron and placed it on the brick mantle above the blocked fireplace.

Helen, Steve's six-year-old sister, appeared midway down the stairs, her little face pressed between the white balusters.

"Go back upstairs. Go back to your room, dear. Steve will stay with you."

"Where are you going, Mommy?" Her voice trembled.

"I have to get your father." She exhaled and frowned. "I have to get him, now."

"Don't go, Mommy." Steve saw a frightened prisoner holding onto the bars of her cell.

"I'll go, Mom. I'll get him." Careful never to confront his father, Steve weighed the risk to his mother. "Pop almost never hits me."

He surprised himself with his words. An awkward silence fell over them all.

"I'm sorry, Mom."

Stroking his cheek, Mimi offered him a weak smile. "You're growing up. You want to protect me." Biting her lip, she added, "But you're too small yet. You go upstairs with Helen. I'll be back soon."

"He won't hit me, you'll see. I'll go get him. I'll stand by the door and make him come home with me." The boy considered himself expert at escaping his father's wrath, not yet old enough to realize his only defense was his invisibility. In the drunken man's presence, both children were quiet as frightened mice. "I'm going to go."

"No." Mimi closed her eyes and sighed. "Stay here and watch your sister." Opening her eyes in time to see the screen door swing shut, she shouted, "Steve! Come back here this instant!"

By the time she reached the door, he was already out the front gate and standing on his pedals, racing toward 6th Avenue.

"Oh, my God."

She would never catch him on foot. Folding her arms, she prayed for the best.

Determination drove Steve to the door of the Lucky Shamrock tavern, his father's favorite hangout, housed in a sad green building on the corner of 6th and Pine. Leaning his bicycle against the painted brick wall, he stood for a moment holding the handlebars. After gathering his courage, he stepped in front of the door and waited. It was a difficult threshold to cross. When the door burst open, releasing an inebriated sailor into the street, the boy ran and slipped through door before it shut. He sought to blend into the woodwork of the smoky room, hoping that his eyes would adjust to the dark and allow him to spot his father before someone tossed him out on his ear. The fog of cigarette smoke helped keep him obscured, but it burned his eyes and made him cough. He went unnoticed by the crowd of boisterous drinkers and their harried servers. Then he caught sight of the unmistakable wire brush of brown hair and the lightweight gray sports coat. Perched at the bar, his back to the door, thirty feet of drunken revelry separated the boy from his unpredictable parent. Frightened in spite of himself, Steve considered running away, but a sense of duty kept him glued to the narrow floorboards. Fear and indecision left the boy in limbo and staring dumbly at his father's back.

"Hey, Sam—that your kid?" The man sitting next to his father had spotted the boy. The short, ugly fellow with a pockmarked face who lived at the end of their street regularly drove his drunken father home.

"What?"

"Turn around, look."

Turning his head, bloodshot eyes blinking against the smoke, Samuel Bodowski snorted, "Yeah. That's one of my bitch's pups."

"Christ, man—that's no way to talk about your boy."

"Ain't worth a shit, Frank." He gulped a shot and banged on the counter for another.

"Maybe you should go see what he wants. Something could be wrong at home."

"Something's always wrong at home." Sam took the shot from the bartender's hand and drained it in a single motion. "Hell, I don't even know if he's really my kid. That bitch will open her legs for anyone."

"C'mon, Sam. That ain't true. Mimi's a good woman. You know that."

"Fuck her and fuck you, buddy."

"Fine. Be an asshole. You can find your own way home." His friend reached for his beer.

"Fine. Okay, fine." Standing, he scooped up his cigarettes and change, spilling some of both onto the greasy floor. "Who needs you, anyway?" He cursed the patrons as he staggered through the obstacle course of crowded tables.

A shiver of fear hit the boy, but he didn't panic. Rocking back and forth on his toes like an infielder waiting for the crack of the bat, Steve ran his tongue over his gums.

The rawboned man with hollow cheeks bent over close and, in a mocking tone, asked, "Your mother send you?"

Recoiling from his father's acrid breath, Steve took a step backward. "No, Pop. I came here to bring you home." He balled his hands into fists to keep his fingers from trembling.

"All by your lonesome, huh?" He seized the boy by the arm and walked him out the tavern door into the brilliant sunlight. "Jesus, Mary, and Joseph." The drunkard squinted and lowered his head. "It's still the middle of the fucking day." Shoving the boy several feet down the sidewalk, he shielded his eyes and said, "Go tell your mother I'm coming home, but not because she sent you to do her dirty work." He belched and blinked several times. "It's because I'm ready to come. You go tell her that, you little shit." Swiveling his head side to side, he lost his balance but caught himself on the wall. "Where's Frank? Where's the car? Oh, right. Fuck him. I'll walk." He staggered along the sidewalk in the general direction of his house, stopping every few yards to steady himself.

The boy hopped on his bike and raced home. Running into the house, he found his mother in the kitchen stowing the ironing board. Gasping, he said, "Mom. I found him at the tavern. He's walking home."

"Oh, good Lord." She wiped her hands on her apron. "You catch your breath." She hugged him around the shoulder. "You found him, did you? How far gone is he?"

"He seems pretty bad. He'll be here soon. You know it's not that far."

"Of course, I know." She patted him on the arm and said, "You go upstairs with your sister, now."

"I don't want to. I'll stay down here with you."

"I'll be all right. He'll be a little sore that we got him out of there, but he'll be happy when he sobers up and sees there's some money left. At least, I hope there's some left. Anyway, you go up now."

"No, Mom." Pulling away from her, Steve said, "I'm going to stay right here." He had summoned up the courage to go to the tavern, and now he would take the next step and be present while his mother dealt with the vicious alcoholic.

"We don't have time to argue." She picked up a large spoon and shook it at him. "Now, you march right upstairs."

Steve backed away and crossed his hands in front of him.

"Oh no, no, no." Mimi threw the spoon to the side and gathered up her boy, hugging him. "I'm so sorry, I would never hurt you." She kissed him on top of the head. "Never."

A car door slammed and they heard Sam Bodowski shout, "Thanks for the ride, bub."

She held her son at arm's length. "Go upstairs, now."

He pulled away and ran into the living room just as his father stumbled up the front steps and threw open the screen door.

"Okay, I'm home. What's the big goddamned emergency?" He noticed the boy standing with his back to a tall stack of ironed laundry. "Well, lookee who's here."

His wife rushed into the room, holding a rolling pin.

"That for me, old girl?"

She managed a smile and asked, "Are you feeling all right? Did you have a hard day?" She glanced at her son.

"Oh, you don't have to act nice just because he's here with us. You just want the money, don't you?"

Modulating her tone, she answered, "It's important, Sam. We need to pay the bills."

"We need to pay the bills," he mocked.

"Sam, please take it easy."

"Don't get your girdle in a bunch. I just want to lie down, that's all." Holding his hand to his chest, he burped. "Whew, I'm not doing so good." He slumped against the doorframe.

Mimi looked at her son. "Why don't you help me get your father upstairs?"

Uncertain what to do, the boy reached out and took his father by the wrist.

"There you go." She took his other hand. "I know you don't feel well, Sam. We'll just help you up the stairs."

Sam straightened and struck his son across the face with the back of his hand. The boy reeled, collapsing backward and striking his head against an end table.

Mimi screamed and ran toward her fallen child. From her room, little Helen echoed her scream. Crouching next to her boy, Mimi pointed the rolling pin at her husband and shouted, "You rotten bastard. How dare you strike my son?"

"Your son." He leaned in and sneered, "That's right—your son, not mine." With that, he snatched the wooden utensil from her outstretched hand and swung it like a bat. The blow landed full against her temple sending her sprawling on the worn carpet. Mimi lay motionless. "Whore. Get up, damn it."

The boy opened his eyes, but the entire world had narrowed to the edges of his blurry vision. Something pressed against his face, but he couldn't lift his arms to move it. Then it was gone. Blinking, he could see a person sitting next to him. A body convulsed in waves. Slowly, he realized his father was shaking his mother by the collar of her housecoat, cursing at her, demanding she respond. Eyes shut and mouth open, the insensible woman seemed to agree to every command as her head flopped against the violent motion. Powerless to move, the boy watched as his father hurled a final curse and let her go. Mimi fell backward, her head smashing against the floor. Rifling through her pockets, the man discarded keys and buttons, keeping the few coins he found. He reached into her shirt and filched the ironed dollar bill. Smirking, he stuck it into his pocket.

Steve tried to say something. His mouth moved without emitting sound. His arms were as dead as old sticks.

The angry drunk stood and nudged the poor woman with his foot. She did not respond. He mumbled something and then staggered out the front door, steadying himself against the wall as he went.

The world spun around the boy as he slipped into unconsciousness.

# Chapter Twenty-Two

## Remembrance of Things Past

The refrigerator shuddered as the condenser came to life. Bodowski, seated at the small kitchen table, mourned the loss of his concentration as he shouted toward the bedroom of the efficiency apartment. "Jesus, Nancy. You've got to get that thing fixed. And how about we turn down the radiator?"

A muffled reply came from behind the door. The detective, clad in undershirt and slacks, grunted and returned to his thoughts. He rapped out a beat with his pencil in rough symphony with both the whirr of the condenser and the classical music crackling from the old radio next to the window. The bedroom door swung open. Nancy, hair down but still wearing the day's makeup, shimmied into the room barefoot, wearing a smile and a red silk kimono.

"Ta da."

Engrossed by the case folder, Bodowski hardly acknowledged her presence. "Mm-hmm."

"What are you, dead?" She pulled out one of the four thinly padded chairs and sat opposite her boyfriend. Moving the forgotten bottle of beer that sat on the table untouched every night, she asked, "Is it time for the bottle to go back into the fridge?"

Thumbing through the pages, he sighed.

Nancy smelled her wrists, one after the other, then closed her eyes and moaned, "This perfume is heavenly. They say it drives men wild." She leaned across the table and stuck a hand under his nose.

He brushed it aside.

Sitting back with a plop, Nancy blew air through her lips. "Apparently not."

"It's not you." He shuffled through the array of papers and folders.

"Good to know. Who is it, then?"

"What?"

"Who's getting your attention?"

"You're beautiful." Returning to the paperwork, he added, "But it's that little girl we found in the ditch."

"Ho boy. I lose out to a dead kid. You know, I thought about her all afternoon, but I told myself I'm not going to think about her tonight."

Realizing his error, he sat upright and beckoned. Smiling anew, Nancy got up and danced around the table. He hooked her around the hip with one arm and pressed the side of his face against her thigh. She rubbed the top of his head with one hand, enjoying the sensation of touching his thick brown hair.

"Why do you do it, Nancy?" He peered up at her. "Why do you put yourself in this position?"

"What position?"

"C'mon. A divorced woman in the civil service living with a man in her apartment off post? How long do you think you'd last if the brass got wind of it?"

"Three months and not a peep." She rubbed the nape of his neck. "You and I work in an office full of detectives and no one has figured it out."

"Mavis knows."

"She does?" Surprised, she ran her hands over his arms. "No, she doesn't."

"Afraid so. I can tell, believe me."

She eyed him for a moment and frowned. "Do the other agents know?"

"Melcher." He smiled at her exaggerated concern.

"Oh. Any others?"

Laughing, he pushed her back. Holding her by the hips, he said, "Don't worry about Mavis. She couldn't live without you. And Mel? Hell, he'd lay down in traffic for me. The others wouldn't give a damn even if they did know. Looks like you're stuck with this gumshoe."

"Well, you must be doing something right." She grabbed his wrists. "You're with me."

Drifting for a moment, he said, "It's the damnedest thing. No missing persons reports, and the just plain strange condition of the body. And the calluses? Where is she from? Cutting up her face—that's the only part I get."

Nancy backed away and swung his outstretched arms back and forth. "You know, that isn't very romantic talk. Also, you'll notice I'm wearing the kimono and not the warm terrycloth robe with the matching fuzzy slippers."

"So I see."

"You're a detective. What does this outfit signify, hmm?"

"Huh?"

"You need to drop the case for a little while—at least for tonight."

He nodded.

"You're thinking about it again—the case."

"Sorry for being such a boor, kid. Give me a few minutes." Bodowski stood up and resumed his search through the small maze of paperwork scattered over the tabletop. Nancy moved back to her chair and sat with a thump. "This unfinished report by Doc Larson is full of errors—typos. Look at these reports you dug up about the domestic violence calls. It's amateur work at best."

"You fellows clear your share of cases." She sighed and played with the sleeve of her kimono.

"Sure. Most are so cut and dried the MPs could handle them. But no civilian prosecutor could get a conviction on half of this crap. This is a murder, and my experience has been that the perpetrator tries real damn hard to avoid detection." He lifted up a handful of paper and dropped it on the table.

"Sloppy paperwork like this ain't gonna hack it. Say, what about the missing files?"

Nancy wore a quizzical look.

"You know. The Judge Advocate's case files against those two enlisted men that that warrant officer—Nowak—accused of possessing kiddie porn? I want to read those before I speak with him, but they're missing."

"You're going to question Nowak after all?"

"I've been thinking about it since this afternoon. I'm giving LeMarc a hard look, but I can't just slide on this Nowak character. You never know."

"They're not missing—the Nowak files. They were checked out late this afternoon, but with no name on the log. We'll just have to wait until they're returned."

"I'm flying blind here, Nancy."

"Didn't Palls tell you to lay off?"

"Not exactly."

"What, exactly?"

"I told you before. He wants to clear our people, and by that he means don't look too hard and make sure the mess gets handed over to the locals."

"I dug up anything I could think of that seemed like it might point to someone. One of ours."

"I'm glad for it. You're doing your job. Palls is just trying to wish it away. It suits him to keep Fulbright out of harm's way. The colonel needs to be free of any messy situations, such as having a child killer loose on his watch. He gets his star and Palls moves up the ladder. It's the master plan."

"Don't they care about justice?"

"Watch out, girl. Talk about justice gets me randy." Bodowski smiled but kept reading.

"Good. From now on, I'll just quote John Stuart Mill to set the mood." Nancy held up a wrist and addressed it. "Goodbye Chanel."

"Hey. Are you throwing your college degree at me?"

"And why should I apologize for spending my daddy's hard-earned money getting an education?" She waited, but he did not acknowledge her remark. "Honestly, Steve, you're an incredibly bright guy. Why didn't you go to college? Was it the money?"

Still busy, he answered, "I joined the police so I could dodge the draft."

"Really?"

"No, not really. I didn't have two nickels to rub together. After high school, I did odd jobs, biding my time until I could join the police department."

"So what about the draft?"

"Childhood asthma—cleared up enough that I could become a cop, and then a soldier, or something like a soldier."

"You're heads down on this. I've never seen you so intense. We don't have anything to go on at all and here you are, intent on finding something."

"It's what I do. Back in Tacoma, there were hundreds of men on the force but only eight of us in Homicide. I was a member of the Murder Police. I want that feeling back. I need to run down the worst and get a little something back for the dead. I can't think of a better thing to do."

"Well, I guess there's a bit of the idealist in you."

He looked away from her. "I can't get it all back. I blew a good thing—that's for certain. I just want to do what I can." A look of resignation settled over his face.

"I'm no dummy." Nancy clutched the bottle of beer by the neck and inspected the label. "You never take a drink. Every night you take this out of the fridge and set it on the table. Before we go to bed, you put it back, unopened." She let go of the bottle. "It's an alcoholic's ritual. But it's your business."

Bodowski sat back and took a deep breath. "I was going great guns, knocking cases over like bowling pins. I got free of Cranston—you remember me talking about him. I had the world by the tail. Hell, I was looking to nab a gold shield before I hit thirty." He stalled for a moment. Closing his eyes, he faced upward and rubbed his head with both hands.

Nancy leaned forward as if to coax him.

He slapped both hands onto the table. "Damn—I don't even remember what set me off. At first, I'd hoist a few with the boys to celebrate breaking one; then it got to be several and, before I knew it, I was closing the bar. I'd stagger home or drive like a blind man. I was lucky I didn't kill someone. Pretty soon, I was hammered at work. I had to switch partners more than once because nobody wanted to work with a lush. A lush—that's what Palls called me today. He was right."

"But you cleaned up. Look at you now."

"Yeah, but back in the day, I did some damage. I have to live with it."

She offered a sympathetic smile. He stood up and grabbed the bottle. Walking to the radio, he set the beer on the console and turned to face her. A piano concerto faded into the ether as the station drifted off frequency.

"It got so I was away from work more than I was on—usually sleeping one off. I'd done a lot of good in the first four years I had my tin shield, so I got cut some slack. One day when I made it into work—still half in the bag—I caught a case with a child as the victim, a boy, maybe a year old. Turns out, Mom got tired of all the crying—probably because she was drunk, and a mean one at that. Anyways, this loon who was loaded to the gills got it into her head to stick the kid in the bath with the hot water running—something about teaching the 'brat' a lesson. Long story short, she passes out on the tiles and wakes up only to find, well, you know."

"Oh, my God."

"A friend of hers stops by and discovers the scene. We get the call. I get there the same time as the uniforms. My new reputation precedes me, and one of them accuses me of being looped. I take a swing at him before going upstairs. Once I get up there and see what's what, I light up a smoke. I get dizzy from the booze and sit down. Somehow, God knows why, I think I'm putting out my cigarette in the toilet. Well, it turns out it was the clothes hamper. Within the hour, the house is up in smoke, including the baby's corpse. Two firemen got hurt, but they recovered." Bodowski leaned over and tuned the station to the Armed Forces Network. "I think I've caused enough trouble to last a lifetime." Picking up the bottle, he walked over and deposited the lukewarm item in the refrigerator.

Nancy got up and hugged him from behind, kissing his back.

Smiling, he said, "Gave up drinking and smoking the same day. How many guys you know have done that?" He turned and kissed her hard on the lips.

She whispered into his ear, "Let's go in the bedroom."

"Too far." He picked her up and carried her to the small sofa by the door.

# Chapter Twenty-Three

## Double Kross
**Thursday**

"Ten-hut!"

The agents stood and came to attention as Major Palls strode into the squad room. Mavis and Nancy sat up straight. Trailing behind the little man, obscured in the morning shadows of the hallway, Bodowski could make out the lithe figure of Herr Leutnant Kross. Palls waved a hand.

"As you were."

The detective remained standing as Palls led the German toward his desk. Kross took a chair from against the wall and seated himself, though the others continued to stand.

Approximating a civil tone, Palls said, "Herr Kross, you're well acquainted with Agent Bodowski, of course. Bodowski, I want you to cooperate and extend him every courtesy. He has a lead in the case with the girl, and it involves locating a GI and maybe some questioning." Palls sniffed. "You're going to have to be present. You follow?"

"Of course, sir."

The lanky German smiled at the major. He looked quite at home, methodically removing his gloves and crossing his legs.

"Herr Kross, I need to speak to the detective on some official business. Please excuse us for a second."

Palls and Bodowski stepped into the hallway. Once out of Kross' line of sight, Palls stopped and glared upward at his subordinate.

"I don't want any fuck-ups here." His sharp whisper produced spittle. "I got to put up with this faggot's request and that shit-eating grin—allied cooperation and all that. And who knows? Maybe, just maybe, he's got a solid lead." He looked back to make certain they were alone. "You let this play out. You help him if it looks like it's going someplace, you see? If it does, then you take over and haul in the fish. This is our little pond. We catch and fry our own." He broke off and walked to the stairwell. Tugging at his uniform jacket to smooth out imaginary wrinkles, he turned and said, "When you're done, get rid of him."

"Yes, sir," Bodowski acknowledged and held a salute. Ignoring the formality, Palls spun and descended the stairs.

The detective could not fathom Major Palls' changing attitude toward the handling of the case. Returning to the squad room, he risked a glance toward his girlfriend. She met his gaze and then looked at the German detective.

"Well, Kross." Bodowski sat hard, earning a loud squeak from the wooden chair. "What brings you here?"

"It may be nothing, but with this nasty business concerning the poor little girl, one does not like to leave any stone unturned." The German smiled. "You never know what might slither out."

"I'm all ears." He saw Herr Leutnant carried a leather satchel.

Kross opened the flap and produced a piece of graph paper adorned with a crude penciled sketch of an Army unit insignia. "Is this in any way familiar?"

Recognizing the design of the 135th Maintenance Battalion, Chief Warrant Officer Nowak's unit, Bodowski answered with restraint. "I think it belongs to one of the units over at First Brigade." Snatching the sheet from Kross' outstretched hand, he held it up for all to see. "Hey. Anybody know this?"

Mavis and Nancy soaked it in for a second. They looked at each another as one of the other detectives chimed in, "Yeah, that looks like the insignia for the one-three-five."

"There you go, Kross. It's the one-three-five Maintenance Battalion over at First Brigade. What's the deal, anyway?"

"There is someone over there with whom I would like to have a brief chat, perhaps clear up a few things."

"Anybody in particular?" He felt like kicking himself for waiting until today to question Nowak.

Twenty feet away, the two women strained to overhear the conversation.

"An officer, tall and out of shape, with black hair."

"How are we supposed to pick him out, Kross? Have all the tall, dark officers at the one-three-five do pushups for us—see who punks out first?"

Nancy coughed to disguise her laughter.

Unfazed, Kross replied, "I believe that recognizing a substantial paunch on a very tall officer in a single unit will not prove to be an insurmountable task."

Standing, Bodowski pulled on his raincoat and grabbed the spiral notebook off his desk. "Over to the one-three-five it is." Looking to Nancy and Mavis, he added, "Going on a fishing expedition with our German friend. Going to need those files I requested earlier. You remember? I need you to put a rush on it." Addressing Kross, he bowed while sweeping a hand toward the door. "Lead on, MacDuff."

"Lay on, Macduff, and damned be him who first cries 'Hold! Enough!'" Kross beamed. "I didn't know you were a fan of the Bard."

"Who?"

The detectives left the squad room and headed across the parking lot. The headquarters of the maintenance battalion, located in a renovated warehouse, sat several hundred meters from the Provost Marshal's office. Bodowski suggested they walk the short distance despite the cold morning wind and mist. As they neared their objective, the American blew on his hands and glanced at Kross, who tightened the fit of his gloves.

"Where'd you get this lead?"

"Sources. You know."

"No, I don't. What sources?"

"I believe that Major Palls instructed you to cooperate, not interrogate."

"Do you have access to our reports? Is someone feeding them to you? Cooperation works both ways, you know."

The German stopped. "Come, come. What's all this, then? Have I not been helpful? Did I not have those crime scene photos to you so quickly they were still wet with fixer?"

"I appreciate that, I do. But what gives? This is my beat and I want to know how you got the lead."

"You said just now, 'access to our reports,' so I assume you have interest in someone at this unit as well."

"I was just reaching, you know, just trying to draw you out. I want to know what's going on here. Can you at least let on as to what you're going to ask this guy once we find him?"

"I'm not certain, and I won't say anything until I size him up, as you say." In perfect deadpan, Kross added, "I am loathe to unnecessarily besmirch the reputation of an officer."

It was all the American could do to keep from bursting into laughter.

Entering the unit headquarters, Bodowski asked to see the battalion sergeant major.

"Why are we not speaking with an officer about finding this man?" Kross asked.

"Would you rather get something done or die a slow death waiting?"

Kross smirked. "Some army."

"Good enough to fuck up the Wermacht."

Herr Leutnant looked down his nose at his counterpart. "Of course, in this case, we'll need to depend on quality rather than simple quantity."

Bodowski decided to let it go.

Following a few queries, and with the German close on his heel, he found himself standing before the unit's top kick, a hard man in his forties with thick silver eyebrows.

"What's the deal with the civvies, fella?"

"CID." The detective flashed his badge. Pointing his thumb

at Kross, he said, "This is a local. The Provost Marshal has requested your cooperation." He decided he would make Kross work for the name. "We need to identify one of your officers."

Kross broke in, "Tall with black hair."

Taken aback, the sergeant major asked, "You an Englishman? I spent a few years myself on the unsinkable aircraft carrier—back in the day, of course."

"Tall with black hair," Kross reiterated.

"They all got black hair, I think. As for tall, well, I think we got two fairly tall ones."

"And, my good man, a bit of a paunch."

"What the hell's a 'paunch'?"

"A swollen abdomen—a large gut."

"Still two." The Sergeant Major shook his head. "Of course, one of them has been on leave for the past week. The other runs the battalion motor pool—Nowak, a CWO3. You want I should give him a call?"

"No, no. Please, what is a CWO3?"

"A chief warrant officer three. A warrant officer is a kind of no-man's-land between enlisted man and commissioned officer. Is this going to affect our operations? Nowak in trouble? This is the guy who pressed the kiddie-porn beef on those two lowlifes that worked in his section. Both of those assholes are history. We got a clean operation here. One of those sick bastards got hung out to dry by the Judge Advocate."

"No trouble," Bodowski reassured him. "Nowak might have witnessed something unrelated. Just need to ask him a couple of questions. No big deal."

"Well, okay. But watch your feet over there. He ain't got his shit together, and that goes for his motor pool too. Right out into the courtyard, then turn left and go about two hundred mikes. When you get to the head shed, ask for the section chief."

Once outside, Kross commented, "I never fail to be amused by the argot of the American military man." The detectives walked to the motor pool in silence.

The "head shed" was little more than a glorified trailer. As rusty as the chain-link fence surrounding the vehicle compound, the cheerless box housed a crowded office. Entering the single room, the detectives observed several enlisted men working cheek by jowl. Near the radiator at the far end of the trailer sat Henry Nowak, head down, working behind a stack of manila folders. A clerk standing next to the door intercepted the pair.

"Can I help you gentlemen?"

"Thanks, need to speak with your chief. The sergeant major sent us over."

"Sure." Bemused by the civilian clothes and Kross' general appearance, the enlisted clerk pointed to Nowak. "That's him. Hey, Chief, you got visitors."

Not looking up, Nowak snapped, "Visitors? Where?"

"Right here, Chief."

"What?" The warrant officer lifted his head just enough to catch a glimpse of the two detectives. Startled, he spoke out lest one of the policemen announce himself with his badge. "No problem. Hey, it's too damn crowded in here, and all we're going to do is bug these guys on the phone." A sudden bout of nerves made him talkative against his nature. "We'll go outside." Sidling through the thicket of desks, Nowak grabbed his cover and field jacket. "Follow me."

Outside the windowless trailer, the three stood for a moment on the adjoining metal grate while Nowak prattled on about the weather. Kross retrieved a cigarette from his silver case, squeezed it into his holder, and cut off the tall man by clearing his throat.

"CID." In his practiced manner, Bodowski flipped the badge open and closed. "And this is Leutnant Detectiv Kross, Geistburg Polizei."

"How can I help you two?" Nowak rubbed his hands together and sniffed at the cold.

"Herr Kross would like to ask you a few questions."

"Okay." Nowak stamped his feet. The grating rattled in protest.

Kross, employing his usual methods, said nothing as he lit his cigarette. He watched as the cold wind obliterated one of his smoke rings.

"Your commander owes you a debt of thanks—unless, of course, you have already been so honored."

"Pardon?" Nowak looked at Bodowski. "You said he was German, right?"

"Yeah, he's German. Please answer his question."

"What question?"

"I guess it was not a question so much as a statement of what's owed you. Seldom do we acknowledge those who expose themselves to quash the insidious vices that gnaw at smaller men."

"What the hell's going on here? What's he talking about?"

"I speak of those two you had sent away due to their vile habits. How is it you came to know of their despicable sexual perversion?"

"Oh, those guys? Judge Advocate's got all my testimony. You can just read it for yourself. It wasn't more than any other man would do if he caught wind of that shit." Nowak folded his arms and moved around too much to justify fighting off the chill.

"Please. Just tell me in your own words, briefly."

"All right." Shaking his head, Nowak continued, "Couple of privates, Henderson and Wilford—turns out they liked the hard stuff. You know, kiddie stuff." The warrant officer bent forward as if relaying a secret. "Those two were sick. They had themselves their own little perverted group. I caught them. Not both right away, mind you. First I got Henderson. Then I got Wilford a while later."

Bodowski itched to ask the man some very pointed questions, but he was not going to do that while Kross was present. He figured he'd return on his own once he had obtained the Judge Advocate's transcripts.

"Well, Mr. Nowak, that's laudable, commendable. But with what exactly did you catch them? What manner of vice did they hold?"

"You mean the pictures? The dirty pictures? Yeah, they both had them. Say, why are we going over old ground, huh?"

"Small photos, like you might carry in your wallet? Hmm?"

"No. A big picture. An eight-by-ten, you know."

"Each man had just one?"

"Yeah, that's right. Jesus, this is all in the reports." Nowak put his hands behind his back.

Kross and Bodowski glanced at one another.

"And the depictions? What image was depicted on each photograph?"

"Oh, I don't know. It's hard to remember."

"Come, come. The course of two men's lives has been inalterably changed over those images. I'm certain you must remember."

"I—"

"Chief, I'm going to need you to answer his question."

"Pictures of kids, you know." Folding his arms, Nowak avoided looking at the detectives. "Kids without their clothes on."

"Boys or girls?"

"Oh girls, definitely girls." Nowak, his face glowing hot, asked, "What the hell's going on here? I catch some sick bastards and then get the third degree from you two?"

"Hey, simmer down," Bodowski said.

"Mr. Nowak," Kross began, employing a soothing tone, "please forgive us for this difficult moment. You see, one of the perpetrators of this terrible crime remains on our soil in your military prison."

"Yeah, so?"

"Well, the good people of Geistburg may wish to punish him further for his perversion once he is released from American custody. I needed to test your resolve in case you are called upon to testify in our courts. Our defense attorneys are notorious for badgering prosecution witnesses."

"Oh." Calmer, Nowak asked, "So this was just a test to see if I would make a good witness?"

"You could say that."

"We done here? I got a motor pool to run."

"Say, Chief, I have a quick question." Bodowski knew he should wait until Kross was out of the picture, but he wanted answers.

"Yeah?"

"How'd the inspection go?"

"Inspection?"

"Yeah, you know—the one you got called out to get ready for in the early hours yesterday."

"Some kind of dumbass joke. Wait'll I catch the asshole who pulled it."

"A joke? I don't follow."

"I get woken out of a sound sleep—two, no, wait, zero-three-hundred yesterday. I got told the IG was springing a surprise inspection on the motor pool in the next few hours." The tall man's nervous energy found a new outlet in anger. "I get down here in the dark and work like a fucking dog. Then I step outside to stretch for a moment, and I don't see another damn car except for the OD and his runner. It dawns on me that there isn't going to be any inspection. Someone was screwing with me."

Kross began to speak, but Bodowski held up a hand to forestall him. "Mr. Nowak, did anybody see you?"

"How do you mean?"

"From the time you left your apartment after the call until you got back home, who saw you?"

"Christ, I dunno." He searched the sky for an answer. "Nobody. I was here by myself. Wait—the gate guards saw me."

"They stopped you? They talked to you?"

"No. They just waved me through, you know. That was here, on post. Over at the housing area, they had that damn readiness drill. They looked in my trunk, but I didn't talk to anyone."

"Yeah, sure. No big deal." He smiled to put him at ease. "Just one more question."

"Yeah? What?"

"No idea at all who called you about the inspection?"

"Never heard the voice before—kind of mumbled his name. I didn't catch it. It sure wasn't anybody in Battalion that I know. Say, what's this got to do with anything?"

"Just filling in the blanks. Cop stuff. Well, that's all for me. What do you say, Herr Leutnant? It's your show."

"I think we have what we need. Again, sorry for the little test, but it was necessary."

"Humph." Giving the detectives a wide berth, Nowak walked to the trailer door and stopped. "I'm going to have to testify in a German court? Is that for certain?"

"No, my good man. Not certain at all. This is one of those just-in-case scenarios."

The word *scenario* gave him pause. For a moment, Nowak looked as though he was going ask a question. Instead, he turned and entered the trailer.

"For Christ's sake, Kross. You read the case files on this guy, didn't you? The Army's own case files. Shit—I haven't even seen them yet. How the hell did this happen?"

"Come now, don't let the pot boil over, especially if you're not certain of your facts." Kross pulled his half-smoked cigarette from the holder and replaced it with a new one. "We're on to something here. Don't you think? His inspection alibi is so inept it borders on the comical."

"We'll get to that, goddamnit." Bodowski faced the German detective. "First, tell me what happened with the reports."

Despite Bodowski's nose within inches of his own, Kross answered as he would a casual inquiry. "Sorry, old sport, but I've not read any case files regarding the edgy Mr. Nowak."

Bodowski studied Kross's face but could not detect a crack in the façade.

"Allow me to expound. Yesterday, following our final meeting, I went right to work. I followed up on a lead of my own—"

"What lead? Who?"

"Tut tut. For the time being, I must insist that it stay confidential. I don't wish to compromise the ongoing local investigation of an unrelated crime."

"Go on. Get to it, damn it."

"As I said, I followed a lead that produced the insignia I showed you and a person, shall we say, of interest? And, old boy, it was your office that led me to this place."

"How did you know about the two GIs Nowak busted?"

"Could you step away so I might light my cigarette?"

He backed off a few feet, allowing Kross to light up and exhale a stream of smoke into the cold wind.

"The two GIs?"

"His own sergeant major gave me what I needed to go down that path. Don't you remember?"

"What about when you said one of them is still in Germany?"

"A little white lie." Kross shrugged and smiled. "I took a chance that he might not know full disposition—it really was quite a chance. I just got a bit lucky. Oh, and the main stockade for Seventh Army is in Mannheim, correct?"

"And the pictures?" Bodowski grew uncertain over his own anger.

"Just paying attention. The suspect indicated 'a big picture,' singular. I deduced each man probably possessed a single photograph when he was found out." Kross turned to leave. "Are you coming?"

Bodowski did not respond at first. Staring at Kross, he mulled over the events of the past few minutes. "I'll bet a month's pay that bastard likes nothing more than getting a gander at little girls in their birthday suits. You could smell that the guy was wrong."

"I completely agree with your assessment. Our case is still in its infancy, but I feel we should pay some real attention to this fidgety man and his utterly worthless alibi."

"You know, we're still just looking down alleys. We don't have a lot to go on here. Like you say, our case is just starting and murders can take a while, especially ones where you don't know shit about the victim. Funny you happened on this guy so quickly." By dint of hard experience, he had grown wary of coincidences.

The German cleared his throat and looked around. “There a loo about?”

“There are some portable toilets over by the motor pool gate.”

Kross excused himself and walked toward the conveniences. Bodowski turned up his collar against the cold drizzle. Suddenly the door to the motor pool trailer burst open and the clerk with whom they had spoken earlier emerged, slamming the door behind him. Muttering unintelligibly, he stomped past the detective, who seized the opportunity with Kross indisposed.

“You pissed at something?”

“Yeah.” Moderating his tone, the clerk continued, “I mean, yes sir.”

“Don’t worry about that.” The detective waved away the clerk’s concern over military protocol with the flick of a hand. “I just want to ask you something.”

“Shoot.” The young man retrieved a pack of cigarettes and offered one to Bodowski, who declined.

“I want this to be in confidence. We’re conducting a serious investigation.”

“Sure. Anything.” The clerk lit the cigarette.

“What do you think of Chief Nowak?”

A worried look came over the man’s face.

“Hey, no sweat.” Bodowski tried to put him at ease. “You say what you want. No way this gets back to him.” He held up three fingers and smiled. “Scout’s honor.”

The clerk looked around and leaned forward. “The guy’s a fucking prick. You sure I’m not going get my ass hung out to dry?”

“Not going to happen.”

“He’s a shit-for-brains, too.”

“What do you mean?”

“He’s been whining nonstop since yesterday about someone jerking his ass around on that fake inspection. He’s blaming us for his stupidity.”

“You got any inside dope on that inspection call? Honest, you can tell me—I swear you won’t get into trouble.”

"Nah. Someone here must have pulled a fast one. Ha. If I find out who did it, I'm going to buy him a beer."

"Sounds like Nowak's a head case."

"Yeah, he thinks he got over on that shit with Wilford. But a lot of us know better. Oh, sorry—maybe you don't know what I'm talking about."

"I know about Wilford's case. Go on."

"Kiddie porn, my ass." The clerk took a long drag of his cigarette and exhaled through his nose. "Wilford was the original babe-hound. He loved the skirts, and he loved them big and busty. Kiddie shit. Fuck that. You can't hang around with a guy for a year and not know that."

"You're saying Wilford might have been framed?" Bodowski retrieved his notebook and leafed through it until he found a blank page.

"Look, I don't want to get in trouble here."

"Like I said, it ain't going to happen." He glanced toward the portable toilets.

"I can't prove anything, you see?" The clerk pointed the butt of his cigarette at the trailer. "I think it's the chief who has all that sick stuff—those pictures that keep cropping up."

"What did Wilford do to get in the lurch with Nowak?"

"He kept dropping dimes on Nowak's ass with the sergeant major."

"Over?"

"Over how this motor pool is the dirtiest, shittiest-run motor pool in the whole fucking Seventh Army. Hell, I'm ashamed just to be working here."

"What about Henderson?"

"I didn't know Henderson. I think he worked on the mechanic's crew."

Bodowski noticed Kross stepping out of the portable toilet and pausing to light a fresh cigarette. "Anything else you can tell me about Nowak?"

"Every now and then he disappears for a couple hours and tells me and the other guys we got to cover for him. The prick."

"Where does he go?" The German was moving toward them now.

"I don't know, but one of the guys said he saw him driving downtown once—didn't know where."

"Here." He scribbled the CID telephone number on a small card and handed it to the clerk. "Do me a favor. If Nowak disappears again, give me a call. I'm Bodowski. Just leave a message if I'm not there."

"Sure. Glad to." The clerk gave a quick thumbs-up and walked away.

"Say, old sport, wasn't that the young fellow we met in the trailer?"

"Yeah." Bodowski jotted down the name from the man's uniform patch. "Just crossing T's, you know."

"What did he reveal to you?" Kross watched the young man as he trudged toward battalion headquarters.

"That he didn't know jack. In any case, you can't expect him to badmouth his section chief to a stranger."

"Hmm." Kross blew a smoke ring that remained stubbornly intact in the dying wind.

# Chapter Twenty-Four

## Fort Stewart, Georgia: Monday, November 12, 1956

"Claire? I'm home."

"Daddy?" The small voice came from his daughter's room.

Finding that his wife was not in the kitchen preparing lunch, Nowak threw his keys to the floor and plopped on the couch. He unlaced his combat boots, muttering to himself about his wife's oversight.

"Claire?" He stood. Boot tongues out and laces dragging on the floor, he called her again as he approached the master bedroom at the end of the hall. From the doorway, he saw her, the apron still wound over her dress, lying asleep on top of the covers. He opened his mouth to complain but then hesitated, considering whether it would be simpler just to grab lunch at the base snack bar. On his way back to the living room, he looked in on Charlie. The three-year-old lay motionless on the floor, surrounded by a forest of toys, his legs twitching in a dream.

The final stop along the way was his daughter's room. With his finger pressed to his lips, Nowak opened the door and peered in at his five-year-old, sitting on top of her pink bed sheets and playing with two wooden horses. The girl pressed her own finger to her lips, recognizing the sign for quiet. Nowak smiled at Susan and winked. She covered her mouth with both hands to suppress a giggle. A dark yearning washed over him—the same desire he had felt watching grainy movies of little girls forced to perform acts of sexual depravity. Somehow, he had separated his daughter from that eddy of perversion, lying to himself that she would not be a target for his twisted urges. After all, they were only pictures—ghosts on film—not real children debased by diseased men. He had never touched a child, not in that way. But now, at this very opportune moment, a storm swirled through his mind.

"We have to be very quiet," he whispered. "Mommy and Charlie are taking a nap."

"Okay." Unable to command a whisper, Susan rasped out her compliance.

Nowak closed the door and sat on the bed next to her, gently pulling on her brown curls.

"Mommy just do these for you? I haven't seen you in ringlets before."

"Yes, Daddy." Susan grew excited. Outside of her daily bath, a chore for which he always seemed available, he rarely spoke with her alone.

"C'mon, now. Stay quiet. Mommy works real hard."

"I know, Daddy."

"What are you playing?"

Susan gave her best impression of a whinny.

"Horsies, right? You're playing horsies."

"That's right." She danced the toys in an animated fashion.

He moved in close. The aroma of soap residue in her hair excited him. An arc of sexual desire surged through him. His throat tightened as he surrendered to his obsession.

"Let's play another game," he whispered.

Another person said it, not him. His mind turned inside out as he obeyed this inner voice.

"What game, Daddy?"

"This game doesn't have a name. But you can't tell anybody else about it. It's a secret, a secret game."

"A secret?"

"You know what a secret is?"

She nodded.

"Okay. Now, remember, you can't tell anybody else, not Mommy or Grandma or Grandpa or anybody."

"Why not?"

"If you tell about our secret game, Daddy will have to go away. You don't want me to go away, do you?"

"Oh no, Daddy." She stifled a cry. "I don't want you to go away. I'll be good. I won't tell anybody." Tears welled in her blue eyes.

Nowak stood up and walked into the hallway. He could just make out the sounds of Claire's gentle snoring. Stepping back into his daughter's room, he closed the door and held his finger to his lips to reinforce his demand for quiet. Giving in to a smile, he unbuckled the web belt of his fatigue pants.

Charlie awoke to the sound of a thump against his bedroom wall. Muffled sounds came from his sister's room. A moment later, the noises stopped. The little boy wiped the sleep from his eyes and resumed his earlier game with the German hand puppets his father had given him the previous Christmas.

One room over, Henry Nowak, hands trembling, pulled up his pants. Teeth chattering, he looked down at his child.

"Oh, Christ. Oh, Jesus."

The voice inside him had vanished, leaving the sad, shocked father to deal with the aftermath. Falling to his knees in front of Susan's body, he clasped his hands into a tight ball and banged them against his forehead.

"Bring her back to life. Oh, God, please, please, please. Oh God, help me."

He looked up but found only the bare ceiling with its single domed light. In a fit of panic, he imagined his own death was imminent—it was just a matter of seconds before final judgment would occur. He could not breathe. He would die as she had, choking for air. Bursting from her room, he barely had the presence of mind to keep the door from slamming open.

Even in his panicked state, some part of him attempted to exert control. Eyes darting, he paced with manic energy around the living room. He imagined his impending doom. The brass buckle of his loose belt clacked against the buttons of his fatigue pants as he lurched back and forth, the fear stabbing at him.

He stopped and forced himself to inhale. It felt like trying to fill a heavy leather balloon. Gradually, the panic subsided and he breathed easier. What remained was fear—real, visceral fear. He wondered if his wife had heard them, if she was awake and hiding in her room, biding her time until he left so she could call the MPs. The thought forced involuntary laugher.

"Shut up."

Shocked he had said it aloud, he covered his mouth as though it had a life of its own. Tiptoeing through the hallway, he observed Charlie playing with some toys. The little boy, happily busy, did not look up. Peering into the master bedroom, he saw that Claire had rolled onto her side, facing away from the door. She was still asleep. Nowak moved back into his daughter's room, surprised in spite of himself to see that she had not moved. Death was new to him.

He tried to focus on finding a way out of his predicament. What little self-control he had mustered evaporated as his thoughts ran toward prison and worse. Then an idea struck him. Claire had scolded Susan for playing with the bags from the dry cleaners ever since she'd read a magazine article warning of the suffocation danger to young children. Rushing to the hall closet, he tore a bag off one of his dress uniforms and returned to Susan's room. He knelt and opened his daughter's mouth. Reaching in with two fingers, he fished out the handkerchief she had choked on during their brief struggle.

"Why, honey? Why couldn't you just do what I asked?"

He placed the bag over the child's body, paying special attention to press it close to her head, to twist the voluminous bag around her arms. They would say she had become entangled. Straightening up the room completed the staging of what the medical examiner would later deem an unfortunate accident. His fear ebbed as he went through the motions of covering up his crime.

Nowak left her room and slumped onto the living room sofa. A bout of the shakes overwhelmed him, which made the simple act of lacing his boots impossible. Several minutes passed before he could regain full control. He spent the time concocting the final portion of his deception. Boots laced, he stood and straightened his uniform. Retrieving his key ring from the floor, he removed the apartment key and tossed it under the coffee table. He opened the front door and closed it quietly behind him as he stepped out into the deserted stairwell. From the sill above the doorframe, he located the spare key and locked the door. The key returned, he took a deep breath and shook his shoulders, like an actor preparing for his entrance. Then he pounded on the door and shouted for Claire. Hearing her faint response, he knocked again for effect.

"Just a minute." She opened the door blinking sleep from her eyes. He rushed in and began his performance.

"For crying out loud, Claire. What were you doing? Sleeping?"

"Is that a crime?"

"I was standing out in the hall. You know how that looks? I felt foolish."

"Oh, Henry, don't make a federal case out of it." Rubbing her eyes, she asked, "Why didn't you use your key?"

"Hell, I must have lost it this morning when I was fiddling with my keychain."

"Well, you could have just used the spare key."

He screwed up his face. "Damn, I forgot about that." Sitting on the living room sofa, he unlaced his boots.

"Gosh, I got so tired. Sorry." Stepping into the hall, she said, "I'll get the kids and start lunch."

Despite the knot in his guts, Nowak's hands had stopped trembling. He felt he could survive the coming storm.

# Chapter Twenty-Five

## Drunken Master

The attack came out of nowhere. Bodowski reacted instinctively, throwing both hands up to cover his head as the initial blow glanced off his left temple. Before he could recover, the assailant, who had ambushed the detective from behind, caught him full force with his other fist. Bodowski reeled and slammed against the brick wall of the Provost Marshal's building, banging his head and tearing a gash into his scalp. Sergeant Cramer LeMarc, wearing his parade dress uniform, seized the addled man by his collar and threw him headlong onto the lawn.

"You talk to my wife behind my back, you piece of shit?"

LeMarc stalked toward Bodowski, who rolled up into a ball to defend against the anticipated kick. The burly sergeant brought his foot down hard on the detective's right thigh but his victim moved before it could do any real damage, and LeMarc temporarily lost his balance as his boot slid off. Regaining his footing, the red-faced drunk leaned over his victim, his Medal of Honor swinging about his neck on its long blue ribbon.

"Get up, you fucking coward. I'm going to teach you to fuck with my family."

Still on the ground, Bodowski pulled his sap, then opened up all at once and raised the rubber-coated metal bar to strike at LeMarc's head. The enraged man swatted his hand away. Bodowski jerked the automatic from his holster with his other hand and brought the butt of the gun down hard across

LeMarc's right knee. The squat man howled in pain as he fell back onto the ground.

Two MPs exiting the building witnessed the final few moments of the attack. One of them ran to control LeMarc, who writhed on the ground, grimacing and holding his knee. The other helped the detective to his feet.

"What the hell was that all about?"

"I don't know."

"You're bleeding." The MP steadied him. "I'll take you to the dispensary."

"Okay." Watching as the other MP turned LeMarc on his stomach and pressed a knee into his back, Bodowski added, "Cuff that sonofabitch and take him to holding. Put him in the cage, but make sure he's by himself. This guy'd kill whoever was in there with him."

The MP helping Bodowski stopped once he glimpsed the conspicuous medal that had twisted around on its ribbon and now lay on the prone sergeant's back.

"Hey, he's wearing the Medal of Honor. Stimson, you see that?"

"Don't get all glassy-eyed, boys," Bodowski admonished. "Does this look honorable to you?"

The MP drove the detective to the dispensary at the main post hospital and deposited him in the waiting room. The young man offered to stay, but Bodowski declined and instead asked the MP to alert his office to the incident, emphasizing that he wanted LeMarc to remain in custody no matter who tried to spring him. After several minutes spent walking off the knot in his thigh and checking his bloodsoaked handkerchief, a nurse appeared and took him in to see the doctor, who stitched Bodowski's scalp and handed him a sheet listing the symptoms of a concussion.

"Jesus." Bodowski rubbed the back of his neck. "Nausea, headache, fatigue, irritability." He scanned the full list and quipped, "I got most of this on a normal day."

"Just take it easy. I'll write you a profile script so you can take off from duty."

"Do me a favor, Doc, and leave it undated."

"You're in law enforcement, right?"

"It'll be our little secret. Can you point me to a phone?"

Nancy, flustered by the news of the assault, broke several traffic regulations on her way to the hospital. Spotting her injured boyfriend standing in the waiting room, presumably calling her for a ride, she ran up behind him and grabbed his shoulder. He spun around, surprised, and almost lost his balance.

"My God, Steve. Look at you."

His hair shot out in all directions beneath the narrow headband of white gauze securing the large bandage to the back of his head.

"What happened?"

"Sorry, Nancy. I guess I'm a little touchy right now."

"They say LeMarc came after you." She brushed at his wild thatch of hair.

"I've had some time to think about this while I was cooling my heels here. I'd say there's a good shot LeMarc's hiding something, with his kids or his wife—or something worse." Still limping a bit, Bodowski walked with Nancy to the parking lot. "Of course, maybe he's just seen too much. Trying to drown all that death in booze could drive a man nuts."

"What are you going to do?"

"You mean, after I take a half-dozen aspirins? I'm going to investigate him thoroughly. I've got to make sure."

# Chapter Twenty-Six

Near Munsan, Korea: Saturday, June 29, 1952

"Word is they're going to ship you stateside next week." The soldier checked the ammo magazine of his carbine. "Why's a blue-ribbon hero like you sticking your neck out on patrol? They could get any dogface to do this. You ain't the last squad leader left in Korea, you know."

"Shut up, Peterson. You want the fishheads to find us?" Buck Sergeant LeMarc signaled to the column of a dozen men strung out along the dusty road to close ranks and join him. Using a map pulled from underneath his flak vest, LeMarc pointed to a small red triangle and then to the wooded ridge a few hundred meters from their position. "G2 wants us to confirm that there's a possible enemy lookout just over there, like it shows right here on the map. Loudmouth here can walk point."

"Fuck you very much, Sarge."

"Anything to sew your trap shut. Okay, now listen up. We ain't here to engage—just to reconnoiter, savvy?"

The men nodded their assent.

"Markenville, Chavez. You hang back with the Browning. If you got to open up, try not to blow Peterson's ass off."

"Man, I can't wait for you to rotate."

"All right, let's get it done."

Minutes later, Peterson reached the crest of the ridge and signaled for the squad to follow. The other men ventured several dozen meters up the hillside, placing themselves in an exposed position. Peterson stood up and removed his helmet to wipe away the sweat from the liner band. A single shot rang out and echoed off the granite outcrops along the ridge. LeMarc and the remainder of the squad hit the ground. No one could tell from where the shot had originated. Peterson stood frozen for a few seconds before collapsing into the dirt.

"Oh shit—Sarge, is he okay? Did he get hit?"

"Shut the fuck up! Anybody see where it came from?"

Prior to the shot, the men had advanced up the hill in a wide arc, keeping several meters between them with LeMarc holding the center and the Browning team bringing up the rear. The two machine gunners set up their position while the sergeant, still on the ground, struggled to remove his ammo belt and vest.

"Sarge! What the hell are you doing?"

"Watch your heads, damn it. Don't do nothing unless I give the signal, and bring my shit along with you. Johnson, if I go down, you get everybody back and tell the LT we drew sniper fire, but we got no twenty on the objective. You hear me?"

"Check, Sarge."

Free of encumbrances, the squad leader leapt to his feet and ran uphill. When he reached the midpoint of the ridge, another shot tore through the humid air and blew up dust where it hit, no more than two feet behind him. LeMarc realized the shot had come from an outcropping to his left and, while still on the dead run, pointed to the mound of granite with an outstretched arm. The Browning crew opened up with their thirty caliber, raking the hell out of the earth surrounding the layer of rock. A squad member affixed an M7 grenade to his rifle and took careful aim. The resulting explosion behind the granite face sent rocks and dirt raining onto the open hillside. The sergeant got to within feet of where Peterson lay and threw himself flat on his belly. Inching forward, he called out the unlucky private's name. The man neither answered nor moved. LeMarc sidled up and jerked him by the shoulder. Peterson's head flopped to the side, exposing the gaping hole in his left temple. For the next few minutes,

LeMarc maintained his position while Corporal Johnson and the other men advanced to the outcropping. They found the sniper's torn body sprawled on the far side of the rocks.

Reforming his small unit near the top of the ridge, LeMarc ordered two men to stay with Peterson's body and guard the rear. There was a small hut on the other side of the ridge, and he led the remainder of the squad past a pen full of bleating goats and up to the front wall of the structure. At his direction, two soldiers crashed through the rickety door. Hearing screams but no gunfire, LeMarc rushed in after them to find his men pointing their rifles at a small Korean family huddled on the earthen floor. An older man, perhaps the grandfather, prattled as a middle-aged woman squeezed two small children, a boy and a girl, to her chest.

"Ain't much of an enemy position, Sarge."

"Don't be so sure. Could have been this old slope's boy that wasted Peterson."

"What do you want us to do with them?"

"Nothing for now. Set up a guard rotation with your section until I can figure out our next move."

The old man, dressed in rags and wearing clogs made of tire remnants, placed his hands together and bowed repeatedly to LeMarc. The sergeant surprised the two soldiers by spitting on the man and kicking him to the floor.

"Fucking zipperhead."

For the next hour, while the unit rested, the unceasing cries of the Korean family echoed through the mountainous terrain. LeMarc, sitting alongside his corporal on a log in front of the hut, became more agitated with every passing moment.

"Christ sake, Sarge, you need to calm down. What's wrong with you? You look like you're fixin' to explode."

"We're going to take the geezer and the woman back over the ridge. We'll take them to G2 so they can question them. But we ain't going to make it to base by nightfall. Too many slopes in the trees for us to go after dark."

"You want us to set up camp?"

"Yeah, about five hundred meters back the way we came. Let's go."

LeMarc stood up and shouted orders at the unit.

"What about the kids, Sarge?"

"What about them?"

"They're only about six or seven. Shit, who knows how old them little slopes is? Leaving them on their own just don't seem right. We could stay here. We got a hut and all. Why go lay out on the ridge?"

"You heard me, goddamnit. Now move!"

"Sure, Sarge, sure. Anything you say."

Corporal Johnson undertook the task of separating the prisoners. The woman collapsed in anguish, certain she would never see her children again. Her plaintive cries penetrated Johnson so deeply that he stepped out of the hut for a moment and forced himself to take several deep breaths.

With their Korean captives in tow, the unit set up camp a half kilometer from the hut. Two members of the squad wrapped the body of Private Peterson in a poncho and hauled it down the ridge to lie next to the living.

Hours passed, and still the prisoners cried and begged as they huddled together amid the squad. As midnight approached, two soldiers got up to relieve the guards.

"Chavez, stand down. We've all had a tough day. I'll take this one," LeMarc said. "Besides, I'm getting' tired of hearing them fucking slopes whine."

"Okay, Sarge."

The stocky man grabbed his weapon and walked up the ridge. He disappeared into the darkness. Moments later, the guard he relieved walked into the dim light of the camp.

"Damn. You guys see that? What's gotten into LeMarc? He just took over my guard mount."

"Hey, Johnson, I hear you was with him when he pulled the big deal."

"Yeah."

"Well, c'mon. Give us what you seen."

"We're in a ditch and run out of ammo during a firefight. Some slope throws in a grenade and Sarge jumps on it. Of course, it didn't go off. After that, he runs out while the shit's flying and starts dragging back weapons and ammo off bodies. He must have done it half a dozen times. Every time he goes out, he's shooting slopes who's charging him—a regular fucking John Wayne."

"They say he's going to get the Medal of Honor. Man, that's one brave motherfucker."

Johnson peered into the darkness toward LeMarc's position. "Brave? Sure. I know he saved my sorry ass. But while it was going on, it seemed more like a crazy stunt to me—just like what he did today."

Half an hour before the next change of guard, Johnson ordered Chavez to relieve the sergeant. With dawn nearing, he knew LeMarc needed to plan their return to base. Chavez ran back into the encampment a minute later.

"He ain't there! I can't find him!"

"Take it easy. I'll go back with you."

Chavez and Johnson hiked uphill to the guard position near the midpoint of the ridge, but they could not find LeMarc. As they whispered their concerns to each other, first light illuminated the mountains and revealed a figure walking toward them from higher up on the ridge.

They brought their weapons to the ready. Hearing the safeties click off, LeMarc spoke.

"Hey, boys, those ain't for me, are they?" He came up to them. "How come there's two of you?"

"How come you left your post?"

"I didn't leave my post. I thought I heard something going on up the ridge or over on the other side where the hut is. I went to take a look. Guess it was just the goats. If you listen real close, you can almost hear them."

Despite the meager light, Johnson detected a strange look on LeMarc's face.

"Sarge? We heading out soon?" Chavez asked.

"Right now."

"What about the kids?"

"What about them?" Sniffing at the air, he asked, "You guys make coffee?" He turned and strode toward camp.

Chavez looked at Johnson, then fell in behind LeMarc. The corporal stayed put. He recalled the pitiful cries of the children from the previous evening as the unit pulled out, taking their grandfather and mother with them. Now the only sound he could make out was the bleating of the goats.

# Chapter Twenty-Seven

## Catching Up Is Hard to Do

"What in the world happened to you?" Mavis watched as the bandaged detective limped to his desk and began rifling through the papers scattered on top.

Nancy caught the older woman's eye. "You know that man they've got down in holding?"

"Yeah. I heard they have that hero fellow, LeMarc."

"Well, he attacked Steve right outside. And in broad daylight, no less."

"Oh my. Are you going to be all right?"

Bodowski waved her off.

"Better let him be."

"You know Major Palls is looking for him," Mavis said.

"He's looking for Steve?"

Bodowski lifted his head. "What? He wants to see me now?"

"Yes. He wants you to go with him and brief the colonel."

"Goddamnit, this is all I need. I was going to grill LeMarc."

"That's going to have to wait. When the runner gets back and finds you—"

"I got it, thanks." Bodowski turned his attention to the other detective in the squad room. "Hey, Delancy?"

"Yeah?" The man didn't lift his head, buried in a copy of the *Stars and Stripes*. "What do you need?"

"You worked the canvass yesterday for the dead girl. You handled building N142, apartment 306, the Nowak family—or was it someone else who took it?"

Delancy dropped the newspaper. "Ain't it in the report?"

"Nothing in the report says who caught N142."

"Let's see." Fishing out his notebook, Delancy thumbed through a few pages. "Apartment 306. I gave it a one grade—moderate suspicion. C'mon, ain't that in the report?"

"Yeah, I know it's in here. I just want you to think for a minute. Do you remember that interview?"

"Sure. Nice lady, right out of *Ozzie and Harriet*. Neat apartment, too, real clean." He referred to his notes. "She says her old man got a call around two or three in the morning, and he got into uniform and took off. Says he didn't get back until around, uh, seven."

"Bodowski? Hey, Bodowski." The enlisted runner for the battalion CO's office appeared in the squad room doorway. "Jeez, man. You look like death warmed over. Major Palls is looking for you. He wants you to meet him at the colonel's office. You'd better hop to it. The major's been waiting, and he ain't happy."

Bodowski waved to acknowledge the runner's message as he moved toward Nancy's desk. Despite several aspirin and the shower of concern from his girlfriend on the ride back from the hospital, his head felt like it would split at the seams.

"Nancy, whatever you do, find those missing case files for Nowak. Something's going on and I need to find out what."

"Oh, the Nowak files? I got them right here," Mavis said.

"What?" Nancy asked. "All of them?"

"Sure. I got the two Judge Advocate's case files and even Nowak's personnel file. Can't keep these too long. You know how they are over there."

"I don't get it. Somebody returned the case files just after I left to pick up Steve?"

"A clerk from the Judge Advocate's dropped them by not ten minutes ago."

"Who cares how we got them?" Bodowski put a hand to his forehead and grimaced.

"You're just going to keep pushing yourself, aren't you, Steve?"

"I know what I'm doing, Nancy. Mavis, give them to me." He grabbed the manila folders and rushed out of the squad room.

"Why don't you insist that he go home? He's a mess."

"I think you'd have to shoot him to get him to stop."

Ducking into the utility closet across the hallway from the squad room, Bodowski pulled the chain on the single bulb dangling from the ceiling. He cleared some shelving space on one of the tall racks and spread out the manila folders. Others had a head start on Nowak and he needed to catch up. Frustrated by the sheer size of the Judge Advocate's reports on the child pornography cases, he skipped to the findings and resolution sections. Both the accused drew Undesirable Discharges, but only one caught jail time. Private Timothy Wilford had been sentenced to six months in the Mannheim Stockade.

"Hey, where's Bodowski?" filtered in from the hallway. "The major's going to have a stroke."

Time was running short. Leafing through Nowak's personnel file revealed nothing of interest until he discovered the deceased dependent form: DAUGHTER: NOWAK, SUSAN R, DOB 5-OCT-51, DECEASED 12NOV56, COD: ASPHYXIATION. The investigating officer had determined the cause to be accidental. Bodowski knew this warranted further scrutiny, but right now, he had a date with the top. As he was closing the file, Nowak's current address caught his attention.

"Winterville N142, APT 306," he read aloud. He already knew that, but this time something about it clicked. That Nowak resided in the Winterville Housing Area did not raise a flag—most low-ranking officers lived on the north end of the complex. But it dawned on him that the buildings numbered in the hundreds faced the potato farm. Nowak would have a clear view of the spot where they found the body. Checking to see that the hallway was clear, he rushed back into the office, tossing the files into his desk drawer.

"Steve? What are you doing? The major's got men all over the building looking for you. Why aren't you up there?"

Bodowski winked at Nancy and left the office. His leg was feeling a little better as he scaled the steps to the third floor. Rubbing his thigh, he remembered the knot he'd received years ago outside Bell's Tavern in Tacoma. He pushed the memory away as he entered the Provost Marshal's outer office.

Palls flicked at his cigarette, not even pretending composure as he shouted, "About goddamned time. What the hell happened to you?"

"Had to fend off an attack."

"What? I didn't hear about this? What attack?"

The intercom on the secretary's desk pinged and she announced, "Gentlemen, the colonel's ready for you."

"Jesus—you can't go in looking like that. At least pull off that idiotic bandage."

"It's holding the other bandage over my stitches."

"Gentleman, please," the secretary said.

"Let's go, Bodowski." Palls grabbed the doorknob to the inner office and stabbed a finger at the detective's nose. "Do not embarrass me. And leave Kross out of it."

They came to attention standing on the expensive Persian carpet in front of the colonel's wide teakwood desk. Crowded with small statuary, tobacco boxes, and a brass nameplate embedded in dark wood that read WILLIAM MARION FULBRIGHT, the desk created a sense of distance between the men and its owner. Plaques and photographs plastered the wall behind the colonel's chair. The room's décor smacked of self-congratulation. Struck by the contrast between Palls' tiny, crowded workspace and the colonel's extravagantly decorated office, the detective smothered a grin.

Rising from his plush leather chair rimmed with brass buttons, the large, heavyset officer smashed out a cigarette in a crystal ashtray. "Good to see you, Randolph. Please be at ease. Don't stand on ceremony."

The colonel's manner differed from that of any officer in Bodowski's experience. He had the strange thought that the big man was a bad actor hired to play a colonel, but he was getting the part all wrong.

"So this is Sergeant Bodowski?" Fulbright rounded his considerable desk and extended a hand to the detective, an action almost unheard of between a field-grade officer and an enlisted man upon first meeting. The gesture did not faze the young detective, who returned a firm handshake and recalibrated his impression of the colonel from actor to politician. Squeezing the older man's fleshy hand sent a renewed wave of pain to the back of his skull.

"Did you want our briefing, sir?" Palls rocked forward on the balls of his feet.

"Of course, Randolph." Still facing Bodowski, the colonel added, "That's quite a bandage on your head."

"Yes, sir. Took a few blows during an altercation with a suspect."

"A suspect in the case I'm most concerned with?"

Palls turned to him. "Well, answer the colonel. How did this happen, Bodowski?"

Fulbright jumped in before the detective could answer. "Let's just hold on. I don't want to get off track with Steve. It is Steve, isn't it? Or do you prefer Steven?"

Bodowski noticed the open personnel file on the colonel's desk. "Steve's just fine, sir." A handshake was rare, but an officer addressing an enlisted man by his first name was a new one to the detective.

"It's good to see a man able to smile, in spite of the difficulties he faces." Turning to Palls, Fulbright asked, "What have you got for me?"

The little man seemed ready to burst, he was so happy to oblige. "Lack of ID—no missing persons report. We still believe the girl's local."

"A little German girl?"

"Almost certain."

"Excuse me, sir?" Bodowski addressed Palls.

"What?"

"We can't rule out her being a dependent."

"Very little chance with no missing persons reports. It's been more than twenty-four hours."

"We might also consider the possibility that the victim may not be a local, sir—especially given some of the findings."

"Young man. Steve. Do you think it's fruitful to dwell on the slim chance of her being American, or, what? A foreigner? Why not go with the odds? Isn't it most likely that a victim in our jurisdiction is local? Doesn't that make sense, in the absence of solid evidence to the contrary?"

"Well, it's not that simple, sir."

"Bodowski! I think the colonel is trying to give you the benefit of his knowledge." Palls glared at the detective. "Listen up. You follow?"

"Now, Randolph, we don't have to come down hard on the sergeant." The colonel reached into one of the several tobacco boxes on his desk and retrieved a cigarette. "He is a detective, much like you when you were just starting out, and he's trying to do his job. But of course, he doesn't have your many years of military experience." Fulbright lit the cigarette using an ornate gas lighter disguised as a pistol. "You'd be wise to follow the direction of Major Palls in this matter, young man."

"Yes, sir."

Palls jumped in. "As I was saying, sir, we can consider the girl a local. It's probably just a matter of time before the Polizei produce a missing persons report."

"Randolph. You've omitted the most important finding concerning the girl."

"What's that, sir?"

"Why, that it'll be the devil to identify her. The poor child's face was all cut up."

"A terrible thing, sir."

"Go on, please."

Palls cleared his throat and began reading from his notes. "Victim suffocated—probably subjected to some form of sexual molestation; had marks showing that she might have been restrained. Canvass of the Winterville housing area produced no specific leads, but," he looked up, "thanks to Bodowski here, and with a little help from the Polizei, we have developed a viable suspect." Palls grinned and turned to the young detective. "Tell him about Nowak, Sergeant."

"Chief Warrant Officer Henry Nowak, motor pool officer at the one-three-five Maintenance Battalion over at First Brigade, sir. We questioned him this morning regarding an odd coincidence concerning some cases involving child pornography."

"Yes, Steve. Please go on."

"He's responsible for fingering two guys at different times for possessing illegal pornography—photos of kids. I have my suspicions about him. Just a gut feeling about the kiddie porn being his own. That's about it, sir."

"Young man, do you believe in coincidences?"

"Never met a good detective that really did, sir."

"A child attacked—sexually attacked. We know that the vile scum who, who..." He made a show of searching for just the right word. "...slather over those awful photographs are often the very same men who molest children." He looked to Palls. "Isn't that a fact?"

"No doubt of it, sir. Both crime statistics and experience tell us that a man like this is a top candidate for molesting children." He smiled.

"Steve, you need to stay on this man, this Nowak character. Randolph, you provide every resource to our young man here. I want to see a solid case against this fellow, post haste. This is a terrible business. Everyone's sitting on a bayonet." The colonel put out his cigarette and stared at Bodowski. "Can I count on you, Steve?"

"Of course, sir."

With the meeting concluded, the two men left the colonel's office and walked downstairs. Standing in the hallway in front of his outer office, Palls spun and poked the larger man in the chest.

"Don't fuck this up, you hear me?"

"Wouldn't think of it, sir."

"I want this asshole Nowak wrapped up in a tidy ribbon by the beginning of next week, you follow?"

"Even if he's not the right guy, sir?"

"You sonofabitch. If you open your mouth one more time, I'll have your stripes. Do you understand?"

"Yes sir."

"Forget by the end of the week. You get enough on this bastard in the next twenty-four hours to put him in the hopper, or else you'll be scratching your ass on traffic duty. Now get out of here and make it happen." The major stormed into his office, slamming the door behind him.

Bodowski stood in the hallway, allowing the events of the day to permeate his aching skull. Slowly, he returned to his office and plopped into his chair. Nancy moved to stand next to him while he shoved a few papers around on his desk.

"What happened, Steve?"

"A big dog-and-pony show. Palls put on a little drama to make sure the boss feels good about the case. It was all about Nowak." Bodowski sighed. "Look, he's probably good for something, but I just don't see a hard connection to this crime. All this crap with Kross thrown in—well, it all just seems too convenient."

"What are you going to do?"

"What I always do. Follow the best leads and ignore all the bum steers—no matter how much brass is attached to them."

# Chapter Twenty-Eight

## The Bearer of Bad Memories

Bodowski gobbled two more aspirin and washed them down with a slug of lukewarm coffee.

"You've been sitting here for a while," Nancy said. "You really should go home."

"No. I'm okay. Thanks," he answered, rubbing his neck.

"It looks like the contact number for Monica LeMarc's sister is bogus."

"Did you do a directory search for a real one?"

"I got someone checking into that right now."

"How'd we do on his daughter's dental records and fingerprints?"

"None on file."

"What?"

"It happens."

He mumbled under his breath and returned to pouring over the numerous folders stacked before him. Nancy returned to her desk, answering Mavis's questioning look with a shrug.

Bodowski glanced at the clock. It was almost fifteen hundred hours—LeMarc would be frothing about his incarceration by now. Picking up a couple of the files, he walked to Nancy's desk and talked over her shoulder.

"I'm heading down to interview LeMarc in holding before some brass nob springs him. Palls doesn't need to know. But if he comes around asking, I understand you've got no choice." Including Mavis in the conversation, he continued, "I would appreciate it if you could reassure the major that I have plans to hit Nowak with a surprise grilling tomorrow morning."

"The major knows about Sergeant LeMarc being arrested, doesn't he?" Mavis asked.

"I think if Palls had wind of it, we wouldn't be having this conversation."

"Steve, you know we're both out at seventeen thirty today." Nancy swiveled and looked at the only other detective in the room. He sat at the far end of the large room, reading the *Stars and Stripes*. Her voice low, she added, "Delancy's got night duty."

Straightening up, Bodowski resumed speaking in full voice. "Well, I better get going. The suspect isn't going to grill himself."

"Why don't you save it for tomorrow? Go home and get some rest."

Delancy, his face still buried in the sports section, asked, "Got somebody in holding you need stretched out? Want me to go down and close a case for you?"

"That'll be the day. Just keep reading."

Bodowski headed out of the office and descended the stairs to the grim concrete maze of rooms that comprised the detainee holding facility. When he reached the basement, he banged on the large metal door. The slider opened to reveal a pair of eyes and he held his badge up to the slot. A second later he heard a heavy metallic scrape. The door swung wide and an MP in fatigues stepped back, allowing him to enter. As he signed the roster, he handed over his automatic and requested that the MPs deliver Sergeant LeMarc to an available interrogation room.

"So you're going to talk to the big hero, huh? Ain't the first time he's enjoyed a short stay here in gray-rock hotel. I'll tell you, though, I never seen him mostly sober before. It ain't pretty. Say, what the heck happened to you?"

"Just a quiet room, okay?"

"Oh, they're all quiet. You can't hear diddly-squat after you shut the door." The MP squinted at him. "You know, I think I've seen you at formation. That's a real get-over you and your pals got, not having to wear uniforms."

The two men walked down a long cinderblock hallway illuminated by a string of bare bulbs housed in thick wire cages. Taking a left turn at the end of the hall, they passed several green metal doors, each hosting a tiny observation window reinforced with embedded wire mesh.

"They say the SS used these rooms to question witnesses, if you know what I mean. Brrr. Gives me the willies just thinking about it."

"Don't let it get to you." Bodowski understood the power of the place, how the Nazis had designed it to fill their prisoners with dread.

"Here you go." The MP stopped midway down the second hallway and unlocked the thick steel door. No stranger to the accommodations, the detective stepped into the small, forbidding space. A substantial bare metal table bolted to steel supports occupied the center of the room. Welded onto the side of the table opposite the door was a single steel hoop. Three folding chairs, stacked upright, rested against the far wall. Overhead, a wire cage identical to those in the hallway covered two hot incandescent lights. The MP whistled. "Man, I wouldn't last five minutes in this room. I got claustrophobia."

Bodowski grinned. "Me, too."

"No shit? How can you sit in here and not go crazy? It's like being in a damn concrete box."

"It's all about who's calling the shots." He unfolded a chair and sat at the table with his back to the door. Placing the folders on the table, he said, "You could do it, too—just as long as you kept control of the interrogation. Power is a funny thing."

"You can have it, man."

The MP walked away, leaving the door ajar. Bodowski leafed through the folders and turned all the files pertaining to Nowak face down on the table. A few minutes passed before the detective heard the sound of a door opening, followed seconds later by a loud clang as it shut. He heard footsteps and a man shuffling. An MP pushed open the door to the interrogation room.

"Got your man here. How do you want to do it—him locked down or me in the room?"

LeMarc, wearing a torn uniform shirt, grass-stained dress pants, and flip-flops, hobbled into the room with an ice pack taped to his right knee. The MPs in charge of holding had removed his hat, jacket, belt, shoes, socks, and personal items, including his Medal of Honor.

"You can leave him in here. You don't have to lock him down."

"C'mon, Agent, you know the drill. If I'm not in the room, he's got to be locked down."

"All right. Go ahead."

Leading the prisoner to the table, the MP opened a folding chair and placed it across from Bodowski. LeMarc sat without prompting. The MP produced a small padlock and used it to secure the sergeant's handcuffs to the welded steel loop.

"Can't get the new fucking cuffs through the loop. I can be right outside. Otherwise, I'm going to grab a smoke. I'll come back when you say. He ain't going nowhere."

"No problem. Take your break. Come back in a few minutes."

"You got it."

The MP left, closing the door behind him.

The master sergeant, thickset with powerful arms, exuded an aura of physical strength, though thanks to a decade of heavy drinking LeMarc appeared much older than his thirty-six years. Close-cropped red hair framed the tough and finely cracked skin of his ruddy face. His large nose burst in a swirl of blue, spidery veins. Lowering his head to his cuffed hands, he rubbed his face.

Bodowski leaned back. He adjusted his bandage and then threw an arm over his chair.

"Hey, pal. I do that to you?" LeMarc sat back as far as the lock and chain would allow.

"You don't remember?"

"Maybe. I don't know." He shrugged.

"You throw a lot of punches you don't remember?"

"I don't remember what I had for fucking breakfast. How

am I going to remember every time I take a swing at someone?"

"I can tell you what you had for breakfast, pal—a drink and nothing else."

"How the hell would you know?"

"Because I'm a drunk," Bodowski declared, "and drunks, real drunks, forget to eat but never forget to drink."

LeMarc bent over and wiped his forehead on his sleeve. "You? A drunk? Ha."

"It's been a couple years since I had a drink, but I'll always be a drunk." It felt therapeutic to say it, even to LeMarc.

"Jesus, what is this? You from AA or what?" LeMarc looked up and winced. "I'm burning up under these goddamned lights. So if you ain't here to charge me or spring me, then just twelve-step your ass out of here and let me get back to my cell."

"Do you know who I am?"

"Yeah. You're the dickhead that snuck around me to talk to my wife. She described your ass pretty good." He rattled the cuffs against the table.

"Wait a minute. It's tough to threaten someone when you're pinned down like that." The detective retrieved a small black case from his suit jacket and unzipped it to extract two dental probes. Bending over the table, he lifted the small lock and inserted the probes into the key slot.

"What the hell are you doing?"

"Let's see if I've still got it." Working the probes, he squinted while giving the lock a little English. It popped open. "What do you know." The lock dropped to the floor and LeMarc lifted his cuffed wrists over his head, grimacing as he stretched. He bent over and grabbed his injured knee.

"What's to stop me from paying you back for this?" He rubbed his knee for a second. "You damn near busted it."

"I figure you're going to be more interested in what I have to say than in picking another fight."

"Damn thing hurts like the devil."

"Sorry about that. I meant to crack your skull, but you were just too fast for me."

Offering his upturned hands to the detective, he asked, "Why not uncuff me?"

"That'd be against the law."

"You hide behind the law? The law don't mean shit to me."

"Why should it? You're the black tape man. You can ignore the law when the man says you're untouchable."

"What's on your file? Pink tape? All you got to do is stand tall when the shit flies and you could get yourself some black tape too. Of course, in your case it'd probably be yellow."

"You're quite the chatterbox once you've sobered up. It's only been a few hours. You dry out pretty fast."

"That's my curse." LeMarc ran his tongue over his teeth. "I need to keep my tank full, else I lose my buzz quick."

"Wouldn't want that."

Through bloodshot eyes, the squat man sized up his opponent. "So you're one of those fancy Army cops that don't wear uniforms. That good for getting snatch?"

"I have to read this aloud." He flicked a fingernail against the small card he held in one hand. "Article 31 of the UCMJ says you can have an attorney present while we talk to you. And you should understand that we're investigating the death of a little girl we found near Winterville yesterday. Anything you say could be used against you in a court martial." He glanced up at LeMarc, keeping his expression neutral. "I have to say this to everyone I talk to. It's no big deal. We just need some information. You don't mind helping us out, do you?"

"A kid died?"

"Yeah. You okay with what I said?"

"I got a choice? Go ahead and ask me anything you want, but I didn't kill no kid. What's this about? I kick your ass and you want to ask me about some kid?"

"Who's Frau Mueller?"

"Where the fuck did that come from?" LeMarc looked for answers on the bare walls of the room. "I thought we were here to talk about me smacking you. What the hell do you want with me, anyway?"

"Who's Frau Mueller?"

"You talked to that ugly bitch I live with. Why didn't you ask her?"

"Who is she?"

"She's the goddamned cleaning lady. What'd she do—steal some fucking pennies from an officer's wife?"

"She hasn't cleaned your place in a long time."

"So?"

"How many kids you got?"

"What?"

"You heard me."

"You got my fucking personnel file sitting right in front of you. You know how many kids I got."

"Answer the question."

"Three. There—how'd I do? Want to check the file to see if I got it right?" Red-faced, LeMarc bent forward. "You know, maybe I'll just keep my mouth shut. Yeah, that's the last goddamned question I'm going to answer. I want to go back to my cell." Craning his neck toward the small window in the door, he demanded, "Where are the shithead MPs when you need them?"

"Want a drink?"

"Goddamn right I want a drink." He changed his tone. "Say, you don't have a flask on you, do you?"

"Dry as a bone." Bodowski smiled.

"Fuck you. Fuck you and your goddamned questions. I hear one more thing out of your mouth, so help me God—"

"What are your kids' names?"

"Motherfucker!" With that, the prisoner jumped his feet and charged around the table, fighting his limp. Bodowski stood to meet the assault. The master sergeant steamed into the detective, pinning him against the wall. Even though he was pinned by the heavy man's weight, Bodowski kept his impassive expression, coolly holding the handcuff chain away from his throat. No more than an inch separated their faces.

"You already got some time coming for your little trick this morning." He sounded calm despite the physical strain. "If I say anything, this business gets you two more years. That means Leavenworth."

"So, what?"

"You do six months up at the Mannheim Stockade—no sweat. You're out in three and only short a few stripes. You're a big hero. Guards will smuggle in booze. Nothing to it." Bodowski shifted and caught some breath. "You know your medal won't mean shit to the humps running Leavenworth. Just imagine—three years in isolation and nothing to drink. After your stretch, they hand you a dishonorable discharge before you start your next career: selling your ribbons, one at a time, for a shot of booze."

"Maybe I should just kill you now and get it over with."

"You're good at killing, aren't you?"

LeMarc eyed him for a moment. He backed away and asked, "What do want with me? I didn't kill no kid. I don't even know what you're talking about. Goddamnit, come out and tell me what you want with me!" It was almost a plea.

"Sit down." The detective rubbed his hands where the chain had left a deep impression in his palms. The assault had only exacerbated his headache.

LeMarc limped back to his seat.

"What are your kids' names?"

LeMarc muttered something under his breath and then, resigned, answered, "Tony, Tammy, and Marc."

"That their birth order?"

Thinking for a second, he responded, "Yeah."

"Where's Marc?"

"What?"

"Answer the question."

"Hell, I don't know. It's late. It's after school, ain't it? Home, I guess."

"And where's Tammy?"

"Fucking wife." He shook his head and bit his lower lip. "Shipped her off to her sister's in Dayton."

"Dayton?"

"Yeah, Dayton fucking Ohio."

"What's her name?"

"Who?"

"The sister. Your wife's sister in Dayton, Ohio."

"How the hell should I know?"

"You don't know your sister-in-law's name?"

"I never met her." Cheeks reddening, he asked, "What's with the goddamned twenty questions?"

"Your wife ever mention her sister to you?"

"You mean before I hear about Tammy going there?"

"Yeah."

"No."

"You're telling me you've been married for, what," he referred to LeMarc's personnel file, "sixteen years? And, in that whole time, your wife never mentions she has a sister until just a few weeks ago?"

"A few weeks? Hell, a couple of days ago."

Bodowski held up the folder, hiding the dependent transfer form while he scanned it for dates. "You black out a lot?"

LeMarc shrugged.

"You get so wasted you can't remember signing something?"

"Hey. Give me a little credit, buddy."

"Tammy go by boat or plane?"

"How am I going to know that?"

"Did she go to Rhein Main or Bremerhaven?"

"Hell, all I know is that bitch said she put her on the train."

"Train?"

"Behind my back. Don't that beat all?"

"Your wife put a ten-year-old girl—alone—on a train for a port of departure from a foreign country?" He moved forward. "Figuring out the German railway system, switching trains, catching a ride to whichever base from the Bahnhof, checking in with personnel—I could go on and on. I don't think she did. You get it?"

"Yeah." More perplexed than angry, he added, "I ought to know."

"Yeah, you ought to, but you don't. Jesus. You haven't even stopped to think about this."

"I—"

"Why'd your wife put in for the girl's transfer?"

"Huh?"

"Here, check this out." He thrust the 9034 into LeMarc's face.

"What's that?"

"It's called a 9034—a dependent transfer form. This one's made out for one Tamera LeMarc and signed by both you and your wife."

"Piss off. I didn't sign nothing of the sort."

"Oh, I believe you. I have no doubt that your wife forged your signature."

"Dirty bitch."

"Jesus, LeMarc." The detective laughed in amazement. "You been stoned for so damn long you didn't even have enough sense to question your wife's bogus story about how your kid left." He shoved the form back into the folder. "Got any idea why your wife wanted to ship your daughter off?"

"I...I don't know. Christ sake, I'm burning up in here."

"Maybe the missus figured it was just a matter of time before the drunken monster she lived with was going to do something."

"What are you saying to me?" LeMarc's face grew bright red.

"A drunken pig like you—a wife-beating, child-terrorizing son of a bitch. I've seen it too many times—too many times not to see it in you."

"Shut your goddamned mouth."

"You get fucked up enough and angry enough, well, pussy is pussy."

LeMarc's eyes narrowed. "I'll kill you."

"She wanted to get her out. It was the only way to save her."

"Cocksucker!" LeMarc bolted to his feet and charged the detective, but Bodowski got the edge on him, rounding the table first. This time it was LeMarc who found himself pushed up against the wall.

"Maybe it went down another way. Got any thoughts on that, hero?"

LeMarc, despite his raw strength, could not free himself from the taller man. "Goddamnit, let me go."

"Maybe you caught wind of your wife's plan." The detective pressed his advantage. "Maybe you decided to give your daughter a little going-away present."

LeMarc struggled to no avail.

"I saw your place. I saw that you like to sleep it off on your daughter's bed. Bet it happened all the time. I guess you couldn't live with the shame. So you snuffed the life out of her and cut her up so we couldn't identify her. Then you toss her like so much garbage into that ditch just a ways from your apartment. No wonder there aren't any completion forms on your daughter's rotation. She never left, and your wife's helping you to cover it up."

LeMarc's face went ashen. "What?" He stopped struggling, his arms going limp as he slumped into the wall. "My little girl? My little girl's dead? No, that ain't possible. She ain't dead."

Bodowski grabbed him by the arm and pushed him into his seat. "So where the hell is she?"

"No, no. You don't understand. She left on a train. She's heading for the States." Confused, he rubbed his forehead and looked to the detective for reassurance.

It struck Bodowski that LeMarc was truly at sea over what had happened to his daughter. Disappointed, he walked back to his side of the table and kicked over his chair.

The prisoner did not react. Distraught, like a man who loses something and struggles to retrace his steps, LeMarc lowered his head and muttered to himself, too quietly for Bodowski to pick out the words.

Startled by a sudden impulse to kill his prisoner, the detective placed his hands on his hips and took several deep breaths. His head throbbed.

The MP signaled his return by tapping on the glass. Bodowski retrieved the padlock from the floor and reconnected the confused man to the steel hoop. Opening the door, he said, “He’s all yours.” He stepped past the MP and stood in the hall. Taking another deep breath, he bent over, hands on his knees, and exhaled.

# Chapter Twenty-Nine

## Tino and the Goons

"He's heading out."

"What? Now?" Bodowski held the telephone receiver away from his ear. The loud crackle compounded his headache. "Are you sure?"

The tinny voice on the other end cut in and out. "You told me to call you when the chief—Nowak took off, right?"

"Yeah, but I meant when he was headed off post. Did he say he was headed off post?"

"I know he is. He said he had to run home first, and then he would be gone for a while running errands. That's the same old bullshit he feeds us when he's going into town."

"Has he taken off yet?"

"Uh huh. He left a minute ago, but you might be able to catch him at home."

"He actually goes home first?"

"I think so. At least, that's what I heard."

"Thanks." Bodowski hung up the receiver and snatched his raincoat off the rack. Holding the slim case folder in his mouth, he struggled to get his arms through the sleeves.

"Where are you headed? You just got back from the interrogation with LeMarc." Nancy stood at her desk. "I thought you were going home."

Mavis stared at the folders on her desk, pretending not to listen.

"Home, Steve. To your quarters—to take it easy?"

"Got to go. I have a chance to see what Nowak does off post." Pulling a black watch cap from his desk drawer, he walked to the door. "Sign me out as a tail on Nowak. I'll try to get back… shit, what time is it?" He glanced at his watch. "Damn, it'll be dark in less than an hour."

"Oh, wait," Mavis piped.

"What? I have to get going."

"Robertson—the new agent? He called in. Said he had something for you, something to do with a request from Melcher."

"What's he got?"

She read from a legal pad. "Slidell's gone on leave—search of quarters came up empty on the knife—won't be able to contact him for a couple of days." She looked up. "This means something to you, I take it."

"Goddamnit." He raced out of the office.

"What are you doing? You've got to slow down." Nancy's words bounced off the empty doorway.

"The way he's been hurt," Mavis said, "he shouldn't even be on duty."

Nancy leaned back in her chair and closed her eyes.

"Are you all right?"

After a beat, Nancy answered, "No, I don't think so."

Bolting through the massive front door of the building, Bodowski ran across the gravel parking lot, bypassing the vehicle assigned to him by Provost Marshal's office. He jumped into his own car, an older model Opal Coupe with a slipping clutch. The aging engine whined its disapproval as he sped over the wet cobblestone streets that separated Woodford Kaserne from the Winterville housing area.

He pulled up to the apartment building just in time to see Nowak step into his car. The detective shielded his face as the man performed a U-turn in his sedan and drove past. He caught a glimpse of the car as it rounded the wide street and headed toward the housing area entrance.

Trailing at a safe distance, he followed Nowak as he veered from the road leading to the Kaserne and drove toward the center of the ancient city. As they approached the mercantile district, he found himself several cars behind the speeding sedan. Twice he had to run red lights in order to keep up.

Nowak passed the city center and turned onto a side street, pulling over opposite an Apotheke, a drugstore. Bodowski managed to find a parking spot on the same street, but he was unable to see Nowak through the parked cars separating them. The detective strained to see out either side of his small, cracked windshield. Nowak emerged from his car and hurried across the narrow street, glancing both ways. Pressing up to the large window of a bakery shop, he cupped his hands around his eyes and peered inside.

"What's he doing over there? 'Utz Backerie.'" Bodowski scribbled the address in his notebook.

As if ducking a punch, Nowak pulled back from the glass and ran back to his car. Three men walked out the bakery and headed down the street in the opposite direction. Bodowski saw two of the men dressed in the fashion typical of German detectives, hatless and wearing cheap gray suits under long leather overcoats. The third man, an odd-looking character with black, oily hair, covered his barrel chest with a brown American bomber jacket and sported a pair of silver-tipped cowboy boots. It was hard for Bodowski to get a good look, but he thought he saw earrings.

Nowak waited until the trio had rounded the corner before jumping out of his sedan and walking into the bakery shop. A few minutes passed before he re-emerged holding a hollow cylinder protected by a cover of butcher paper. The tall man tossed a large pretzel against the curb and jogged to his car. Grabbing the driver's side handle, he stopped and looked in Bodowski's direction. The detective froze. He could tell by the man's eyes that he was looking past him at something else. Nowak got into his car and the detective exhaled. The sedan pulled out and disappeared down the narrow street.

Figuring Nowak had gotten what he came for, Bodowski did not pursue him. Instead, he prepared to go into the bakery, removing his wallet, badge, and holster. He fitted the black watch cap to conceal his head bandages and got out of the car. As he crossed the wet cobblestones, he wondered what business the other three men had conducted in the shop. One thing was certain: no one was shopping for baked goods. The bell above the door signaled his arrival.

"*Guten Tag*." A squat, bald-headed man stood behind the counter and peered over his glasses at Bodowski.

"*Guten Tag. Sprechen Sie* English?"

"I understand English."

"Are you the proprietor? The owner?"

"I am Herr Utz, yes." He eyed him. "We do not get many Americans in this part of town. Most of our baked items are no longer fresh. I am sorry. It is so late in the day."

The detective pretended to busy himself with the candy and whatnot that lined the store shelves. "Your English is pretty good."

Utz gave a half smile. "Well, I had to learn it in school, you understand."

"Sure, sure. Say, what if a fellow wanted something besides bread or candy?"

"Please, what are you asking?" Utz cleared his throat and gathered up several rolls of butcher paper.

"You know—something like my pal gets here."

"What are you doing here? Who sent you?"

"My good buddy Nowak. You know him. Hell, he was just in the shop a minute ago. He took off before I could say hi. He got some of the good stuff, I'll bet." He leaned over the counter. "I want some of that too. *Verstehen*?"

The two German plainclothesmen passed by the shop window. Utz, his eyes growing wide, shouted in their direction. Surprised by the outburst, Bodowski bolted upright. The two men rushed into the shop and, seeing the American, questioned Utz in German. The shop owner let loose a verbal fusillade. The two men seized Bodowski, who feigned shock and offered no resistance. Strong-armed out into the street, they bent him over the nearest car hood and, while one man held the detective's hands behind his back by squeezing his thumbs together, the other rifled his raincoat, jacket, and pants. Bodowski grimaced at having his right cheek pressed against the cold, wet metal. He sensed the frustration of the man who searched him when he came up empty-handed. The cop holding him stood him up to allow the other man to inspect his waistband. Producing the sap, he shoved it in the detective's face and rattled off something in German.

"Hey, what can I tell you?" he responded, smirking. "I forget to ditch the sap."

"*Was sagst du? Sprechen Sie Deutsch*?"

"*Nein*, asshole." The American was in no position to act smart, but the manhandling and his roaring headache had gotten to him.

"*Er kann Deutsches nicht sprechen*." Herr Leutnant Kross appeared and repeated the phrase. Bodowski, always surprised by how deep his voice sounded when speaking his native tongue, acted as though he didn't know the man.

Both cops chattered at Kross. One of them held up the sap and waved it in Bodowski's face.

"*Sie liess ihn los, jetzt*." Herr Leutnant stared them down.

The two cops looked at one another and shrugged. The man holding Bodowski by the thumbs let go and shoved him in the back; the other threw the sap onto the car hood. Kross exchanged a few more words with the two men before they saluted and walked away. The detectives watched in silence as the men rounded the nearest corner.

"Impressive." Kross smiled as he fit a fresh cigarette into his holder. "So what did you do, old sport?" He lit it and added, "Steal a pretzel?"

Wiping the wet grime off his face with a handkerchief, Bodowski answered, "Just trying to steal a little information." He brushed the wrinkles from his sleeves. "I think we've got something here."

"What do you mean?"

He picked up the sap and inserted it into his waistband.

"Those two assholes are on that little twerp's payroll." He motioned toward the bakery shop with his head. "Oh, and thanks for pulling my fat out of the fire. Say, how is it you happen to be here just in the nick of time?"

"I was following Nowak. Then I noticed you following him as well."

"A regular chain of fools." Bodowski grimaced and rubbed the back of his neck.

"There's some bulk underneath your watch cap. A bandage?"

"Suspect took a swing at me."

"Well," Kross blew a smoke ring, "you're more right than you know about payoffs. We've been watching this establishment for some time. It's part of the ongoing investigation I referred to earlier."

"That shopkeeper is pushing kiddie porn, isn't he?"

"Yes, but you knew that as soon as you saw your Mr. Nowak come out of there with his precious treasures."

"What about those two apes?"

"Detectives out of our vice squad. We believe they are protecting the owner. We have them under scrutiny as well."

"Jesus." Bodowski massaged his temples. "What are you guys waiting for? How come you haven't clamped down on this business?"

Kross took him by the arm and walked him several meters along the sidewalk.

"Best we not stand in front of the shop. The less the shop owner sees of me, the better. As for the diminutive man's continuing operations—well, let's just say that German justice, though harsh, comes slower than you might think. All in good time. All in good time."

"It doesn't take a math whiz to put two and two together on this one." Bodowski searched his pockets. "Nowak's getting his porn fix here. Maybe this is also a place where he can order up something even more special—say, a real live girl? I didn't like the creep for the girl—at first—but I'm coming around a bit on that."

"We have no proof, yet, but we're certain that the extent of the operation goes beyond procuring pornographic images."

"There we go." Bodowski fished out a small ring of keys. "I can't believe they missed these. Look, I'm going to get permission to search Nowak's car, but I don't want to tip him. So we'll grill him tomorrow and hold him while I secure the order for the search."

"I'm right with you, Herr Bodowski."

# Chapter Thirty

## Every Boy Loves a Carnival

"I'm going. You gotta go with me." Charlie Nowak danced around his meek friend.

"I don't know. I'll get a beating if my dad catches me," Marc said. He touched the spot on his ribs where a blow delivered by his drunken father the previous week had sent him sprawling onto his bedroom floor.

The two stopped, allowing other children to push past them on the narrow path. Charlie faced his friend. "Aw, jeez. I can't go by myself." Trying a different tack, he said, "A whole bunch of the guys said that they were going over there this afternoon after school. I'll bet they're there already."

"My dad says the gypsies are just a bunch of criminals."

"It's a carnival. C'mon, it'll be a ton of fun!"

"As much fun as your big idea yesterday about jumping into the ditch?"

"I'm going. If you're my friend, you'll come with me. Who cares about a bunch of old gypsies anyway? When did you ever see a carnival that didn't have gypsies?"

"How about the Red Cross carnival last summer?"

"Are you joking? That was for little kids—just a bunch of crappy baby rides. This is going to be the real thing."

"I don't know. Principal Mathers said the gypsy camp was off limits to all dependents."

"That's how you know it's cool—when grown-ups say it's off limits."

"Well…"

"See? You really want to go. You just don't wanna get caught. Tell your mom you have to help me with a special project for school. I make up that kind of stuff all the time when I want to duck something at home."

"We won't be there long, will we?"

"Heck no—just till dinnertime."

"I dunno. I need some money."

"We'll both go home and get some quick. Then meet me over by the fence at the far side of the field. Okay?" Charlie, willing his friend's approval, bounced on his toes like a boxer.

Marc sighed and nodded.

"Great. I'll see you in a few minutes!"

Charlie ran and skipped toward the housing area, laughing as he went. Marc watched him for a long moment before dragging himself home.

Half an hour later, Charlie paced at the appointed spot. Marc, shuffling his feet, appeared in the waning light of afternoon.

"We're going to get into trouble, sure."

"Bull! We're going to have a great time, that's what. C'mon."

After passing through a wooded area, the two came upon a low wooden fence that marked the city limits. The gypsy encampment sat in a clearing on the other side. Squatting on what amounted to public land, the gypsies took great pains to comply with local ordinances. However, once the Polizei got wind of their arrival in town, they would harass them until they left. The traveling Romani clans, comprised of no more than forty or fifty individuals, used carnivals as a means of generating income. What worried the locals was the minor crime wave that always seemed to accompany the bright lights and colorful booths.

"Wow, Marc. Look. It's so neat." The boys stepped into the clearing and gawked at the garishly lit carnival rides crowding up against one another. The kaleidoscope of hot, colored lights blinked out of sync with the steady beat of scratchy rock-

and-roll music. American dependents mobbed the stomach-churning rides.

"Geez. Everybody's here already." Charlie snorted. "I hoped we'd be the first." Recovering, he added, "C'mon, I want to go on that whirly thing."

The excited boy and his cautious friend lined up behind dozens of youngsters, many of whom shouted rudely at the kids already on the spinning ride. An old woman sat off to the side on a three-legged stool and worked a large metal bar that controlled the drive mechanism. Her ancient face collapsed into brown, leathery rolls over her toothless jaw. The slim cigar protruding from the center of her concave mouth looked like someone had jammed a stick into a rotting pumpkin.

"Take a look at her," Charlie whispered to Marc. "She must be a hundred years old."

A thin young man wearing an apron with several large pockets walked along the queue of children, relieving each of them of their small red tickets.

"Charlie, we don't have tickets—just money."

"Aw, crap. I'll bet we have to get tickets first."

They dropped out of line and walked between the rides toward a small table where a young couple sat behind stacked rolls of tickets. A heavyset man in a greasy blue parka stood next to them. He glowered at the young customers stepping up to exchange dollars for a bout with dizziness.

"You can use for both," the woman said, shaking a roll of tickets at the boys. "How many you want?"

"What?" Charlie asked.

"I think she means we can use them for the rides and the games." Marc pointed toward an unbroken line of gaming booths that ran parallel to the rides. After purchasing a few dozen tickets, Charlie and Marc took a moment to watch the action and marvel at the sheer otherness of the gypsies with their ruddy complexions, gaudy jewelry, and exotic clothing.

"You boys love to make the fun, no?"

Startled by the booming voice, the youngsters jumped.

"Oh ho." The large middle-aged man in the leather bomber jacket and blue jeans laughed. "Not be scared." He slapped himself on the thigh.

"What do you want, mister?" Charlie demanded. "Me and Marc are just thinking about going on a ride, that's all."

"Do not worry. You do not do nothing wrong." The man's black eyes, set against the dark olive skin of his face, almost disappeared when he turned away from the lights. A single large gold ring in either earlobe glinted, as did the silver tips of his black cowboy boots.

"Where are big brother or big sister? They here with you?"

"No, mister."

"Your mutti or father?" The boys grew wary of the gypsy's manner.

"No."

"How about these kids. You know these kids?" Marc noticed his scraped knuckles. Charlie, never taking his eyes off the man, reached out and grabbed Marc by the arm. He stepped backward with his young friend in tow. The barrel-chested man stretched out his arms as if anticipating a bear hug, but before he could continue with his unnerving questions, a young, heavyset woman appeared behind him, shouting for his attention.

"Tino!"

The two spoke briefly in a language that the boys did not understand, and then the woman pointed toward the forest. Tino disappeared through the back door of the nearest booth, cursing as he ran. The young woman melted away into the crowd.

"Geez, Marc, what did that guy want? I could barely understand him."

"I don't know."

Turning to go, the boys came face to face with their tormenters from the day before, the two high school boys who'd confronted them at the ditch.

"Crap sake," muttered Charlie, "I can't win today."

"Hey, fatass. Where's your brother now?" The sneering teenager looked around for Tony.

"Leave us alone. Is everybody going to screw around with us?"

"I don't know what you're talking about, you little pissant." Cal stepped forward and poked Charlie in the forehead with his finger.

"Ow. Leave me alone."

"You got my pants all wet—my buddy's too. You and your little girlfriend here are going to pay up. I think all those tickets ought to do just right." Cal grabbed Charlie by the arm. "Mitch, get a hold on the other little jerk."

Charlie managed to break Cal's grip. Slapping his friend on the arm, he shouted, "Run!" Marc burst into action and followed Charlie as they fled along the short midway. The teenagers, in hot pursuit, could not make up ground as the panicked youngsters weaved through the obstacle course of patrons crowding the narrow path. Rounding the final booth, the boys dashed into the forest.

"Marc! Over there." Charlie, panting, pointed to a large van and trailer mixed in with the other vehicles parked in the wooded area just a few dozen meters behind the gaming booths. The boys slipped under the trailer and waited. Within seconds, they witnessed two pairs of feet passing within a meter of their hiding spot. Charlie held his breath. The only sounds he could hear to his fore were the raspy twangs of a rockabilly tune and the footfalls of the irritated teenagers. Behind them, deeper into the woods, someone was shouting. Marc was as silent as the grave.

"Fuck it, Cal. We're never going to find them out here. It's getting too damn dark."

"The hell with them. Let's go."

The boys waited several minutes to make sure the teenagers had not laid a trap for them.

"Okay, Marc. I think the coast is clear."

Just as they began to crawl out from under the trailer, someone ran up from the other direction. The boys ducked back under the vehicle and wriggled around to find a pair of small, bare feet standing not a foot from them. Both boys held their breaths, listening with trembling ears to the sounds of someone gasping for air. Then two cowboy boots adorned with silver tips stepped into view. They heard a stifled scream as the bare feet rose out of view. The cowboy boots backed away and disappeared. Seeking reassurance, the boys reached out and took each other by the arm.

The crunch of leaves and twigs beneath the boots stopped. A door slammed, rocking the trailer. Scrambling out from beneath the vehicle, the boys ran back toward the clearing and the whirling lights of the carnival.

# Chapter Thirty-One

## Someone to Tell Your Troubles To

"For crying out loud, what did you think you were doing?" Tony kicked aside some clothes, clearing a path in the boy's bedroom.

"Don't be mad," Marc said. "Charlie and I just wanted to go on some rides."

"You know you're not supposed get near the gypsy carnival when it's in town." Tony glared at the boys in turn. "It's off limits. What if you got caught? You know Dad would've kicked the crap out of you. And what about you, Charlie? What would your dad have done?"

"Nothing." Charlie bounced up and down, impatient to get on with the story. "He doesn't care. Anyways, that's not what's important."

Tony brushed the candy wrappers and dirty clothes off the lower bunk and sat down. "Okay, what's the big deal?"

The two boys looked at one another before Charlie said, "We saw something really strange over there."

"I'm listening."

Thirty feet away, Monica LeMarc leaned against an aging gas stove, her eyelids drooping. She barely noticed the unintelligible whine of Charlie's voice passing through the door of her sons' room. The phone rang, and she fumbled the receiver. Clearing her throat, she answered, "Master Sergeant LeMarc's residence."

Back in the boys' bedroom, Tony's eyes were wide. "Charlie, are you kidding? You're not lying to me, are you?"

"Heck no." The excited boy looked at his friend, who nodded in confirmation.

Tony stared at the boys for an instant before declaring, "We gotta tell the MPs."

"That's what I was thinking," Charlie said.

"But who do we call?" Tony got up and looked out the window. "What do we tell them? We think somebody's been kidnapped, or killed, or what?"

"I don't know. Maybe we could ask your mom."

"Where you been, on Mars? Fat lot of good that's going to do."

Monica opened the door a few inches and said, to no one in particular, "Your father's in custody." Pausing, she added, "Again," before closing the door.

The boys fell silent. Tony sighed. "At least we won't get to hit for a while."

"C'mon, guys! We gotta tell someone."

Tony looked up at Charlie dancing back and forth on his toes. Despite his own kit of troubles, the teenager felt a little sorry for him.

"Okay. You gotta tell your mom we're going on post. It's a school night. Do you think she'll let you go?"

"No sweat."

"Marc? You with us?"

"Okay."

Following a quick call to Charlie's mother, the three hopped on their bicycles and traveled the short distance through the misting darkness to the Kaserne. Due to their family's constant turmoil, Tony and Marc already knew the way to the Provost Marshal's command. The trio entered the building and stood fidgeting before the desk sergeant.

"Well. What brings you boys out on a cold night? A school night, I might add."

"Sir, my little brother and Charlie saw someone in trouble."

Only a brief description of the incident was enough to convince the desk sergeant that an investigator should hear their story. After bouncing from one MP to another, they wound up in the CID office, where Bodowski, fresh from his misadventure tailing Nowak and anxious to update his notes, had agreed to hold the fort for the scheduled duty officer. Standing in front of his desk, the boys cooled their heels while the detective washed down several aspirin with a swig of cold coffee.

"So, the desk sergeant says you kids saw someone get hurt?" He glanced at the boys before returning to his notes.

Tony started to speak, but Charlie cut him off. "Are you a real detective?"

Bodowski chuckled.

Again, Tony tried to speak, but Charlie was full of questions. "Geez, mister. You're all banged up. What happened to you?"

"Boys, I'm pretty busy here." He looked up at the three and winced as he adjusted the makeshift headband that held his bandage in place. "If you got something to say, spit it out."

Tony finally got his chance. "My little brother and Charlie, here, saw a kid getting hurt. Charlie, you tell him what you saw."

Bodowski half listened to the excitable boy, barely absorbing the story and believing less until Charlie mentioned the barefoot girl. Suddenly the boys had his full attention. He thumbed to an open section of his notebook.

"Can you describe this gypsy character?"

"He was a big old guy, older than you. The lady called him Tino."

Bodowski nodded. "Okay, Tino. Go on."

"He wore a jacket just like Gregory Peck in *Twelve O'Clock High*, and he was almost fat. And he had big black eyes and spoke crummy English with a strange accent I never heard before."

"Anything else?"

Marc cleared his throat and tugged on his earlobe.

"Oh yeah," Charlie said, "I almost forgot. He had two giant gold earrings, just like a pirate. Also, he had on shiny black cowboy boots with metal tips."

Bodowski had that feeling you get when something good falls into your lap.

"How about you, kid? You're letting your friend here do all the talking. Is there anything you want to say?"

"No, sir," Marc said. "Except that everything Charlie said is true. I would have said more. I guess I'm just worried about my dad."

"What's happened to your father?"

"He's under arrest," Tony interjected.

Marc hung his head.

"Sorry, kid."

"Oh, it's okay, mister. It's happened a bunch of times before and he always gets out pretty quick. He's a war hero, so as soon as someone on the general's staff hears he's in trouble, they make sure all the charges get dropped."

Astonished and already knowing the answer, Bodowski asked, "Is your name LeMarc?"

"Yes, sir. I guess you heard of him, huh?" Tony, eager to pretend that some vestige of pride still existed for their family, announced, "He won the Medal of Honor, you know."

"Yeah." Sensing the boy's sadness, he added, "I know."

"I'm Tony and this is my little brother Marc. And Charlie."

"Got a last name there, Charlie?"

"Nowak, sir. That's spelled N-o-w-a-k."

What?

"Nowak."

What seemed like an extraordinary coincidence regarding LeMarc's sons became an astounding one with the addition of the Nowak boy.

"What's your address, son?"

"I live in Winterville in building N142, apartment number 306, sir. My building is just across the street from Marc and Tony. Is everything okay, mister? You're looking at us real funny."

"Sure. Thanks for coming in and telling me about this, boys. You did the right thing. You'd better get home before it gets too late. I'll call if I need anything. Stay away from the carnival, okay?"

The boys said goodbye and left.

The phone rang.

"Agent Bodowski, CID."

"Why, Herr Bodowski, what a delight."

"What do you want, Kross?"

"Any news on the girl's identity?"

"No, and I don't have a missing persons report. You?

"Unfortunately, no. Poor child. You'd think she'd be missed. Pity."

"Any other leads on your end?"

"No, old sport, and that's a pity too. You uncover any more evidence on your Mr. Nowak? He's a likely-looking scoundrel, isn't he?"

"Hold on a minute." Pressing the receiver between his shoulder and his ear, Bodowski flipped through the notebook. "Yeah, I got a chance to scan the Judge Advocate's records of his testimony earlier. What with all we saw today, he comes off as pretty shaky. I guess I could see him planting those photos on the two GIs—probably covering up for himself."

"It makes him look better for it, don't you think?"

"Look, Kross. Planting a few shots of kiddie porn doesn't make him a killer. Of course, there's that business about the accidental death of his daughter several years ago." He felt loathe to admit that Kross and Palls could be on to something. "You've really narrowed in on this guy."

"Well, I guess that will all come out in the interrogation."

"Yeah. If there's anything to it, we'll find out tomorrow."

"I appreciate the tenuousness of the connection. After all, they are just dirty pictures, and as for his daughter, well, terrible accidents do happen. However, I, like yourself, am not fond of coincidences. Also, I would remind you that consumers of that filth are in the statistical forefront when it comes to committing sexual crimes against children."

"Save the speeches, Kross."

"Let's be honest. At this time, do we have any other suspects? Until we do, I feel, as does your Major Palls, that we should continue to focus our energies on this fellow. By the way, you really should surrender the forensic evidence you've been secreting."

"What evidence?"

"I'm reading it right here on your Dr. Larson's report. Ping-Pong balls. Does that ring a bell?"

"Hey, it just slipped my mind. I wasn't holding out on you."

"I believe you, Herr Bodowski. You know we have much better facilities for forensic analysis. Perhaps you could bring the evidence with you when we meet to speak with your Mr. Nowak. Of course, I will need you to leave word with the gate MPs to allow my entry on post."

"Yeah, sure." Palls' standing order to cooperate left him no choice in the matter.

"Cheers."

Bodowski hung up and then phoned Melcher to catch him up on the latest developments. The two talked for several minutes as the detective used his partner as a sounding board. Afterward, he leaned back in his chair and stared at the wall, lost in thought.

The agent on duty returned from his trip to the snack bar.

"Hey, Bodowski—you look like somebody just hit you with a two-by-four. Anything happen while I was gone?"

"So much that I don't know where to start."

# Chapter Thirty-Two

## A Nickel Slug for Your Thoughts

"Shit."

Bodowski had dropped the case folders onto the welcome mat while fumbling with the keys to Nancy's apartment. Muttering, he squatted and collected the errant paperwork. The pain in his skull was almost debilitating now, and he was forced to pause several times during his chore. He stood and inserted the key into the lock just as Nancy opened the door.

"Sorry. I'm late."

Nancy wore a paisley-decorated kitchen apron over her work clothes and an oven mitt on her right hand. She stepped back and gestured toward the sofa.

"It's about time you got here. You're hurt. You've got to slow down."

Bodowski walked over to the coffee table, dropping his folders on top of the magazines already littering the surface. Still wearing his coat, he plopped onto the sofa and leaned back, grabbing his head in both hands.

"Hold on, I'll get something for that." Nancy walked into the kitchen, returning moments later with an ice bag. "Here, maybe this'll help."

He took the bag and nodded in thanks. Placing it behind his neck, he leaned back and closed his eyes.

Nancy watched him for several minutes while he neither moved nor made a sound. At last she said, "He needs to eat" under her breath and moved back into the kitchen, returning with a plate of pot roast. She waved the hot food under his nose, then pulled the dish away just as he lurched forward.

"What the..." Bodowski rubbed his eyes with the palms of his hands.

"I didn't think you would fall asleep." She set the plate down on the coffee table. "You know, it's not raining in here."

Standing, he grimaced and held the back of his head with alternating hands as Nancy helped him out of his raincoat. She placed it over a hook on the coat rack and then took him by the arm as they both sat on the couch.

"Christ!" He rubbed his temples.

Nancy inspected the blood-soaked bandage. "This has to be changed. I'll be right back." She got up and walked to the bathroom.

"Hey, got any more aspirin? I ran out on the way over here."

"Coming."

He pushed at the folders spread over the tabletop. "I got nothing but headaches."

"What's that, Steve?" The young woman approached the sofa, fresh bandage and aspirin in hand.

"Headaches. You know. I got nothing but headaches."

Nancy dropped the aspirins into his outstretched hand and dabbed at the wound with some sterile cotton. She replaced the soiled bandage underneath the supporting head wrap. "There. I'll clean you up after you eat. You say 'nothing but headaches'...I take it a lot has happened since earlier?"

"I'll say." He threw the aspirins into his mouth and chewed. "Two years. I've waited two years for a homicide, and here I am, so screwed up I can't tell my ass from a hole in the ground."

"C'mon. You seem to be making good progress on the case." Rubbing her arms, she added, "I just wish you wouldn't push yourself so hard. You keep this up and, well, I don't know what."

"I can't stop myself." He bent over and sniffed at the food. "I told you before. This is who I am." Sitting back, he pressed his head into the ice bag and continued, "You'd figure my biggest headache's from LeMarc bouncing my skull off a wall. Truth is, it's all the coincidences and strange behavior that's really getting to me. There's so much craziness going on, it's hard to know where to start." Leaning over, forearms on his knees, he asked, "How about I eat right here? I'm not sure I can make it to the table."

"Okay, Steve." Nancy got up and walked toward the kitchen. "I'll be right back with a fork."

She returned quickly with flatware and napkins. As he picked at his food, Bodowski ran through all the facts again, putting the whole puzzle to Nancy's sympathetic ear: the strangeness of the body dump, conveniently right on the jurisdictional line where it would cause the most trouble; the missing knife, the condition of the corpse, and the mercurial leads he had on Nowak and LeMarc, both of which seemed to be going sideways. Nancy shook her head, worried by his recklessness, when he described his encounter at the bakery, but even she couldn't hide her surprise at the story of the three boys showing up at the station, the dependents of his main suspects handing him a tale about the gypsies that, if true, felt like it had the potential to crack the case wide open. Bodowski did his best to fit a few bites of pot roast in around the words, but the chewing made his head ache and it wasn't long before he leaned back into the bag of ice, surrendering the plate to Nancy.

"What about LeMarc? Did everything go okay when you went down to talk to him?"

"The jury is still out on him. I came down hard, but he didn't give up anything. I walked away thinking he doesn't look so good for the murder. You have to understand: this guy's seen more than his share of death. He lives at the bottom of a bottle, his wife is fried, he goes ape at the drop of a hat—he damned near strangled me—plus he has a kid he can't account for. Maybe there's a crime in that, but I got another idea on that whole business. He's one violent asshole, but I don't think he's our asshole." He leaned back and pushed the ice bag under his neck. Closing his eyes, he said, "On the way over here, I got to thinking about why I'm so hopped up about going after LeMarc, and I think it's more than just feeding my ego."

"What do you mean?"

"I've mentioned my father, right, at least in passing?"

"I remember."

"Well," he opened his eyes and sat forward, "he wasn't just a shoe salesman. He was a goddamned drunk shoe salesman who liked to take out his frustrations at being a failure on my mother. Regular beatings."

Nancy reached out and touched his forearm.

"It got so bad, that I, well, I mean, my poor mother—" He rubbed his eyes. "Hell, maybe LeMarc just caught some of the payback I could never give my old man."

"Steve, you have to stop this. Go in and wash up—take your mind off the case for a little while. I'll put on something soothing."

Exhausted, the detective stood and stumbled into the bathroom.

Nancy tuned the radio to the Armed Forces Network before carrying his half-finished plate back into the kitchen. Halfway through scraping the leftovers into the casserole dish, she stopped and threw the serving spoon into the sink. She sighed and stared at the wall clock, watching the minutes of their night tick down. She washed her hands and wandered into the living room, toward the radio.

"Tonight, ladies and gentlemen, our classical hour features—wait, wait."

Surprised by the announcer's abrupt change of tone, she stood back from the set.

After a few seconds of dead air, the man spoke, his voice trembling. "Ladies and—oh my God, President Kennedy has been shot. I repeat, President Kennedy has been shot."

# Chapter Thirty-Three

## The Blustery Wind
**Friday**

"When were you going to tell me, huh?"

"For Christ's sake, Mel, calm down."

"You jaw at me over the phone last night and don't mention one word about LeMarc smacking your skull off a brick wall." Melcher raised his voice to speak over the noise as they entered the packed auditorium. "Man, this isn't some minor scrape."

"Kennedy getting shot is going to make our work tougher."

"Don't change the subject."

"I'm going to be all right."

"Yeah, you look it."

"Can you men in the back hear me?" Colonel Fulbright stood on the stage of the base movie theater, arms akimbo. He shouted above the heads of the soldiers who crowded the room. "Show me a sign, you men in the back."

In contrast to the hundreds of MPs dressed in combat uniform, the small CID contingent stood along the back wall in their customary civilian attire. Melcher, standing next to Bodowski, raised his hand and signaled in the affirmative with his index finger. He spoke out the side of his mouth to his partner. "I should be using a different finger for this guy."

"Check out the uniform," Bodowski said. Fulbright had accessorized his battle fatigues with a pair of silver-handled revolvers on either side of his web belt. "Is there a camera crew around that I didn't see?"

"Men, this is a difficult time. Our president has died at the hands of assassins unknown. There could be a conspiracy at work." Holding his hands behind his back, Fulbright strutted across the stage. "We are on alert and will continue to be until further notice. You men know what that means. If word comes down that the Soviet Bloc had anything to do with this, well, it could mean war. I won't kid you. Another world war could begin in a matter of hours, or days at the most."

Bodowski glanced at his watch. Zero four-fifty hours. The unabated throbbing in his head kept him awake despite the debt of two sleepless nights. Fulbright's considerable production of hot air did nothing to lessen his fatigue. He wondered how such a man could rise to become one of the Army's top law enforcement officers.

"Many of your brothers-in-arms are already on duty in the cold darkness of this dreary November morning, guiding the movement of the convoys and other such—" Having lost his thread of thought, Fulbright looked over to Major Palls, who stood just offstage, away from audience sight lines.

The little man mimed the movement of large vehicles. He then held up his hands, signaling one and five.

"And, well. Let's see." Fulbright continued his boring monologue. "Guiding the movement of the convoys that carry mechanized equipment and, of course, directing the inflow of armored vehicles from 'I' Corps and Fifth Corps." Pleased, he smiled.

Meanwhile, Bodowski's thoughts drifted toward the case and the impending interrogation with Nowak. He was mulling over the implications of the alert and what impact it might have on the investigation when something spilled out of the colonel's mouth that caught his attention.

"During this alert, all normal duties are suspended. You will report for ready status at your go-to-war assignments. That is all, men. Make me proud."

The detective's jaw clenched. He knew the order would derail the case, forcing the CID contingent into combat uniform and onto convoy detail.

Major Palls came on stage as the colonel stepped off. "Attention!" The men stood in unison and he added, "Dismissed." The little man pointed over the milling crowd—and in spite of all the people in the theatre, Bodowski knew that crooked finger was meant for him. The detective sighed as Palls signaled him to come up on stage.

"You want me to go with you?"

"C'mon, Mel—I appreciate the offer, but do you really want any part of what that asshole has to say?"

"Good point. I'll wait for you here."

Bodowski fought through the remaining crowd in order to join Palls, who waited with folded arms.

"Take your own sweet time, Bodowski. As you can see, nothing's going on."

"Sorry, sir." He saluted.

Palls returned his salute, after a fashion, barely flicking one of his hands. "You can forget everything the colonel just said. None of it applies to you."

"Sir?"

"You stay on the case. This is too important to interrupt, you follow?"

"No uniform?"

"You're wearing it. And you can forget your go-to-war assignment. I had you cleared."

"I'm going to need Melcher."

"Okay." Palls shrugged. "What the fuck. You got him. I'll tell the operations officer." He pulled out a pack of cigarettes and popped one into his mouth. "You'll pursue the case, all right, but you better realize there ain't a damn thing I can do about keeping the krauts out of it." He lit his cigarette and continued to speak as smoke poured out of his mouth and nose. "By the way, I know I made myself crystal clear yesterday when I said I wanted to see a ribbon wrapped around that asshole, Nowak." Palls stared hard at the detective, his face twisted as if he had just tasted something acrid. He tossed the lit cigarette aside and it bounced off the hardwood floor in a shower of sparks. "Do you think I'm fooling around here, pal?" Palls leaned forward and pointed a finger at the detective's forehead. "You know, I was going to mention it later, what with this assassination hullabaloo and all, but there's something else that recently came to my attention. You're not being square with me or the krauts."

"How's that, sir?" Bodowski chewed the inside of his lip.

"I get a call last night—interrupted my wife's canasta party—from Kross's boss, what's his name. He says you're holding out on evidence. That true?"

"Christ, sir. Our pathologist found it during his examination. I already agreed to share it with Kross. I don't understand why he had to get his superiors involved. It was all arranged, Major."

"Look. Nobody knows who that kid belongs to, so, as much as it irks the shit out of me, they got a right to see the evidence. You make sure the faggot gets it today."

"You want me to surrender the evidence?"

"No, just let him take it for a while. Make some arrangement to get it back. I don't want to hear any more shit about not playing ball. You follow?"

"Yes, sir."

"That's the spirit. And lose that god-awful headband. Jesus, all you need now is to stick a feather in it." Palls sneered at the detective as he turned and strode toward the edge of the stage. Stopping at the stairs, he shouted, "Hey, cheer up. Maybe we'll go to war with the reds over Kennedy—that'll take your mind off things."

# Chapter Thirty-Four

## Cat in a Hot Concrete Box

"Thanks for coming by, Mr. Nowak."

Bodowski motioned to the chair across from his desk. Herr Leutnant Kross, arms folded, sat on the edge of the desk just behind the detective. The rain tapped against the grimy windows of the CID office.

"I don't know what I'm doing here. I only came because I was ordered." Nowak surveyed the otherwise empty office.

"Mr. Nowak, please sit down," Kross said. He pointed at the chair with his cigarette holder. "You really should remove that rain slicker. It can't be very comfortable."

"Why am I talking to this English guy?" Fidgeting, he sat down and gripped the armrests.

"He's German. I told you that."

Both detectives stared at Nowak until he broke the silence.

"Deserted here, huh?" He tried to appear casual as he looked around the room. "Must be that everybody's on alert over Kennedy. They are over at my unit." Noting Bodowski's bandage, he tapped on his own temple. "What happened to you?"

The detective gave him a stony look.

Nowak cleared his throat. "The alert's got everybody running after their own tails." Nervous laughter overtook him, and he coughed to cut it off.

"You okay? Need a glass of water or something?" Bodowski never took his eyes off the tall man in his wet raincoat. "All the agents are on MP duty, and I sent the ladies out for a break to give us a little privacy. If they come back early, we're going to have to go down to the detention area to continue the interview. I just want to give you a heads up."

"Why would we have to do that?"

Kross jumped in. "The indelicate nature of the subject matter."

"Yeah," Bodowski said. "That." The trio fell silent again, the Americans frowning and the German beaming his trademark grin.

"Goddamn, it's hot in here." Nowak stood and removed his raincoat.

"Got a hook right behind you." The detective motioned with his chin.

Nowak fumbled with his slicker, dropping it to the floor twice before hanging it from the coat tree. His hands trembled. While the man's back was turned, Kross motioned to Bodowski that he wished to speak with Nowak alone. The American ignored him. Often, the young detective took cues from Herr Leutnant, but recent events had put him on guard.

"Case of the dropsies, Nowak?"

"I'll be fine." He fell into the chair. "I should be with my unit. I know it's an alert-in-place, but what happens if my unit gets inspected? Now, why exactly—"

"Hello, Bodowski, Herr Kross." Mavis greeted the detectives as she walked into the room. Nancy entered next, right on cue,.

"Good morning everybody. Sorry about coming back so early, but they closed the snack bar on account of the terrible news. Do you want Mavis and me to go somewhere else for a while?"

"No, no. You and Mavis got a job to do." Looking at Kross and then Nowak, he said, "We need to let them get to work." He stood and picked up several files from his desk.

Kross stood up as well.

"I hate to do this," Bodowski said. "I know it's a real dungeon down there, but we need to head out to detention and finish this up. Shouldn't take any time at all."

“Why can’t we just talk here or go to another office?” Nowak crossed his arms.

“C’mon, it’s standard operating procedure. Hell, I don’t write the rules.”

The young detective grabbed Nowak’s coat. He walked toward the office door and stopped, waiting for the others. “Say, Nancy. What’s the personnel situation like this morning?”

“Skeleton.”

“Heck,” Mavis added, “less than that.”

“That’s right.” Holding up a sheet, Nancy read, “You, me, Melcher, and Mavis are the only four out of CID, and then there’s the desk sergeant and his runner downstairs and whoever they got down in detention.” She smiled and set the paper on her desk. “Oh, and Major Palls. I saw him come in on my way back from the snack bar. Otherwise, this place is a ghost town.”

Bodowski addressed the other men. “You fellows wait over by the stairwell for a second?” Kross and Nowak left the room.

“Not a bad performance on our part, if I do say so myself,” said Mavis.

“Is Melcher on the car?” he asked.

“Yes,” Nancy answered. “Mavis and I saw him wait until Nowak got in the building. He went right to work with one of those skinny sticks.”

“Slim Jim.”

“In any case, you’ll need to sign the search form.” She retrieved a form from her top desk drawer and held out a pen to Bodowski. “I’ll fill in the rest and get the right signatures.”

“The date?” He approached Nancy.

“You know I’ll take care of that. I just need your signature.”

He signed the document and strode toward the door. Stopping, he snapped his fingers. “If Melcher strikes gold, tell him to give me about five minutes before he barges in, okay?” He wheeled and sped out into the hall to join the other men.

Descending the stairs, he felt Nowak’s nervous energy but detected nothing from the enigmatic Kross. At the lowest level, he hammered against the large metal door, just like before, and as before the sliding window opened to reveal a pair of suspicious eyes. Holding up his badge, he said, "Agent Bodowski, CID, and two. One's a German national cleared for entry by Major Palls." The slide shut and the door opened in a single motion. The MP guard, dressed in full battle gear, pointed at the dank, narrow hallway.

"You here for interrogation or for the prisoner?"

He signaled to the MP to stop talking, careful to hide the movement of his hand from Nowak.

"Did he say interrogation?"

"Just part of the protocol, Nowak. That's for suspects. Believe me, this isn't an interrogation. It's an interview. There's a world of difference."

"Yeah, sure," the MP repeated with uncertainty. "An interview." He looked at the room sheet. "Number eleven okay? It's the one down off the left after the T."

"So it's not an interrogation?"

"No, no, of course not." Kross faced Nowak and spoke in a soothing manner. "Just think of this as further assessment of your utility as a witness."

The detective signed the book and handed over his automatic. "How many of you down here today?"

"What? Are you kidding? Just me and Walinsky, and he's out on break. Everybody's up on the bricks today. Hell, we only got one prisoner. You know the one—that LeMarc character?"

"I'm glad to hear that. I figured they would have sprung him once the word got out."

"He's already called his CO about a half-dozen times. I seen that drunk down here a bunch of times before, and they always fish him out right away. I guess what with all the shit hitting the fan, they ain't got around to him yet."

Once the men were clear, the MP shut the door. The loud clang made Nowak jump.

"Sorry, sir. It ain't nothing but the door."

"LeMarc been any trouble?" Bodowski asked.

"At first he was a house on fire, just like usual. But he's been sober quite a while. Hell, he's so quiet now I go back and check on him every hour or so just to make sure that he ain't hung himself or something."

Bodowski thought to kick himself for encouraging the guard. He knew it would only make matters worse as they prepared to grill Nowak. He read the MP's name tag. "Calvert. You can give me the key to the room. I'll take it from here."

The soldier held up the large key. "Sorry there, sir. No can do. SOP says we have to be keepers at all times. Top sergeant shows up and I ain't got the key? I'm staring at an Article Fifteen."

"No sweat. Lead on."

"You ain't planning on taking the German national here with you into interrogation—I mean, interview?"

"Yeah. Believe me, Major Palls has insisted on it."

"I don't know."

"You want me to find the major and bring him down here just so he can see what's holding up the show?"

The MP blew air through his lips before answering, "Okay, but he has to surrender any weapons first."

Kross drew back his leather coat to show his empty hip holster. "I remember the procedure from last year's taskforce."

"Okay, then. If you'll all follow me."

After depositing the three men in the interrogation room, the guard assured them he would leave the door unlocked. Bodowski tossed the files onto the large metal table and sat on a folding chair with his back to the door. He motioned to Nowak, who grabbed a chair from the far wall and sat opposite. Kross stood behind Bodowski, arms folded, leaning against the wall.

"I don't see why we need to be in here." Nowak held onto the steel ring welded to the table. "This is a horrible place. Isn't this for criminals?"

"Do you feel like a criminal?"

"No." With all the umbrage he could muster, he added, "I'm a good man and a good officer."

Bodowski was on, calculating the effect of every movement on the suspect. He leaned forward and coupled a weak smile with the act of resting his chin on his hand.

Nowak caught his breath.

"You know why we're talking to you, right?"

"Like what the German fellow says—seeing if I can be of further help on that awful business with the photographs, right? I mean, what else could I know?"

"So this guy, Henderson," Bodowski leaned back and lifted one of the several files from the table, "he's the first one you caught with pornography, huh?"

"Yeah, that's right."

"What was it?" He opened the folder and scanned a document. "Oh yeah, you caught him with a single eight-by-ten. Hey, isn't that what you told Herr Kross you caught Wilford with—one eight-by-ten?"

Nowak shifted in his seat.

"What'd you do?" He addressed Nowak while peering back at Kross. "Keep all the rest for yourself?"

"How dare you?" Nowak swallowed hard. He jumped at hearing the thunderous knock against the metal door.

Kross turned and admitted Melcher to the room.

Still shaking water from his sleeves, the agent produced the paper cylinder he'd recovered from under the front seat of Nowak's sedan.

"No, no, no, no." The tall man bolted from his chair.

"Sit down, Nowak."

"You can't search my car." He waved an angry hand at the detectives. "You need my permission."

Bodowski frowned as he accepted the cylinder. "Sorry, pal. I saw you acquire this little nugget myself, yesterday, right outside the bakery. I reserved the right to make a probable cause search. Check your UCMJ."

"No, no, no." Nowak, stunned, continued to wring his hands while backing into the far wall.

"What else do you need, man?" Melcher asked.

"Well, maybe you can help process today's latest collar in a few minutes." The detective jerked a thumb at Nowak. "Best you hang around out front until we need you."

"Okie-dokie." Melcher winked at Nowak. "See you in a few, big guy." Exchanging nods with Kross, he left, easing the door shut.

"Now, let's see what we got here." Unrolling the cylinder revealed several eight-by-ten photographs interleaved between large sheets of butcher paper. Nowak closed his eyes and pressed his body against the wall as though attempting to disappear into the unforgiving concrete.

Bodowski's cavalier attitude vanished after examining one of the photographs. "Maybe I need to ask Herr Leutnant here to step out while you and me discuss this further?"

"I—I—" Caught red-handed, Nowak scrambled for a serviceable lie.

"Sit down, goddamnit."

"I—"

"Either you sit down or I charge you on the spot and cuff you to the table."

Breathing rapidly, Nowak moved from the wall to his chair, feeling his way like a blind man. Kross indulged in a chuckle as he placed a cigarette into his lighter.

Changing character, Bodowski held up one of the photos for the German. "You ever see anything like this?"

The German sniffed and lit his cigarette.

"But I…" Nowak choked out the words. His mouth had gone bone dry.

"Article Thirty One of the UCMJ says you can have an attorney present while I ask you about the death of a little girl. What you say can be used against you in a court martial. Now, we can wait while you get a mouthpiece to try and run interference for you, or you can help yourself by talking to me. What's it going to be?"

"I don't, I mean—"

"Good. Let me ask you a simple question." Bodowski leaned

forward on his elbows and stared at the frightened man. "Why did you kill the girl?" He held up the photos, allowing them to spill out onto the tabletop. "Jacking off to these wasn't enough? Did you need a little something more than just photographs?"

"Kill her?" Trembling, Nowak swallowed hard and stuck out his tongue as if he were gagging.

"Ditch the act. We'll sit here as long as it takes." Bodowski pushed the heavy metal chair back from the table and stretched. He grimaced from the headache and added, "Right now, I don't want to know the grisly details. Just why. That's all. Why?"

The room fell as silent as a tomb. Kross blew smoke rings that disintegrated against the cold concrete walls while Bodowski watched the shaken man stare at the table.

Softly, Nowak said, "I loved her."

"I didn't get that." Bodowski leaned forward, placing his hands on his knees. "What did you say?"

Nowak sobbed, his shoulders heaving under the weight of his guilt.

Sensing an opening, Bodowski leaned into the table, forcing his voice sympathetic. "It hurts, doesn't it?"

Tears rained down on the table as Nowak, unable to control the spasmodic movement of his upper body, crossed his arms, holding himself together. "She. I." He could not continue.

Bodowski stood and walked behind Nowak, resting a hand on his upper arm. "She didn't deserve it, did she?"

"No, no."

"Only you can talk for her now. You be her voice. It's the least you can do." He squeezed the man's shoulder. "You want to help her now, don't you?"

Nowak motioned without looking up.

"Just try to talk. It'll make you feel a hell of a lot better to get it out." The detective placed both his hands on Nowak's arms. "Why did you do it? Was she going to tell?"

"She…she wouldn't stop crying."

"You had to stop her crying."

"She was going to wake up Claire. How would I explain it to Claire?"

"Having to explain it to your wife—why, that's not fair at all. All you wanted was to be with her, right?"

"No, I…I mean. I just wanted her to touch me." Nowak's tears were abating, displaced by his self-pity. "She started to cry. That's not right. She shouldn't have done that. All I wanted was for her to touch me."

"It's not fair. All you wanted was to be touched."

"Claire couldn't know. Oh my God!"

"You had to stop her crying."

"I put my hand over her mouth, but that didn't stop her."

"You had to do more."

"I used my handkerchief. I just wanted her to be quiet. She… choked on it, got it into her throat. I didn't mean for that to happen. I was so scared she would wake up Claire that I didn't notice right away." He pantomimed the motion of holding onto someone and covering her mouth.

Unseen by Nowak, Bodowski frowned and shrugged at Kross, confused by the suspect's description of the murder. Jumping back in, he asked, "So she stopped crying."

"Yes."

"Everything was quiet?"

"Yes."

"Claire didn't wake up?"

"No."

"The little girl? What was her name?"

"Susan. My little Suzie."

"Susan?" He glanced in astonishment at Kross, who did not respond. Looking sideways at Nowak, he repeated, "Susan. Your daughter, Susan?"

"Yes."

"When did this happen?"

"Years ago, but I think about it all the time. Every day." The uncontrollable rack of grief returned. "I can't get it out of my head."

Bodowski stared at the wall for a moment. He walked around the desk and opened the case folder.

"The report said she was found suffocated in a dry cleaning bag. Did you do that—after?"

"Yes."

He continued to scan the file. "And the rest of it…coming home, your wife finding the body…you staged all that, too?"

"Yes. Oh God, what did I do?" Nowak slid out of his chair and collapsed onto the floor, losing himself to his tears.

Bodowski motioned to Kross to get Melcher and the guard. Kross leaned out the door and signaled to the detective, who stood only a few feet down the hall, then stepped back into the room and closed the door.

Bodowski reckoned Nowak was now at his most vulnerable and, despite the revelation concerning his daughter, there remained the pressing matter at hand. Sinking into his chair, he leaned under the table to face the warrant officer, whose wet cheek lay against his hands on the concrete floor.

"Henry?"

"What?" The broken man responded between sobs.

"A couple of days ago, in the early morning, you got called out on that phony inspection. Well, that same morning, they found a little girl just down from where you live." He paused. The sight of Nowak convulsing in abject misery made him wonder what could bring a man to molest and kill his own daughter. He reminded himself that Nowak had made a choice that resulted in the death of at least one innocent child, and perhaps another. He screwed himself up to the task. Still in a sympathetic tone, he continued, "Like I said, a little girl, all alone. They found her body just down from where you live. What happened to her? Did she start crying, too?"

"Who?" Nowak, spent, glanced up with bleary eyes.

"The little girl in the ditch along the path near your apartment."

"I don't…I don't know. Who? What are you asking me?" Nowak didn't seem to understand the question.

Bodowski hid his revulsion and tried to coax him. "Henry,

it's time we took care of this business. You sit up, now."

The man returned to his seat, quaking as though every inch of his frame was in agony. "I'm sorry."

Hearing several taps against the metal door, the detective signaled Kross, who relayed a sign through the small window, indicating Melcher and the guard should hold their position. Bodowski folded his hands on the table and leaned forward.

"You've said a lot here, just now—some very important things. You confessed to me about your daughter. Herr Leutnant Kross heard it too. That's all done, but you need to write it down. You know why you have to write it down?"

Nowak, wiping his eyes, stared up at the hot, incandescent lights and ventured, "Because I might take it all back if I don't?"

"No. Most folks think that. I guess they watch too many crime movies. No, it's for you and your daughter."

Nowak, baffled, blinked several times.

"Confessing out loud to Kross and me—well, that's as good as gold in any court and you can never take that back. But by writing it down, you honor the memory of your daughter. You'll see. After you write it all out, you'll feel a thousand times better. It'll really be off your chest for good."

Nowak nodded.

Forcing a pained smile, Bodowski stood and walked to the door. "Henry, give me just a second." He and Kross stepped out of the room. He closed the door behind him and held onto the handle as he spoke to the men gathered in the hallway. "Can't leave him alone for more than a moment." Looking at the guard, he asked, "You got a writing pad lying around out front?"

"Wait," Melcher said. After digging around in his coat, he produced a small spiral notebook. "It's a new one."

"Good, give it to me." Taking the notebook, he said, "He copped to his daughter."

"His daughter?"

"It's in his file—his young daughter died accidentally some years ago. Looks like what really happened is he lost it trying to molest her and then covered it up. A spontaneous confession. What can I tell you?"

"Some men cannot live with the guilt," Kross said with a smirk.

"Jesus, man. What about our case?"

"Mel, you come back in with me. You ask nice if he needs anything to drink. I'll get him started writing. If he wants something, send Calvert here to—"

"Hey, Detective. I gotta watch the front and the other prisoner."

"You do what I say. I'll cover for you with Top if it comes to that, you hear?"

"Yes, sir."

"Anyway, Mel, you sit with him. But don't start any conversations. Just keep him writing. Be good cop. Got it?"

"How the hell are you getting him to write it all down?"

"An old trick I learned from my first partner when I started working Homicide, back in the world." Bodowski smiled. "At first I couldn't believe anybody would fall for a bullshit story about honoring the person you killed, but it works if you get the suspect in just the right frame of mind. Anyway, let's get going. I don't want him to have too long to think. It might occur to him that an attorney would be helpful right about now."

"Wait. You're not going to stay once we get in there?" Melcher asked.

"No—believe me, it's better if I split for a while. Once he gets it down on paper—you make sure he signs and dates it—we'll jump his ass again about our current case. Kross, you wait for us out here, okay? It'll just be a second."

"Of course."

The two men entered the interrogation room, leaving Kross and the guard to stand near the door and watch through the small meshed window as the show inside unfolded. Kross grinned while pressing a fresh cigarette into his holder. A moment later, Bodowski stepped out into the hallway and closed the door.

"He doesn't want anything, Calvert. You can go back to your other duties."

"Yes, sir." The guard walked back toward the entryway.

Lighting his cigarette, Kross asked, "You've conducted quite a few homicide interrogations during your brief career, haven't you?"

"This is my first in uniform, but back in Tacoma I worked quite a few, yeah." Always a little uncomfortable discussing himself, Bodowski felt that twofold with Kross. The German smiled and blew smoke at the ceiling.

"Shall we get some air, old sport?"

"Yeah, sure. Why not? Mel's babysitting that fucker. Hell, Nowak couldn't wait to start writing it all down." He looked toward the holding area. "Give me a minute first. I'll meet you up front."

The detective walked down the corridor to the half-dozen prisoner cells clustered at the far end of the hallway. Upon acquiring the building, the Americans had removed the solid doors in favor of a simple array of steel bars, and as he neared the first cell, Bodowski could see LeMarc sitting on the edge of his cot, head down, rubbing his scalp with both hands. A tray of uneaten food sat on the small metal table bolted to the wall next to the toilet. Bodowski coughed, and LeMarc looked up, startled.

"About fucking time. You going to get me out of here?"

The detective thought about his mother, murdered on the eve of her twenty-ninth birthday. He took a deep breath and then cleared his throat. "That's up to your CO."

"The guard told me Kennedy got shot—that true?"

"Yeah, that's right."

"You looking to pin that on me, too?"

"Sure." Waiting a beat, he added, "If I had to." He shocked himself saying it aloud.

"Cocksucker!" LeMarc snatched the tin cup from the tray and hurled it at Bodowski.

Sidestepping, he managed to avoid most of the cold water

as it splashed down the wall. The detective spun around and strode back through the dark, narrow hallway.

LeMarc leapt from his cot and bared his teeth between the bars. "Charge me, hang me, let me go, or get me a goddamn drink. Do something, you asshole!"

Kross was waiting for him at the guard station.

"You have an interesting method of interrogation," the German said, stepping into the stairwell with Bodowski as the large door clanged shut behind them. They ascended the stairs, exited the building through the first floor and moved out into the inner courtyard. The brisk morning air stung Bodowski's eyes. At least the rain had stopped.

"Yes, yes. Your technique is interesting indeed." Kross brushed lint from his sleeve.

"How do mean, interesting?"

"Come now, old sport. You maneuver him to confess to a crime long past, yet you let up at the moment of truth." Kross looked at his cigarette as though it had become distasteful. He plucked it from its holder and flicked it into a puddle next to an ancient stone bench.

"I've used this tactic before with my fair share of success."

"What tactic is that, hmm?"

Bodowski felt the urge to punch the arrogant man. "If the opportunity comes up, I get the full confession to a crime, any crime, signed and delivered. In this case, we got him to cop to killing his daughter." He squatted and picked at grass turned brown by the rigors of the German autumn. "I let the perp stew for a while, then I come back and leverage the hell out of him to get what I can on the current case." He stood and tossed the handful of decayed grass. "Works better than you might think."

"I liked what I saw at first, but I can't agree with you on this." Kross sniffed. "I would have gone in for the kill."

"Well, it's not your call. Besides, if it all comes out in the wash, what do you care?"

"You're putting our case in jeopardy with this unorthodox method of yours."

"He just copped to killing his own daughter while in my custody. He doesn't know it yet, but he's going to die at the end of a rope in Fort Leavenworth. And maybe we'll get the goods on the girl in the ditch—if he did it, that is."

"Good God, man." Frustration pierced Kross's veneer of composure. "What's it going to take to get you to realize that you have your man downstairs? An obvious pedophile, he's confessed to killing his own daughter whilst attempting to molest her. He surrounds himself with child pornography, and he maintains the most dimwitted alibi I've had the displeasure to hear." The German inhaled to calm himself. "He even lives in sight of the murder drop. He sits upon a silver platter just waiting for you to serve him up." Kross shook his head.

"You're right. This guy's fallen right into my lap. Feels a little too easy."

"Don't make me think you obtuse."

"Okay, you'll have to help me with that one."

"Dense."

Bodowski prepared to lay into Kross, but caught himself. Something was off about the whole affair, and he knew Herr Leutnant was not playing straight with him. He thought it better to get past this for now.

"I'll keep a clear and open mind on this. Let's you and me get some coffee, then we'll head back and press Nowak. Even if he didn't do our victim, he lives in that shitty little world. He's got to know something."

Kross shrugged and pulled out another cigarette.

"Tell me, Kross. How many of those do you smoke in a day?"

"I don't know for certain. Say, eighty?"

Bodowski grinned. "Good thing they're not bad for you."

# Chapter Thirty-Five

## One Death Too Many

Melcher stepped out of the interrogation room and pulled the door closed at his back, handing the notebook to Bodowski. "Here you go."

"Thanks."

"Jesus, what a fucking mess this guy is." He turned and looked through the small observation window. Nowak had buried his head in his arms. "You got anything else for me?"

"We still need to process him." Bodowski scanned the three pages of cursive scrawl. "The MPs are shorthanded today because of the alert. How about you do me a favor and hang in for a while—maybe out front with the guard?"

Melcher patted himself down looking for a cigarette. "You're going to owe me for this. I could be out in the fresh air directing traffic."

Bodowski smiled at the jab.

Kross retrieved his antique silver case and popped it open in Melcher's face.

"Don't mind if I do." Melcher removed a cigarette, and the second his fingers were clear the German snapped the case shut and reinserted it into his coat pocket in a single motion. "Fancy."

"I'm surrounded by smoke factories," Bodowski griped.

"I don't mean to air our dirty laundry in front of our German friend here," Melcher jerked his free cigarette at the Herr Leutnant, "but why wasn't I in on the tail end of the interrogation?"

"Palls insisted Kross be present." Bodowski looked at Kross. "I hope you don't mind us talking in front of your back?"

The German smiled.

"With three of us in the room, he wouldn't have said shit. Believe me."

"Like I said, you're going to owe me."

Herr Leutnant produced the lighter emblazed with the insignia of the defeated American unit and lit Melcher's cigarette.

"Thanks, man." Returning to Bodowski, he added, "Okay. Ring out when you need me." With that, he disappeared around the corner.

"You wait out here too, Kross."

"Beg pardon, old sport?"

"Three's a crowd for this go-round." The detective stood firm. "You just give me a couple minutes and I'll figure out what's what."

"I should be in there with you."

"You can watch through the door. These rooms weren't made for observation, so I figure he won't see you through the little window. You just won't be able to hear much, that's all." He shrugged as if it was of little consequence.

Kross hesitated. "All right. However, if things don't turn out as I believe they should, I insist on taking him back to my station."

Narrowing his eyes, Bodowski resisted the urge to engage. "I'll try to make it brief." He turned and opened the door. "Henry?" He waved the notepad in a gesture of recognition. "How about we talk a little while longer?"

Nowak appeared exhausted, but gave an almost imperceptible nod.

"Great. Great." Bodowski entered the room and pushed the heavy door shut. Sitting, he asked, "You get what you need?"

The broken man did not respond.

"Okay, we'll just get started. First off, I'd like to thank you for this—for standing up." He tapped on the pad.

Nowak mumbled something unintelligible.

The detective leaned forward, cocking his head. "I'm sorry, I didn't get that."

Staring at his hands, the warrant officer asked, "My wife has to know?"

"I won't lie to you. Sooner or later she'll find out."

He covered his face. "I'm so screwed up."

"Just take a deep breath."

"No, I'm telling you I'm all messed up. I—oh God."

"C'mon, now. Let's keep it together here."

Nowak sighed and lowered his head until it almost touched the table. He rubbed his balding pate as he spoke into his chest. "You know, my wife is a little woman."

"Sorry, I haven't met your wife."

"She's real small." He hesitated. "When we—when we do it, I always imagine she's a little girl. Oh my God! Why did I just say that? What's wrong with me?" His head bounced under the force of the renewed sobs.

Bodowski knew this was his chance. "Did your wife hear the call you got for the phony inspection the other night?"

Nowak's tears ebbed. "What?"

"Did she hear it ring? Did it wake her up?"

Lifting his head, he wiped the tears from his cheeks. "What does that matter? Why are you asking about that?"

"Just tell me."

"No. Wait, wait—it did. It woke her up, but I told her to go back to sleep. Who cares?" He searched his pockets.

Bodowski threw out a handkerchief.

Nowak blew his nose. "I want to die." His face contorted into a grimace at the admission.

"It'll be all right, you'll see." Overcoming his repugnance toward the pedophile, Bodowski reached across the table and touched him on the arm. "There's one other child we need to put at peace."

"I don't understand."

"The little girl found in the ditch just behind your apartment. You know, that morning two days ago? She needs rest, too, just like your daughter."

"No, no, no." Nowak bolted out of his seat.

"Sit down." In a blink, Bodowski switched character. "I can still cuff you to this table. Sit." Rising from his seat, he pounded once on the table for effect. "I mean now."

Nowak slipped into his seat like a student late for class. "I didn't do anything to that child. It's not me. How could you think it was me?"

Bodowski blinked. "You killed your daughter after you molested her."

Nowak could not control himself. The tall man's chest heaved. He buried his face in his hands.

"You got caught red-handed with kiddie porn. Hell, you just told me you fantasize about screwing little girls. It's easy to figure: you cook up some bullshit story about an inspection so you can sneak away and stroke your urges, and another child pays the price." Folding his arms, he sat and waited, watching as the wretched man stewed in his own misery. He leaned forward. "Goddamnit, you were man enough to admit what happened to your daughter—"

"Susan. Oh, my little girl!"

"Have the guts—or if you haven't got those, then just have the common decency to help us bury this other poor kid."

Through his tears, Nowak said, "God strike me dead if I touched that little girl." Crossing his arms on the table, he laid down his head and continued to sob in waves, his forehead bumping against the steel ring.

"Hmm." Bodowski kneaded his palm and studied the bare gray walls, choosing his next move. After a beat, he stood and glared at the pathetic man. "You're under arrest for the murder of your daughter, Susan. You recall that I read you your rights?" Nowak did not acknowledge him as he pulled his handcuffs and manacled the distraught man to the table by his right hand. Without another word, he left the interrogation room.

Surprised to find that Kross was absent, he walked to the

front of the guard station. "Where'd Kross go?"

Melcher and Calvert both stood as he approached. The other guard, who had returned from his break, came up from behind.

"He split just a second ago," Melcher answered. "You didn't see him?"

"No."

Bodowski signaled for his partner to follow him upstairs.

"Hey, sir?" asked Calvert, "What do you want me to do with the guy in eleven?"

"He's a felony collar. Toss him into holding and keep an eye on him at all times. Just to be safe, put him through your suicide watch SOP. And don't let anybody talk to him until I get back."

"Okay." Calvert threw a pair of handcuffs to the other guard. "Make it happen."

"Hey, he's already cuffed. Let's swap."

The guard tossed the handcuffs to the detective.

"Sir? I'm going to need some paperwork on him."

"I'll get to it."

Once upstairs, he paused outside the CID office and handed the spiral notebook to Melcher. "Here—tell one of the ladies to type it up. When it's ready, go back downstairs and get Nowak to sign a copy." Handing the writing pad to his partner, he added, "If he doesn't sign the typed copy, at least we got his John Hancock on the write-up."

"You going somewhere? Now I got admin duty?"

"I'm going to talk to Nowak's wife. We have to get this processed. I'm counting on you. Believe me, if there was any time, I'd do it differently."

"I don't know." Melcher mulled it over for a moment. "Go on, man. You've run with it this far."

Bodowski smiled and slapped him on the shoulder. Poking his head into the office, he saw the two women both busy at their typewriters. "Where the hell did Kross go?"

"Right behind you, old sport."

"Jesus." Both detectives started at the sudden appearance of Herr Leutnant.

"How long have you been standing there?" Melcher asked.

"Just arrived. That dumb-show I watched through the little window was nonetheless revealing, but now that the interrogation's ended, Herr Bodowski, I hope you didn't forget about the evidence we discussed?" He smiled and squeezed a cigarette into his holder.

"Oh yeah." The detective fished around in his pockets but came up empty. "Can you believe it?" Bodowski patted himself down.

Lighting his cigarette, Kross frowned. "Now, really, I thought that you and I—"

"Wait." He felt something in his jacket breast pocket. "Couldn't feel it because it was under my holster."

"I hope you have them both."

"Both?" He hesitated in producing the small package.

"The Ping-Pong balls—two of them. Come now."

"Sure." He returned Kross's disingenuous smile as he handed over the bag.

"Light as a feather." Kross juggled the items in his hand before inserting the package into his trench coat pocket. Taking a long drag off his cigarette, he blew another perfect smoke ring. "Looks like your Mr. Nowak lost his courage when the time came."

"How do you know about that?"

"An ear to the door does the trick." Kross flicked the lobe of his left ear. The three men stared at one another. "So, Herr Bodowski. Have you decided on your next move?"

Bodowski pointed a thumb toward the office. "Looks like I got a lot to write up. Probably take me the rest of the day."

"I see. Call me as soon as you decide on your next course of action." Kross spun and walked toward the stairwell.

Melcher opened his mouth to speak as Kross disappeared down the first flight of stairs, but his partner held up a hand to silence him. Listening to Kross's footsteps die in the distance, he turned to Melcher and spoke with urgency.

"I have to make a call right now." He ran into the office.

"What's going on?" Trailing after him, he added, "I like to be in the loop, you know."

"Nancy? Quick, find the number over at the hospital, you know, the medical examiner's number—the morgue?"

Taken by surprise, the young woman fumbled through the papers on her desk looking for the post directory.

Mavis opened the leaf on her top drawer and read from the phone list taped to the surface. "Eight five three five three."

"Thanks." He dialed the number while fishing through the folders and loose papers strewn across his desktop. Picking out a single carbon sheet, he shoved it at Melcher, who held onto it like a vital piece of evidence.

"What's this?"

Listening to the phone ring for the fourth time, he became impatient. "There." He punched the single sheet of paper in the middle. "Right there. What does it say?"

"Let's see." Reading, Melcher brightened. "One Ping-Pong ball, not two like Kross just said. Wait, I don't get it. So what's the big deal? He made a mistake."

"Damn it. That's the sixth ring. He isn't picking up."

"Maybe he's still out to lunch," Nancy offered. "That's Captain Larson, right?"

He nodded to Nancy and turned to his partner. "I need you to track down Doc Larson." He hung up the receiver.

"It'd help if I knew what the hell I was doing."

"Sorry, man, I guess I'm going like ninety. You remember—"

"Hey, I just got it. How does Kross know there are two Ping-Pong balls? That's it, right?"

"Right on target. Yesterday, Kross asks me to hand over the balls. Balls with an 's'—both of them. I didn't think much about it when he asked." He tapped the paper. "I forgot Larson only wrote down one, not two, in his prelim." He rubbed his palm while staring past his partner.

"Now what?"

"Maybe Larson told him, or told somebody else who got word to Kross. You have to find Doc and clear it up."

"What are you going to do?"

"Getting the hell over to Nowak's apartment and talk to his wife before she finds out he's in for murder." He started toward the door but stopped short. "Jesus, Mel, I'm heading every which way from Sunday. Just trust me on this."

# Chapter Thirty-Six

## The Family in Decline

"Oh, my goodness."

Claire Nowak clutched the top of her blouse. Bodowski wondered why he had this effect on women.

"Agent Bodowski, CID, ma'am. May I come in? I have a few questions." He smiled and flipped the badge shut.

"Please." She stood back and opened the door. "You know, I already talked to a CID man the other day. Something to do with that terrible thing that happened out there on the path. Is that what this is about?"

"Like you say, ma'am, one of our agents spoke with you the other day." He produced his notebook. "I just need to follow up on a few points."

"Would you like to sit down, Mr. Bazowski?" She feigned a smile.

"Bodowski, ma'am."

"Mr. Bodowski." She pointed toward the couch. On the far side of the room, through a combination living and dining space, he saw the large picture window that overlooked the potato farm and the path to school.

Sitting on the couch, he unbuttoned his raincoat. "It's not a memorable name."

Claire Nowak took a seat in an overstuffed chair facing him. "Can I get you anything?"

"No, thank you. I'm fine." The detective noticed that none of the furniture matched, typical for the households of low-ranking officers. Opening the notebook to a new page, he asked, "Last Tuesday evening—actually early Wednesday morning, say two or so—were you awakened by a phone call?"

"I—" Uncertain, she searched his face. "I'm not sure. Henry got a call. I mean, he said he got a call. Gosh, I was so sleepy I don't remember. What has this got to do with anything?"

"He did leave, right? Soon after the call?"

"That's right. He got called away to get ready for a surprise inspection. That's what he told me when he got home."

"So, when was the first time that morning you noticed he was gone, and when did he get back?"

"When I woke up—when my alarm went off at five o'clock, oh-five-hundred, you know. He'd already left. That was unusual for him."

"When did you see him next?"

"Just a little later, about half an hour later. At first, he was as mad as I've ever seen him, but he sat down and read the *Stars and Stripes* for a while. That seemed to cool him off a bit. Somebody played a dirty trick on him. The inspection was a phony. He was so out of sorts he didn't even want to go back to work that morning."

"Anything else different or unusual happen?"

"Just all that business with the poor little girl they found. Henry was here when Charlie, our boy, first noticed the MPs. We all watched out the window. It was terrible." She looked away. "I know how awful that can be."

"I see." Scribbling in his notebook, he asked, "Has that happened before? Mr. Nowak leaving in the middle of the night?" He glanced at her. "Not on scheduled exercise or something, just out of the blue?"

"Why are you asking me this?"

"I'm trying to tie up loose—" He heard a toilet flush. "Someone else at home?"

"My son. They sent the children home from school because of what happened to the President."

"Does your husband or son own a Boy Scout knife?"

"What do these questions about have to do with the price of tea in China?" Claire stood and folded her arms. "You don't think Henry's done something wrong, do you?" Although she took a high position, he sensed more desperation than umbrage as she parroted her husband's own words. "He's a good man, a good officer."

"Hey, Mom, what's up?" Charlie emerged from the hallway and smiled upon seeing the detective. "Hi there, sir."

"What? You know this man, Charlie?"

"Sure, Mom." He looked down and sighed. "I didn't tell you or Dad, but remember last night I said me and Marc were going to the snack bar? Well, I'm sorry I lied. Me and Marc and Tony reported some suspicious stuff we saw to the MPs." Realizing that to let on anything else might get him into further trouble, he added, "Just some bad stuff, you know?"

"Mrs. Nowak, was your husband's uniform dirty when he got home?"

"What?" Her veneer of civility melted away.

Bodowski needed to get answers before she shut down. "Dirty. Mud on his boots—that sort of thing?"

"No, No. We are not pigs. He would never run around in a soiled uniform. What on earth do you think Henry did?" Her face went ashen. Rushing down the hallway, she slammed the bedroom door behind her.

"Geez, what's wrong with Mom?" Bewildered, Charlie looked to the detective and pleaded, "Sir, what's wrong? Why is she acting like that?"

Bodowski understood then that she knew about her husband, not with the hard evidence that would convince a jury but in the way only a wife could know. He stepped forward and placed his hand on the boy's shoulder.

"Kid."

He wanted to say something else, something encouraging, but he held back. He knew that when the terrible news about Nowak reached his mother, it would be her job to tell Charlie, and in doing so destroy what his father had meant to him.

"You didn't happen to hear the phone ringing a couple of nights ago—in the middle of the night?" It was a long shot.

"Sure. I got woke up when the phone rang. I think it was two nights ago. It was real early in the morning. The phone is right there on that table." He pointed to the black handset resting on a small table in the hallway. "I got up and answered it. The man said he needed to talk to my father. Dad heard the phone ring too. He came out and took it from me almost right away. Cheese and crackers, he got angry after he hung up."

Bodowski leaned over and set his hands on the boy's shoulders. "Do you remember exactly what the man said to you? Did he give his name?"

"No, sir. He didn't say his name. He just sounded ticked off."

"What time was the call? Can you remember?"

"It was about three o'clock."

"How do you know?"

"I got this neat Mickey Mouse clock and I remember his short hand, the hour hand, was pointing to the side. It glows in the dark. Do you want to see it?"

"You hear what your dad said on the phone?"

"Yes, sir, a little of it. He kept asking who it was, then he got surprised and asked if the guy on the phone knew what time the inspection was."

"What happened then?"

"I got up and looked out my window in the bedroom. I kind of like doing that sometimes when I get woke up. Anyways, Dad was real quiet. I guess he didn't want to wake up Mom. He got dressed in the living room."

"Did you see him leave?"

"C'mere, I'll show you." Charlie led the detective into his room and stood by the window. Pointing down toward the parking lot, he said, "I saw him get into his car, and he drove off over to the gate. See way over there? It's real teensy because it's so far away, but you can still see it. I got good eyes. That night they had guards on it—most nights they don't. And they had extra lights. It was real bright."

Bodowski could just make out the gate over the top of an intervening building. "How long did you watch him—your father?"

"Oh, all the way to the gate, sir. There were a couple of other cars he had to wait behind because they were making everybody open up their trunks."

"You saw him leave through the gate?"

"Yeah. I was bored, so I just watched him. Then I got a big idea and grabbed my binoculars." The boy retrieved a pair of expensive field glasses from a case sitting atop his headboard. "I saw them search my Dad's trunk. He looked real mad, sir. I could see him pretty good."

"May I?"

"Sure, here."

Bodowski expanded the binocular setting to fit the spacing of his eyes and looked toward the gate. "These are good. Where'd you get them?"

"My grandpa gave them to me last Christmas. He's got lots of money."

Despite the great distance, he could read the warning sign on the empty guardhouse next to the gate. "So how long did you watch after your father went through the gate?"

"Geez, I dunno. I must've seen about ten people get stopped and go through." The boy shrugged. "I can't get back to sleep once I get woke up. The doctor says I have some kind of problem with my attention span or something. Mom just says I have ants in my pants."

"You didn't see your father come back through?"

"Heck no, sir. I would have seen him. Why is all this important?"

He handed the binoculars back to Charlie. "Tell your mother I had to go."

"Okay, sir."

Bodowski dashed down the stairs and out into the parking lot, bracing himself for the difficult time that lay ahead. He had a murderer in custody, but Nowak's guilt would not stretch to cover a second killing. He couldn't shake the feeling that Kross was somehow tied up in it. The official sedan roared to life and he took off down the wet pavement, glad to have heard the boy's revelation. He had no reason to doubt the story; experience had taught him that it was rare for a child that age to lie convincingly to the police.

He felt a twinge as he neared the gate. The boy and his mother were hours away from official notification of Nowak's arrest. As to what would happen to them after that...the detective shook his head and put it from his mind.

# Chapter Thirty-Seven

## My Way or…

Bodowski stopped as the MP waved him through the main gate. He rolled down the window, allowing a gust of cold, wet air to burst through the sedan.

"Where are the other MPs? What's going on?"

"The alert's been changed—downgraded." Other vehicles lined up behind Bodowski. "Let's move it along, sir."

When he arrived at the office, he noted the absence of Kross' Volkswagen. Inside, he encountered the desk sergeant sitting vigil.

"Major Palls is looking for you."

"Where is he?"

"Where do you think? Some investigator." The sergeant sneered and returned to shuffling papers on his desk. Bodowski ignored the remark.

The major's secretary was not at her desk. Knocking on the inner office door, he wondered why Palls had not ordered the radio dispatcher to call him in to the office.

"Who is it?"

He shouted sidelong against the door's opaque glass window. "Bodowski, sir."

"Get in here."

With his tiny feet propped up, the little man appeared to sink into the cushions of his office chair. The detective came to attention and saluted but averted his gaze.

"You wanted to see me, sir?"

"At ease." He lifted his small combat boots off the desk and leaned forward in a single motion. "Good to see you covered up that god-awful bandage. How's your head?"

"You want to know how I feel, sir?"

"Hell yeah. I take an interest in all my men."

The detective wondered what had prompted the uncharacteristic display of concern.

"Thank you, Major. I'm still smarting." He removed the watch cap and rubbed the back of his neck.

"I want to congratulate you." Palls placed a cigarette between his lips and struck a match against the side of the chair. Then he rose and walked around the desk to face Bodowski, extinguishing the match and watching as the smoke trailed from his lit cigarette. "Just like that—just like that, we caught a hot case and you were instrumental in getting to the bottom of it."

It was a crude attempt at an analogue, but the detective caught his drift.

"We still have some important work to do, sir."

"That's right, but not you. You've done your part for God and country." He leaned against the desk and exhaled a ribbon of smoke.

"Beg pardon, but what are you talking about, sir? I figure news about Nowak copping to his daughter's death got to you, but that development isn't going to help us solve our current crime."

"Nonsense. You broke that child molester. It was real smart how you did it. The faggot told me you were the man. He said you made it happen. Those weren't his exact words, but you get it."

"Kross talked to you?" The throbbing of his head increased.

"I don't much care for that tone, soldier."

"Kross told you Nowak looks good for the girl?"

"Sir." Palls' good mood evaporated.

"Sir."

"I'm trying to pay you a compliment. Goddamnit, man. You had a big breakthrough." The major returned to his chair and sat forward with his elbows on the desk. "That limey faggot knows good police work when he sees it. I'll give him that. Look pal, you hit a triple and Kross and his cronies are going to bring it home. It's out of our hands now."

"Jesus, sir. Are you telling me that Kross has Nowak? Why would you let him go? For Christ's sake, I arrested him for murder of an Army dependent."

"Hold your fucking horses, Bodowski. Stop and look at the facts." One at a time, Palls unfolded the stubby fingers of his outstretched hand. "The krauts assure us that the girl's a local. Hell, we know she isn't one of ours—no reports, nothing. Thanks to you, we establish that Nowak's got a yen for child porn. Then, of course, he cops to his daughter. All right, I know that little nugget doesn't matter much to the krauts. Finally, he's got no alibi. Man's got means, motive, and opportunity. Krauts need their collar on this one." Taking a long drag off his cigarette, he added, "You know this fucker's going to swing. Too bad we can't kill him twice, the child molesting piece of shit that he is." Palls leaned back, disappearing into the leather folds of his chair. "Hell, I can't stop them from interrogating him. He may be Army, but he killed a local on disputed ground. Our legal agreements with the krauts say that they get a whack at him under these circumstances." Throwing his arms open, he asked, "Why the hell am I explaining myself to you?"

Though he was exasperated, Bodowski took a moment to gather himself, knowing it was a bad idea to push Palls too far. "I got a hunch—no, more than that. Nowak didn't do the girl."

Palls sneered. "What the hell?"

"I interrogated a lot of killers back in the day, sir, and believe me, that surprise of having Nowak turn over for his daughter was according to Hoyle—tears, guilt, you name it. But he flipped out when I started in on the other girl." He turned up a palm. "Why on God's earth would he put a rope around his own neck for his daughter but deny the other girl?" Waiting a beat, he added, "My daughter, sure. A stranger? Hell no." The back of his neck reddened.

"Keep it up, asshole. You're skating on thin ice. One more smartass remark and you'll be looking for your missing stripes. You follow?"

The detective took a deep breath. Shaking his head as if to loosen something that had got a hold of him, he said, "Sorry, sir, that was out of line. Look, Kross is going to get a confession out of Nowak. You know that."

"I sure as hell hope so."

"C'mon, Major. You know what I mean."

"Are you implying Nowak will confess regardless of guilt?" Smashing out his cigarette, Palls sat forward and folded his hands. "Okay, I'll admit that's a real possibility. Those characters working with that limey cocksucker are a collection of tough bastards—a bunch of real thugs. I expect they could strong-arm the Pope into saying he just shot Kennedy." Palls pushed back in his chair. "It's the nature of the beast. Relax, pal. Now that they got him, it's out of our hands—nothing you or anybody can do about it." He studied the young detective for a moment. "You're something, you know that? I have you in here for a simple compliment and you manage to turn it into a fucking soap opera."

Bodowski rubbed his neck and grimaced.

Palls smiled. "I hear LeMarc hits like Sonny Liston."

"So you know?"

"You think I don't know who's in my own lockup?"

"I thought you would have been all over me if you knew, sir. Didn't you put the black tape on his file?"

"Shit, Sergeant, give me some credit." Palls lit another cigarette. "I can't have drunken assholes running around attacking my men just because they're trying to do their job, now can I?"

"I figured with his connections—"

"Fuck his connections. He can take that Medal of Honor and shove it up his ass. CG's pet monkey doesn't mean a thing to me." He took a short drag off his cigarette and spit out the smoke.

For a brief moment, Bodowski wondered if he had just

witnessed Palls showing loyalty to his own at the risk of upsetting a power broker like the commanding general. Then it occurred to him that allowing LeMarc to get away with a public beating would reflect badly on Palls. The angry bluster was for the detective's benefit.

"He's still down there, sir. At least, he was there an hour ago."

"Yeah, he can rot until someone from HQ springs him or fucking Hell freezes up. Say, what exactly set him after you, anyway? I didn't see your report on that yet."

"I been too busy and too damn tired to write it up."

"Well, sounds like it'll be fun reading. I can't wait." Palls swept a hand toward his subordinate as though he were pushing away cobwebs. "Okay, that's all. Why don't you get an early start on the weekend? Screw what's left of the alert. Kennedy ain't going to get any deader. Jesus, just look at you. You won't be any goddamn good to me if you fall apart."

The detective knew he still had a big job in front of him, and keeping Palls out of his hair was going to be a large part of it. "Thanks, sir. I'll be heading out now." He saluted and Palls flicked his hand in response.

He turned to go, but the major cleared his throat.

"Yes, sir?"

"You said something before, something about doubts that Nowak did the girl?" Putting out his cigarette, Palls got up and approached the detective. "Maybe some business about how he reacted during interrogation? That shit is subjective—doesn't carry water. Was there anything else?"

"His alibi."

"Yeah? Hell, he doesn't have one."

Wincing at Palls' foul breath, Bodowski said, "I think he does, sir. At least, it's better than we've been led to believe."

"How do you mean?"

"Two nights ago, the housing area's on readiness drill."

"Yeah, I know. The colonel and I live in the field-grade officer section of Winterville. That readiness shit is a goddamned inconvenience."

"Nowak gets a call around three tipping him to a surprise inspection of the Maintenance Battalion to take place in a few hours. Of course, the inspection's a phony."

"Wait a minute—I thought that story came straight out of his ass. I know he went in and all, but wasn't that just to try and establish an alibi?"

"I don't think he's lying. After the call, he takes off and says he works at the motor pool to get ready for the inspection, and that's just around the time we figure the girl gets dropped in the ditch."

"C'mon. Get it through your head. He's lying to you about the call, that's all."

"No, sir. I think he's telling the truth. You see, I've got a witness—"

"A witness?"

"His son, Charlie—jumpy little kid, about eleven—he answers the phone then turns it over to Nowak. He not only overhears his father on the line, but he watches him go through inspection at the gate. The important point is that he doesn't see him drive back in."

"How the hell was the kid supposed to see all of this? This imaginary call would've come in the middle of the fucking night."

"Binoculars, sir. Best I've ever seen. Kid can't get back to sleep, so he watches his father head out the gate and doesn't see him come back."

"Jesus, the kid's mistaken or lying."

"No, I've been doing this for a while. Even with his attention problems, I could see this boy being a decent witness in his father's defense."

Palls stared at him for a moment. Shaking his head, he returned to his chair. "Kid's jerking you around, that's all." He retrieved another cigarette and lit it. "Looking to protect his old man." He nodded to convince himself.

Stepping to the edge of the desk, Bodowski said, "Why would the kid lie about that? He doesn't know the score about what's going on with his father."

"Let's say, for the sake of argument, that Nowak really gets a call. In that case, he just goes and does his dirty business and then waits a while before coming back in some other way."

The detective leaned on the desk with both hands. "How's it going to read, sir? He gets a call, drives off the housing area, waits a while, somehow acquires the girl, does her, kills her, slices her, strips her, drives back to Winterville, carries the body down the path, drops her in the ditch, and shows back up at the house clean as a whistle—not a speck of dirt. I wasn't in the ditch for a minute before I got mud on my pants, sleeves, you name it. Hell, where's the blood? He'd have to have gotten that all cleaned up too. And he does all this in under two hours." The detective straightened and folded his arms.

Palls leaned forward and looked past Bodowski. "I guess you won't have to worry about that problem if he confesses."

"What?" The detective rocked back like someone trying to see something right in front of his nose. "Sir, I'll give you that Nowak's a murdering piece of shit. Problem is, we got at least one more like him running around."

"You're going to stay on this until you're satisfied, I take it?"

"Yes, sir."

"Nothing I can do about the krauts and Nowak. That's just how things go." Palls stared at the detective for a long moment before asking, "You have any other suspects?"

"Well, not as such, but I've got some good leads."

"Is LeMarc a suspect? Is that why he attacked you?"

"I thought he might be good for it. I talked to his wife about him, and that's why he jumped me." Thinking about it made his head throb. "I interrogated him because his daughter is missing and he was out on a bender."

"So, he's a viable suspect?"

"He's a savage all right, but my gut tells me it isn't him. He'd have been too damn drunk to bring it off, anyway. That was a simple fact I conveniently overlooked because I felt like teaching the guy a lesson. It wasn't my finest hour. Still, I have to clear up the problem of his missing daughter—but I got an idea on that."

"What about the other leads?" Palls appeared interested in earnest—a new experience for the detective.

"Just bits of this and that, sir. You'll be the first to know as soon as I can get something to gel."

Palls narrowed his eyes as if to bring Bodowski into focus. He cleared his throat and asked, "What's your next move?"

"Not sure." Hard-won experience had taught him never to show all his cards. Besides, he had his doubts about Palls in light of his erratic behavior regarding Kross. The detective's antennae were picking up something. "I need some time to think."

The little man searched Bodowski's face. "You do that, Sergeant." His voice had a bitter edge to it. "I'll tell you one thing. Once Nowak—that is, if Nowak confesses to the girl, you'll be shit out of luck."

"I don't think he did it, sir."

"Is it possible?"

"Well—"

"That'll be good enough for the Provost Marshal's office, because truth is, I think he did it." The major blew smoke out the side of his mouth. "You go think about that for a while."

# Chapter Thirty-Eight

## Tell Me No Lies

"I don't care. Find me something, anything." Bodowski rifled through the folders spread across his desk.

Mavis held up a signed report. "Maybe this will help."

The detective walked over and plucked it from her hands.

Nancy stopped leafing through the files on her desk to ask, "Why do you want a report about something that happened at the gypsy camp? You're not thinking of going out there, are you?" Mavis reached over to touch her friend on the arm.

Bodowski held up the paper and smacked it with his hand. "This is just what the doctor ordered."

"Speaking of doctors." Overhearing Bodowski's exclamation as he walked through the door, Melcher added, "I got something for you."

"I'm all ears."

"Larson, that nutcase, claims he hasn't said squat to anybody about the Ping-Pong balls." Melcher crossed his heart. "He said, and I quote, 'I swear by my medical degree, I didn't tell a soul.'" He paused, his hand forgotten over his chest. "You sure this guy's a real doctor? How'd he get to be a captain?"

Mavis chimed in, "Physicians get automatic rank as captain if they join the Army."

Bodowski frowned. "Mel, step over to my desk."

"I think the boys want to speak in private," Mavis said.

The two men walked to the other side of the room and stood with their backs turned.

“If we believe Doc Larson,” Bodowski said, “it could mean Kross knows who killed her.”

“C’mon, man—you’re reaching pretty far there.” Melcher pulled the last cigarette from his pack and held it between his fingers. “I been thinking about this.” He lit a match and tossed the crumpled package into the trash can. “Maybe he just assumed it was two or got confused somehow.”

“No. This is Kross we’re talking about. I’ve dealt with the man a lot. The guy’s as precise as a Swiss watch. He never assumes, and he’s always dead sure of everything he says.” Wincing, Bodowski rubbed the back of his neck. “You have to listen close to him. He gives away a lot, believe me.”

“Well, you’ve had more to do with him than I have.” Melcher shook his head. “I’m just thinking it could all be some misunderstanding.”

“Trust me.” Bodowski smiled and tapped his partner on the chest with the back of his hand. “I’ll be right on this. For what it’s worth, I don’t see Kross having sex with the girl. I’m thinking if he had a part in all this it would be chucking the body.”

“Because of the location? Yeah, man. I see that. If you only have a small window of time to get rid of the body, you can’t bury it. But maybe you can confuse things by tossing the body into the ditch—a place with split jurisdiction.”

“And cutting up the face? That’s classic.” The detective zigzagged a finger in front of his face. “More confusion. It buys time.”

Melcher took a long drag off his cigarette. “It’s like we figured before. Tossing her into the ditch water also screws up the timeline on rigor. All this is starting to sound like someone who knows how to tamper with evidence. What makes you think Kross—if he did any of this—what makes you think he wouldn’t have abused the girl too?”

“It ain’t his cup of tea, Mel. It just doesn’t seem likely.”

“What do you mean?”

“Last year, guys from Battalion busted a couple of GIs for

going to that off-limits Gasthaus by the autobahn—I can't remember the name."

"Are you talking about that big yellow building by the gas station? I've seen it from the road, but I've never gone in."

"That's the place. Battalion hit it twice a couple of weeks apart last year. You know Sergeant Petrov, right?"

"Sure."

"Petrov was lead on the two busts. He staked the place out. He told me he saw Kross getting cozy with some friends at the bar."

"So?"

"All guys."

"All guys?"

"Like I said."

Melcher chuckled. "So Kross really is a fairy. Shit. All this time I thought Palls was just being his usual asshole self."

Bodowski shifted his weight, eager to get back to the subject at hand. "Mel, let's say Kross is a candidate for dumping the body."

"Okay, okay—we're just talking here. What do we have? Number one, body's tossed by a pro, with the washing and cutting—the placement, even."

"A pro without much time—no prep. Keep that in mind."

"Number two, he's looking to pin it on Nowak before he could even know the guy exists. Three, he shows up at this porno dealer just when you need him. Finally, the Ping-Pong ball business."

"And he just snatched Nowak right from under our nose."

"What are you talking about?"

"That fucker Kross stole him—with Palls' blessing—while I was out talking to Nowak's wife."

"Sonofabitch."

"I'm telling you, something stinks on this, Mel."

"So what's Kross's motive?"

"Maybe he's wrapped up in that business with the bakery."

"How so?"

"Maybe Kross is part of the protection racket." Bodowski snapped his fingers. "That makes sense. After I got roughed up by the two Kraut vice cops, he said he was tailing Nowak, but I sensed he was really following me. Maybe he wanted to make sure I didn't get too close to his action." Bodowski paused before adding, "I've been thinking about Palls as well."

"What?"

"Maybe he's got some connection to this business."

"Are you out of your mind?" Melcher's voice dropped to a rasping whisper. "Don't undercut yourself, man. Palls! Christ sake." He glanced at the women to make certain they couldn't hear him. "Frankly, I don't think the little bastard cares enough about the human race to have sex with anyone. Loose talk about Palls could get your ass in a giant sling."

"You two are pretty cozy," Mavis called to them, craning her neck. "Maybe you could let us in on what's going on? We work for the CID too, you know."

"Leave them alone, Mavis," Nancy said. "They're just working something out. You trust us, right, guys?" She stared hard at Bodowski. "I mean, you won't go running off half-cocked or something. You'd tell us, right? After all, we have to sign you out. We have to know where you are at all times."

"Don't worry," Bodowski said. Her tone gave him pause. "We won't make a move unless you're in the know."

Melcher and Mavis understood that the open words masked a private concern.

Bodowski turned away again, dragging Melcher along with a hand on his shoulder. "Mel, I hear you about Palls. I won't say another word until I can line up my ducks."

"This is where you're losing me. Palls just does whatever helps Palls. Handing over Nowak is a shit deal, but it doesn't mean he's in cahoots."

"I'm giving it a little time to percolate."

"Good luck on that. Hey, what's the paper for?"

"Huh?"

"The one in your hand."

"Oh. Remember those boys I told you about, their story about the carnival? This is our ticket to check out that Tino character and the gypsy camp. Says here a GI named Campbell claims his wallet got lifted at the carnival two nights ago."

"Must want his wallet back pretty bad. The gypsy camp is off-limits to base personnel. He'll be staring at an Article 15 if his CO finds out."

"What's important here is that we have a way in."

"Pretty thin for us to head over there. This kind of thing is usually handled by the MP investigators."

"Well, Kennedy's assassination has everybody running around in circles. With the alert going on, the MPs will never get to this before the gypsies split."

Melcher thought for a moment and then smiled. Turning, he said, "Ladies? Sign Dick Tracy and me out at the gypsy camp on the outskirts of town. We're going to follow up on this theft report."

"Okay." Mavis shook her head. Jotting it down, she said, "I'll get the word to the desk sergeant." Nancy folded her arms and turned away.

Melcher walked to the door while Bodowski struggled with his raincoat. The detective paused next to his girlfriend and spoke quietly.

"I've got to do this."

Nancy would not look at him.

Before he could head out, a scratchy female voice caught his attention.

"Hello? This is the CID office, right? It doesn't say so on the door, but the man at the desk said this was it."

Standing in the doorway next to Melcher and wearing an old, tan raincoat and a hat many years out of fashion, Monica LeMarc looked frail and worn. Her bony fingers clutched the raincoat's lapels as she added, "I would like to speak to Mr. Bodowski."

Surprised, Bodowski raised his hand in greeting and called, "Mrs. LeMarc. I didn't expect to see you." Anxious both to leave and to avoid speaking with her, the detective moved toward the door and asked, "Is there something I can do for you?"

"Please, sir." She moved to the middle of the doorway, blocking him more with her desperation than her slight build. "Please, won't you give me a few minutes?"

He could see that she was determined. Still, he had the bit in his teeth.

"Mrs. LeMarc, this is a bad time. Agent Melcher and I—"

"Mr. Bodowski, Please."

"Agent. Agent or Investigator Bodowski will do, ma'am."

"Agent Bodowski." She swallowed hard. "Can we talk alone for just a minute? I know you're busy, but you," she paused, "you must understand how difficult it was for me to come here."

He saw the sadness in her eyes. "Okay. But it can only be for a moment." He turned to Melcher. "I'll see you downstairs."

Mavis grabbed Nancy's arm and tugged her along, pausing a few steps from the pair in the doorway. "Agent Bodowski? We're going to look for a candy machine that isn't broken. We'll be back in a little while." Nancy glanced at him. She seemed about to say something, but thought the better of it. The two ladies left the room.

"Come with me, ma'am." Bodowski took Mrs. LeMarc by the arm and guided her to his desk. The rancid odor of her disheveled apartment clung to her. Bodowski pulled a chair from the neighboring desk and directed her to sit, then dropped into his own chair opposite her and removed his watch cap, placing it between them on the desk.

"Oh my Lord. Did he do that to you?" Monica LeMarc stared at the bandage.

"Yes, ma'am."

"He gets very angry."

"You can say that again." Bodowski rubbed his neck.

"I'm so sorry."

"Wasn't you."

"It's my fault."

"I don't follow, ma'am."

"I've let him down. He asks me to do the simplest things and I can't seem to get anything right. He has to put up with a lot."

"Mrs. LeMarc, I've been doing this for a while. I don't see how his being a violent drunk—a wife-beater, if I may say—I don't see that it's your fault."

This was a tricky area for Bodowski. He avoided talking about abusive relationships. If he kept at it too long, he would remember the smell of liquor on his father's breath.

Monica rubbed her throat. "He was a good man. He still is, somewhere inside him." She retrieved a handkerchief from her purse. "He's been through so much. I don't help him. I don't—" She lowered her head and cried, daubing her eyes with the white cloth. "Please let him go."

"I can't just do that." It was hard as hell to say. A lump had formed in the detective's throat as he recalled the heartrending pleas his own mother had made too many times to get his father out of jail. "He attacked me in front of witnesses. He's in for felony assault. I'm sorry."

She sobbed into her handkerchief. "Doesn't his service count for anything?"

"Of course it does, but it doesn't excuse him. He could have killed me."

"But he didn't. Can't you forgive him? He did so much for his country. He was a hero. Doesn't that matter?"

"He's a brave man, I have no doubt of that. It's that medal that's kept him out of big trouble, but it won't protect him this time. Even his own CO hasn't come to get him. I guess this is the last straw."

Wearing a shocked expression, she asked, "He's not going to jail? To prison?"

"I won't kid you. It's a real possibility."

"Oh no, no." In her distress, she dropped her handkerchief, and both she and Bodowski bent over to retrieve it. Her raincoat opened at the bottom to reveal the same ratty house robe she'd worn when he first met her at home. "What will I do? What will happen to me, to my children?" Her eyes pleaded more than her voice.

Though the woman was clearly already on the edge, Bodowski squared his shoulders, prepared to push.

"Where's your daughter?"

"What?"

"Tamera—Tammy. Where is she?"

"I sent her to live with my sister."

He shook his head. "You and I both know that's not true."

Mrs. LeMarc wiped away a tear and looked down at her feet. "She's safe."

"Why'd you get her out of there? Did he try something with her?"

"No." She straightened and looked him in the eye before repeating, "No. But she's just a little girl. She wouldn't be able to…I mean, I couldn't stop him if—" Stuffing her hands under her arms, she looked away.

It wasn't hard evidence, but it was all Bodowski needed to cross LeMarc off his list.

"Please. You have to do something for him."

He wanted to help her, but he knew the score. If he found a way to let LeMarc walk, the maniac would go back to hurting his wife and terrorizing his children. He could not fix what had happened to the miserable drunk, but he could stop the abuse, at least for a while. All the same, he could not get up and walk out on her. It was not in him. Torn between his desire to help and his eagerness to get on with the case, he looked to strike a bargain.

"I can't promise anything, but I could talk to the Judge Advocate about getting him to a shrink as a part of his sentence. Maybe something can be worked out so he goes to the stockade and gets to stay in the Army. The trick is keeping him out of Leavenworth."

"A shrink?" She acted bewildered. "You think he's crazy?"

"I think he needs to see someone."

Monica stood up and threw her handkerchief at the stunned

detective. "He is not crazy! He's a good man who drinks a little too much. How dare you!" She trembled as she stared at him with wild eyes.

It tore at him. Bodowski stood and pulled on his cap.

"I'll see what I can do. I have to go."

Rushing down the stairs and out into the parking lot, he fought back the feeling that he had abandoned her, one more woman he couldn't save.

# Chapter Thirty-Nine

## Death and the Gypsy

"When the boys told me about the girl this Tino nabbed up, it really got my attention."

"From your description, this asshole is going to be easy to recognize. You think he might be pimping out young girls? I can't imagine that would be a stretch for a gypsy." Steering with his knees, Melcher took both hands off the wheel to light a cigarette.

"How about we arrive in one piece?"

Grabbing the wheel, Melcher shoved the spent match out the cracked wing window. "Sorry, man."

Turning off the highway, they drove several hundred meters along a dirt road flanked on both sides by dense stands of pine forest. They arrived at a large clearing littered with trash.

"Shit, Mel. They're gone. Bastards must have packed up overnight and split."

Melcher stopped the radio car at the edge of the forest.

"No, don't stop here. The boys told me there were some vehicles parked back in the forest. They couldn't see them from the clearing. Maybe the gypsies are still there. Look, see that opening? Drive down it." The car rolled a few dozen meters into the woods before running out of trail.

"Let's check it out, Mel."

Melcher extinguished his cigarette and got out of the car to join his partner.

"I don't see anything but trees."

"Wait." Bodowski pointed toward a clearing. "Look over there."

"You're right, man. There's a couple of vehicles. I can just see them through the trees. There's a big trailer and a step van of some kind." Looking around, Melcher added, "Must be some other way to drive back into the woods."

"The kids said they hid under a large trailer. Maybe we'll get lucky." Bodowski jerked his automatic and checked the safety. Pushing it back into the holster, he said, "Let's go."

"Hey, Sheriff, don't get trigger-happy. We may have probable cause on somebody stealing from a GI, but we're in kraut jurisdiction now."

The rain had stopped, but a cold, biting wind had picked up in its place. Tromping through the wet undergrowth, the men entered the small clearing where the two vehicles sat. They heard nothing aside from the squish of their shoes on rotting pine needles and the wind whistling through the branches of the tall pines.

"Look." Melcher pointed at deep impressions left in the muddy soil. "The rest of them must've bugged out just a little while ago."

"Okay, you go that way around the van and we'll meet up at the trailer."

Melcher nodded, inspecting the cab of the van through the passenger-side window. Bodowski crossed to the far side and squatted by the trailer. He heard a muffled voice through the thin walls. The detective snapped his fingers several times.

Melcher ran to join him.

Bodowski leaned into his partner. "Someone's inside."

"I got it."

Both men moved to the rear of the vehicle. Bodowski placed his hand on the sap in his waistband and stepped to the side, staying out of sight. Melcher stood behind the detachable steps and knocked twice against the windowless door of the trailer. They heard a voice. He gave Bodowski a pained look and knocked again, this time against the metal panel to the side of the trailer. The door swung open to reveal a stout young woman dressed in a sweater and old canvas pants, carping in a foreign language. Clearly expecting someone else, the swarthy woman stopped mid-sentence and tried to pull the door shut, but Melcher had already scaled the two steps and grabbed the side of the open door. Bodowski came around to stand just below his friend. Overmatched, the woman stepped backward and began a nonstop rant, hurling curses at them both.

"She's got somebody tied up in the back. I can see it from here," Melcher shouted.

Both men entered the large trailer, and the spring-loaded door slammed shut behind them. The fetid air was heavy with exhaust from a lone gas lantern. At the far end of the trailer, a young gypsy girl sat on a narrow cot, wrists handcuffed to the frame. The startled child, wearing a dirty nylon parka to cover her tattered cotton dress, pulled her bare feet from the floor and huddled into a ball. The woman flailed her arms, interrupting her tirade to spit at the men. The young girl screamed.

It was a cramped, confusing scene. Bodowski could not get around his partner in the narrow confines. He shouted, "For Christ's sake, get her under control."

"Jesus Christ, lady. Would you shut up?" Melcher's words were lost against the woman's incessant howling.

"Yeah, Mel. That ought to do it."

"Hey, I'm doing my damn best, here, okay?"

Still spouting invective, the woman snatched a crowbar from beneath a pile of tools and took a swing at Melcher, missing him by inches. Stumbling backward, he fell against Bodowski, who just managed to keep them both upright. She reared back with the bar, but Melcher lurched forward and tore it from her hands.

"Holy shit. What's wrong with you?" He spun her and pulled his handcuffs. "Settle down, damn it!"

She angled her head and spat at him again.

"Okay, that's it." Melcher cuffed her wrists and shoved her

down onto a tent roll stored against the wall of the trailer, where she finally stopped screaming and began gulping air.

Bodowski squeezed past Melcher and approached the little girl still hiding under her tortoise shell of oil-stained nylon. Despite speaking to her in a gentle manner, he could not get the child to respond. He thought of his little sister Helen cowering under her covers all those years ago in Tacoma.

"What if you lifted up that parka?"

"I don't want to touch her." The truth was he had a sudden urge to flee the scene—to be anywhere else at that moment. His face reddened at the impulse, but he recovered fast. "Hell, I'm just not sure what to do here. What do you think? You've worked a few child cases, right?"

"Yeah. Maybe you're right—best we get someone down here to take care of her. I'll call the kraut dispatch."

The woman opened her mouth to speak, but Melcher cut her off by raising one sharp finger in her face. She looked daggers at him.

Bodowski inspected the girl's hands, the only part of her that remained exposed. "The marks on her wrists look the same as on our victim." Anger welled within him as he noticed that a second, upper cot on hinges was stowed against the wall above her. "I think they had another girl in here."

An open crate caught Melcher's attention. He rummaged through the contents. The woman rose to her feet and shouted something at him.

"God almighty, what's it going to take to keep you quiet?" Melcher unlocked one of the cuffs and ran it through a supporting bar on the trailer wall. She screamed a curse in his ear while he reattached the cuff to her wrist. "There. You're not going anywhere now." He resumed his inspection of the box, tossing items out onto the floor.

"I'll call it in." Bodowski stood and put out his hand as if to pat the child, but hesitated. "We need to get some people out here pronto." Squeezing by Melcher, he asked, "What are you doing?"

"Aha!" Holding open a brown, calfskin wallet, Melcher read, "Campbell, James R. PFC." Smiling, he added, "Just checking off the boxes. Gypsies picking pockets—who'd a thunk it?"

As he reached the door, Bodowski looked back. "We have to keep a sharp eye out. I don't know who else is still around. There could be more vehicles around and more gypsies."

"No sweat."

The detective opened the door and saw Tino, still wearing his bomber jacket and jeans, walking toward him lugging two overstuffed shopping bags. The man's eyes widened. Dropping the bags, he ran toward the forest.

"Shit!" Bodowski stumbled down the steps and lost his balance as the door slammed shut behind him. Melcher heard the commotion and peered out as Bodowski jumped to his feet.

"It's him. It's that character those kids described—the one I saw—Tino. C'mon, Mel."

With Melcher at his side, he gave chase through the forest. They'd run only a short ways when the detective stopped abruptly and held up a hand toward his partner. Without taking his eyes off the gypsy running between the tall northern pines, he said, "We can't leave them alone too long, in case others are around. I'll run him down. You get back to the car and radio this in. Get whoever you can."

"You sure? This isn't our jurisdiction. What if you get in trouble with this guy?"

"Don't have time to argue."

Bodowski took off on the dead run. Melcher stood and watched his partner disappear into the underbrush past the first stand of pines. Then he turned and raced toward the radio car.

Bodowski kept the fleeing gypsy in sight, but catching up was proving a struggle. Tino was going all out, breaking through the trees so fast he caught his billowy jacket several times on snags and ripped the thin leather. At one point, the detective was so close he could hear the man gasping for air. As they went deeper into the forest, the undergrowth grew denser. It felt like running through waist-deep water.

All of a sudden, the gypsy dropped from sight in the high ferns. Breathing hard, Bodowski stopped and listened. The crisp air stung his lungs. He took a few steps forward, the wet, rotting pine needles compressing beneath his feet. The cold wind blew in small gusts and bit at his cheeks. His eyes focused on the slightest movement. From behind, out of sight, he heard something moving through the forest. He wondered if Tino had managed to circle to the rear. Or maybe it was Melcher.

A twig snapped several meters in front of him as Tino leapt from the dense growth and began wading through the brush.

The detective jerked his weapon and gave chase.

"Stop or I'll cut you down! Halt, goddamnit!"

They broke into a large clearing. The gypsy, popping in and out of sight, ran for all he was worth over the steep hillocks. The detective could not make up ground on the fleeing man. He could see a crowded stand of trees demarking the far edge of the clearing looming over the next hill, and pushed himself to reduce the distance between himself and his quarry. He jumped over the last open rise, but it too late—Tino was gone.

Bodowski searched the stand of dark green pines for movement. He tried to listen past his own labored breathing, but all he heard was only the soft whine of the cold wind through the pine boughs. Still holding his gun, he bent at the waist and dropped his hands onto his knees. After a few deep breaths, he straightened.

His diaphragm seized as he felt the cold barrel of a gun press into the back of his neck.

"No move."

He started to turn.

"*Nein*." Tino jabbed his neck with the gun. He reached around him from behind and pulled the automatic out of the detective's hand.

From of the corner of his eye, Bodowski watched him toss the weapon several meters to the right.

"You think you get better of me? I get behind you, fucker. Move to woods." The gypsy shoved him in the back.

Bodowski's mind raced. He knew the only thing keeping Tino from pulling the trigger was that they were still in the clearing—his body lying in the open would be too conspicuous. He reached into the right side of his waistband, fumbling for his sap.

"What you doing there? Get moving."

Fear clawed at his insides. His best chance was to force Tino to push him again. With the gypsy so close, he might be able to pull out of the way and swing around before his captor had time to react.

"*Xan tu e ruv*!"

Bodowski's muscles tightened in anticipation of a shove.

"Halt."

Spinning, he saw Kross, not a meter behind them, his Lugar pointed at the gypsy's head.

Tino threw up his hands, allowing the small automatic to fall to the ground.

"*Erhalten Sie aus den Grund*."

Tino dropped to his knees.

"*Schnell! Gottverdammt*!"

The gypsy fell forward, arms outstretched.

"Damn, I've never been so glad to hear that bark of yours." Blood rushed in Bodowski's ears as he bent to scoop up the small caliber weapon and stuck it in his raincoat pocket.

"Needling the cavalry? How droll."

The American grabbed his handcuffs and knelt with one knee in the gypsy's back. He gathered the man's arms and locked him at the wrists.

Kross stepped over and picked up Bodowski's .45. He hefted it once, still holding the Lugar in his other hand.

"It weighs quite a bit. A veritable cannon."

Bodowski stood as Kross approached and offered him the pistol, grip first.

"Lose something, old sport?"

He accepted the piece and shoved it into his shoulder holster. A sense of relief washed over him. "You following me again?"

"My, you are the suspicious one." Kross holstered the Lugar and then dug around for a cigarette, his face calm as if he hardly knew how the two had gotten switched in his hand.

"Get up, asshole." Bodowski pulled Tino to his feet. The crisis over, he felt a sting of embarrassment realizing he had allowed the gypsy to outmaneuver him. He dispelled of that feeling by smashing the man's cheek with his fist. Tino staggered and fell to the ground, groaning as he curled in. Unperturbed, Kross squeezed the cigarette into his holder and lit it.

"Thanks, Kross." The detective offered the German his hand.

Herr Leutnant accepted and returned a firm handshake. "*Es machts nichts*, as the old boys say. Think nothing of it."

"I thought I'd had it."

"Wouldn't want to lose you after all the fine work you've accomplished over the past few days."

Though he'd been suspicious of the German only an hour before, Bodowski found himself speaking freely. "I don't know how fine it is. So far I've walked down two dead-end streets, and all I've got to show for it is a rap on the head and this goddamned gypsy making a jerk out of me."

"Come now. You've done a brilliant job in convincing your Mr. Nowak to confess to his daughter's murder. That was out of the blue. We may have prodded you, but you acquired that confession with your skills alone." Kross took a short drag, allowing the smoke to permeate his mouth. "When I get back to my station, we'll resume questioning and see to it that he offers a second confession for that poor child in the ditch."

Bodowski knew it was still possible the German had a connection to the crime, but he took a leap of faith. "Kross, you just said 'we' prodded. You mean yourself and Palls?"

"A detestable man. Sorry to say, he doesn't trust you to get the job done. Frankly, I was shocked that he called me in, knowing the way he feels." He forced the gypsy to his feet. "The major kept blathering on about Colonel Fulbright and how that silly man's reputation would be endangered if we didn't quickly close in on the girl's killer."

"How did you know I was down here?"

"We arrived just moments after you gave chase. Young Melcher took a few seconds to enlighten me. He wanted to stick me with babysitting so that he could run after you, but I told him to follow your orders whilst I trailed you and this miscreant into the bush. Oh, yes—Holzmeier, one of my new charges, is along for the ride. He's back there with your man, waiting for help to arrive."

Bodowski shook his head. "I didn't mean here in the woods—I meant, how did you know I was here at all?"

"I suppose you'd call it a hunch." Kross hesitated. "Lying is so exhausting. Truth is, I followed you, old sport. Rather, one of my men followed you and radioed me once he saw you were on your way to the camp."

"Why have you been following me? This can't be all Palls' doing." Bodowski seized the gypsy by the arm and shoved him in the direction of the vehicles. Kross walked alongside them.

"Just keeping my nose in the game." The German blew a ribbon of smoke. "A fellow like you has a habit of turning over rocks and discovering unpleasant but important things."

"I've got something about Nowak that I think you need to hear."

"Again, I'm all ears."

As they slogged through the underbrush, the gypsy stumbling along in front of them, he told Kross about his recent interview with Mrs. Nowak and young Charlie. He knew he was taking a big chance trusting Kross with his theories—there were still plenty of avenues for Palls and Kross to be working together to screw him over. But the death of the unidentified girl had been eating at him too long, and Bodowski needed a fresh set of eyes.

When the detective finished his story, Kross stopped and tossed his half-smoked cigarette on the ground. The embers made a hissing sound as they died in the wet soil. Then he opened his trench coat and reached for his Lugar, pulling up the leather flap of the side holster. Bodowski slipped his hand under his raincoat and touched the grip of his automatic. Without pulling the weapon, Kross flicked the safety on and then fastened the flap.

"I keep forgetting to do that." He reached into his coat pocket and produced his silver cigarette case.

The detective exhaled and dropped his arm to his side.

Kross frowned while reloading his cigarette holder. "So, Herr Bodowski. You're telling me that you think I'm dead wrong." He flicked the lighter and took a long drag. "You're saying that I've been led down the garden path. And that there really was a call to your Mr. Nowak in the middle of the night. That he did, in fact, leave the housing area and return only much later."

"That's what I'm saying."

"I take it you have an alternate theory of the crime?"

The gypsy mumbled something and flexed his cuffed wrists.

"*Ruhe*!" Turning back to the young detective, Kross said, "And please don't tell me you think *I* had something to do with it."

Bodowski decided to go all in.

"Do me a huge favor and answer the question I'm about to ask you without hesitating."

"A test? Really?"

"Just do it for me, Kross."

The German raised his left hand as though swearing an oath. "Proceed."

"How did you know there were two Ping-Pong balls?"

"Why, Major Palls told me." Kross's grin dissolved into a frown. Dropping his hand, he exclaimed, "*Gott in Himmel*!"

"Yeah, that's right. You read Doc Larson's prelim. He listed only one ball, and that's what you read, right? But he messed up on the report, because he actually found two. Melcher talked to the doc later, and that loon swore up and down that he didn't spill the beans about his screw-up to anyone."

Kross stared at him, nodding to himself.

"The graph paper."

"What are you talking about?"

"When I came to see you yesterday morning, you'll recall I had the drawing of an insignia on a piece of graph paper. It was Mr. Nowak's unit, as it turned out."

"Of course, I remember."

"That clue and the man's general description were fed to me by Major Palls. He said the drawing was from his people—the Provost Marshal's investigators—from a previous case."

"Don't bet on it. Those guys couldn't find their ass with both hands. What's this graph paper you're talking about?"

"This morning, when I went to see the major after you left—"

"To steal Nowak out from under my nose, you mean?"

"Now, now, let's not get off track. When I went to see him, he was doodling on a pad of graph paper. I didn't think anything of it at the moment."

Bodowski rubbed his palm. "He had Nowak in mind the whole damn time. But how did he know Nowak was into the kiddie porn? I mean, not as some phony Sir Galahad busting his own men, but as a buyer of the stuff. Through that bakery?"

"I, too, saw our gypsy friend here emerge from Herr Utz's shop along with those two vice officers. Now that we know he keeps children captive, no doubt for an unspeakable purpose, perhaps he would be willing to help us."

"Let's get him back to the office or your station and put the screws to him. One way or the other, he'll give someone up. Maybe you'll get to close on that bakery operation a little sooner than you expected."

"Perhaps an old field technique might do the trick, and save some time in the bargain." Kross turned suddenly and shoved the gypsy toward a small clearing. Stepping out from the underbrush, the German held the man's neck from behind and kicked him hard. Tino cried out and fell to his knees.

"Hold on, Kross. What have you got in mind?" Bodowski stepped forward, uncertain.

"Just stand back, old sport." Kross drew his weapon and faced the gypsy. "I'll do this in English for your benefit. This rubbish knows how to speak many languages. He undoubtedly steals from every nationality."

Tino pleaded in Romani. His panicked eyes darted to Bodowski.

"Look at me," Kross commanded.

The gypsy lowered his head and whimpered.

"*Gottverdammt*, look up at me."

The gypsy, pleading, raised his head. Herr Leutnant pulled the automatic's toggle lock, chambering a round. Tino held his breath. Kross stepped forward and pressed the barrel to the man's forehead.

Bodowski hoped the wily German was working Tino, but with Kross, you never knew. The gypsy's pleas turned into a whispered prayer.

"How many girls do you have to sell?"

"*Nicht verstehen*." Tino's voice was strained with fear.

"*Auf Englisch*. In English. Say it in English." He tapped the gypsy's temple with the gun barrel. "Stealing from young Americans is your stock in trade. Do not pretend you cannot speak English. Now, how many girls do you have to sell?"

"I do not know what you say."

"I will count to three. If you still do not understand, I will shoot you. One."

"No, no. I had *zwei*, uh, two girls, but only one now."

Bodowski nodded to Kross, who acknowledged.

"You killed the other girl." The German pressed Tino's head back a few inches.

"No! I *miete* girl. What is English."

"Rent." Kross glanced at the young detective.

"Ya, I rent girl."

"To whom. *Zu wem*?"

"No, they kill me."

"I'll kill you, right now. *Im Augenblick*. *Verstehen*? Stand back, Herr Bodowski. The blood will get all over your clothes."

"*Bitte*, no," Tino cried. "They kill me."

"*Xan tu e ruv*!"

"No, no, no, *halten Sie, bitte*. I tell you. Do not shoot."

"Talk fast."

"I rent girl to baker—man who make bread."

"Utz?"

"Ya, Utz."

"How many times have you brought girls to Utz?"

"Many times. Every time we come to city."

"Are the girls for Utz? Does Utz rape them? Rape? *Raub.*"

"No, no. He rent them to others."

"To whom does Utz rent the girls?"

"I do not know." The gypsy swallowed hard.

Kross said something beneath his breath and pressed the gun to Tino's forehead.

"*Bitte*, I do not know. *Schiessen Sie nicht*!"

"The girl you rented to Utz on Tuesday—*Dienstag*? She is dead."

"I do not kill her."

"Who did?"

"I not know. *Kunde*, uh, customer?"

Kross leaned over. "Who killed her?"

The gypsy hesitated. Sweat dripped from his scalp. "Christo, I do not know."

"Did you see the customer? Do you know his name?"

"No. By angels I say, I do not know."

Bodowski jumped in. "Hey, Kross? This guy wouldn't have let it pass for free. He lost half his investment. Yesterday, when we saw him come out of the bakery with the two vice goons, he must have been there for a payoff or to arrange one—a settlement, you know."

"Excellent point, Herr Bodowski." Turning to the gypsy, Kross asked, "How much did Utz pay you for the girl?"

"Pay, uh, three hundred for rent."

"No. How much did Utz pay for the girl's life? The girl you 'rented'?"

"Oh, not hundreds. What is next?"

"Thousands."

"Yes. Ten thousand."

"Marks?"

"Ya, Marks. *Bitte*, I stand up now?"

"You sell out a defenseless child for rape, and then you demand ten thousand Marks when your 'merchandise' is destroyed?"

Tino did not understand.

Kross stepped back and brought the gun to rest at his side. He looked off into the forest as though searching for an answer. Bodowski moved to stand next to him.

"I'm going to ask him a question, okay?"

Kross, still staring into the distance, nodded.

"Listen up, Tino. Did you already get the money?"

"No."

"When are you getting the money?"

"*Halb Vier.*"

"What the hell is *halb vier*, Kross?"

"Hmm? Oh, Three thirty."

"Where?" Bodowski bent to shout in the gypsy's face. "Where are you getting the money? At the bakery?"

"Ya, bakery."

Bodowski glanced at his watch. "We've got to get there. Maybe the killer will show up with the money. You never know. We might catch a break."

Blinking, Kross answered, "Not a moment to lose, dear boy." He pointed his weapon at Tino and flicked off the safety with his thumb.

Tino gasped and began struggling to his feet.

Bodowski moved between Herr Leutnant and the gypsy, pushing the latter back onto his knees. With one hand outstretched to Kross and the other on the gypsy's shoulder, he said, "Okay, man. We need this asshole's testimony. He can help us a lot. We need to keep him in one piece."

An exaggerated frown slipped across the German's face.

The young detective knew he was an instant away from killing the gypsy. He tried to make a joke out of it. "Christ sake.

I already fucked up one career. What'll I do if they toss me out of the Army? Dog catcher?"

"Stand aside." Kross's expression did not soften.

"No. Why the hell would you shoot him now? Think for a damn minute."

"He kept that child penned up like an animal. He sold her innocence. Stand aside."

"Get a hold of yourself. Good God, Kross. I've never seen you like this."

"I won't kill him."

"Oh yes, you will."

Tino tried to get up but Bodowski shoved him down. Buying time, he asked Kross, "What does '*Zan tooey roove*' mean? First this shithead says it to me, then you say it to him."

"*Bitte*, what you ask?"

"Shut your trap. C'mon, Kross, what does it mean, huh?"

"*Xan tu e ruv*."

The gypsy groaned and lowered his head as Kross repeated the oath.

"'The wolves will eat your flesh.' The Romani say it just before they kill you." Kross reached up and touched his own cheek. "I won't kill him, I swear to you."

The three men remained motionless as a light rain fell. Kross broke the tableau by holstering his weapon. In an even tone, he asked, "Would you please step aside?"

"Put on the safety."

"Just step aside."

"Goddamnit, I'm not kidding here. Put on the safety."

Kross pulled the holster flap and did as he asked.

Bodowski lowered his hand, still wary. "We have to get back up there. This piece of shit has to walk. I'm not going to carry him, okay? I don't want to see you pull that fucking Lugar again." He backed away. "I'm right here, Kross. Okay? Just a minute and then we get going."

Kross approached Tino, his hands balled into fists. He stared hard at the muttering gypsy, then looked at Bodowski. "I'm quite all right now. Please do me a favor and get this speck of human waste to his feet." He walked to the edge of the clearing. Stopping, he stood in profile to the American, retrieved a cigarette from his silver case, and squeezed it into the holder. His hands trembled. "I'm all right."

Bodowski couldn't help his grin at the knowledge that even Kross had a human side—something he couldn't hide under the polished exterior. The detective hauled Tino to his feet. "That was a close call, pal. But I expect you already figured that out."

# Chapter Forty

## Sic Semper Tyrannis

The persistent knocking resounded along the narrow back hallway of the bakery. Herr Utz, wiping his hands on his white apron, rushed to the alley door and shouted, "*Wer Sind Sie*?" There was no response other than continued knocking. "*Eine Augenblick, bitte*." He turned the deadbolt and unhooked the chain, allowing Major Palls to rush in, cursing.

"Goddamnit, Utz. We got a problem." He shook water from his raincoat sleeves. "It's always raining. I hate this fucking place. Don't just stand there—close the goddamned door." Utz obeyed and then clutched the man's raincoat by the shoulders. Palls pulled away. "Forget it. This isn't some damn social visit, and I ain't going to be here long. Listen up. I intercepted a call from one of my CID agents. They found the trailer."

"What trailer?"

"What trailer do you think? Christ almighty, they found the gypsy's fucking hideout. They got the other girl and that damn witch that looks after her."

"Ach, *mein Gott*. What does this mean for us?" Utz untied his apron.

Palls retrieved a cigarette from the top pocket of his uniform jacket. "That ain't the worse part of it." He lit the cigarette and continued, "They're chasing that asshole Tino through the woods."

"What?"

"You heard me. The gypsy doesn't know me, and he's only

seen my guys, but he knows you. If they catch his sorry ass, how long do you think it's going to be before he gives you up?" He doffed his fatigue hat, smacking it against the wall.

Utz's eyes darted. He wiped his sweaty palms against his thick corduroy pants. "Maybe they are already coming for me?"

"Not yet. Once I heard about that fucking shit with the gypsies, I got our Polizei friends, Stoltz and Hindschmidt, to run down there. They're hanging back. They'll get a call through to you if anybody heads this way."

"You have to protect me. I pay you for that." Utz sounded panicky.

"Don't tell me my fucking job. Just listen up, and maybe we can get through this." Palls blew a stream of smoke through his nose.

"If your colonel had not killed the girl, we would not be in this mess."

The angry little man shook his cigarette at the shop owner's face. "Don't start pointing fingers. It's over with. He did it, and there's nothing we can do about that. You've got to get hold of yourself and do what I tell you." Looking past Utz, he asked, "Is the front door locked?"

"Yes." The baker folded his arms and hunched his shoulders.

The major produced a thick manila envelope from inside his jacket. "I talked to the colonel. He ain't going to do it again, that's for goddamned sure."

"Why did he have to kill her? He has had many girls before and has not hurt any of them."

"How the hell should I know? Maybe she didn't want to put out. All I know is I get the call in the middle of the fucking night and it ain't an hour later that I'm humping that little gypsy's body over to the ditch. I get to clean up for the old pervert. Good thing we had that patsy Nowak on tap. I figured it'd be easy to confuse the CID, but I didn't count on that fucking Polack checking Nowak's alibi. But that's okay. Faggot Kross and his boys will get a confession out of that asshole even though he didn't do it." Palls handed the envelope to Utz.

"Okay, there's fifteen thousand Marks in there. Keep five grand to give to the boys when they come around for the regular payoff."

"Why don't you just keep it now?"

"That ain't how it works, pal. Our guys got to think they're seeing their piece of the pie before I see mine." He cocked an eyebrow. "If something goes wrong, don't even think about giving me up. The only reason you're alive right now is that this deal is too sweet to kill. I can make changes on the fly if I have to, *Verstehen*? I'm going to do everything I can to salvage it. You pay off Tino if he shows up. The boys'll be watching and they'll take care of him later. If he gets nabbed instead, we'll have to figure a way to kill him in custody. You ditched all the porno, right? Kross or some other asshole is going to raid this place once he works over Nowak. You have to be clean. It'll be your word against his."

Utz nodded. "If you kill Tino, who will procure girls?"

"Don't worry about that, pal." Palls tossed the cigarette to the floor and squashed it under his boot. "I got a good contact up in Frankfurt. We can get twice as many girls at half the cost. This guy is shipping in slopes from Korea. Little slant-eyed bitches ought to put the light in your customers' eyes. Couldn't count on those fucking gypsies anyway, always in and out of town. You just have to wait a few weeks—lay low, right? You tell your johns to beat off for a while, and then we'll take good care of them." He put on his hat. "I'm going to get moving. I don't want to get caught here if the shit hits the fan."

"I'm afraid you're a few moves behind, Major." Kross emerged from the storeroom with his Lugar drawn.

"Sonofabitch." Palls threw his hat to the floor.

Bodowski stepped out from the WC across the hall. He held the sap behind his back. "We got an earful, Major. Thanks for the confession. Kross here is going to take you in. And thanks for the tip on the colonel. By the way, Tino's cooling his heels down at the central Polizei station. He's keeping your two goons company."

Palls grabbed Utz around the neck and pulled the baker in front of him as a shield. Before either detective could reach him, he produced a small automatic and pressed it to the unlucky man's ear. "Get back, you assholes." Spittle flew from his lips as he screamed, "I'll fucking kill him!" Utz gurgled under the chokehold and turned ashen, yanking at his captor's arm.

Bodowski's heart lurched. He dropped the sap and reached for his piece.

"One on me's enough, you Polack shit. If you jerk it, I'll shoot—him first, then you."

"You try anything, you'll be dead." Kross kept the Lugar trained on the major's head. Bodowski could feel Palls' desperation but drew his weapon anyway and pointed it at the major.

"I told you not to do anything, goddamnit." Palls jammed the gun against Utz's head. "I'm getting out of here, and I'm taking this shithead with me. I'm going out that door." He motioned backward toward the alley. "If you follow me, I'll kill this asshole right off, and then we can have a shootout. How's that sound?" He inched backward, dragging his captive. The detectives, guns trained, moved along with him.

Bodowski could barely hear himself over the torrent of blood rushing past his ears. "Give it up, Palls. You're in the middle of West Germany. Where the fuck are you going to go?"

"Screw you." Reaching the door, Palls pressed the handle with his hip and managed to get it open. He backed out into the light rain, his revolver swinging from Utz to Kross and back again.

Palls was so focused on the detectives he was completely blind to the hand coming up behind him until it caught his arm. The two men vanished from the doorway as Melcher swung Palls and his captive into the alley. Utz went flying and Palls crashed head first into the steel door of his coupe. The major collapsed onto the cobblestones, blood pouring from the gash in his scalp. Utz lay on his side, gasping for air.

The detectives ran into the alley. Melcher stood over Palls, grinning. "Thought you two could use a little help."

All three men holstered their weapons. Kross hoisted Utz to his feet and cuffed him, warning the man with a sharp word not to move.

Bodowski walked to Palls and shoved the motionless form with the heel of his shoe. "Fulbright's the guy. Palls blabbed."

"What?" Melcher pulled down his hat to shield his eyes from the rain. "Are you shitting me?" He looked at Kross, who nodded in confirmation. "Jesus—by the time we get done arresting these fuckers, *I'll* be the Provost Marshal."

# Chapter Forty-One

## Walking the Walk
**Saturday**

"The place is crawling with 'I' Corps types, man." Melcher lit a cigarette and tossed the match onto the concrete landing at the rear of the Provost Marshal's building.

"What did you expect?" Bodowski asked. "When you catch a fish this big, everybody wants in." He shivered and turned up his raincoat collar against the morning mist, smiling to himself. The Corps commander had demanded that another officer of equal rank arrest Colonel Fulbright. Several Army sedans sat outside the building, motors running, awaiting the appearance of the high-ranking murderer and the arresting officers. Two enlisted MPs guarded the back door.

"Some perpetrator parade," Melcher said. "Just you, me, and these guys."

"Like I said. They all want in on it, just not in public. I guess they figure it's bad for morale."

"I got to say Fulbright takes the cake as the dumbest criminal I've ever seen. And that's saying something, believe me."

"I don't think it's stupidity. It's something else." Bodowski winced at the pain in his skull.

"Get out of here. Ha." Melcher leaned in close to keep the conversation quiet. "We found the Boy Scout knife in the idiot's desk drawer. Jesus, it was still in the evidence bag. Naturally he claims someone planted it there." He took a quick puff off the cigarette and blew the smoke to the side. "Not to mention he keeps bits of clothing from all the kids he's screwed in a foot locker in his closet." He rolled his eyes. "How his wife doesn't figure it out, I'll never know."

"Mel, I believe there's a lot to be said for the old saw that we only see what we want to see." He waved a hand in Melcher's face. "If you want to keep talking close to my face, you're going to have to stop smoking that damn cigarette."

"And then there's the slew of kiddie porn we found under the back seat of his car." Melcher straightened up and took a long drag off his cigarette. "What the fuck is it with these guys, huh? Why do they have to keep a porn stash in their cars."

"What can I say? The colonel collected trophies. The knife was a prize he won as a Boy Scout. He couldn't let it go." Bodowski paused. "Maybe Palls is the dumber criminal. I mean, look at how he bungled the knife. He intercepts Slidell, then sends him on leave until he can figure out how to cover it up for the long run, but lets the knife get back to the colonel? Stupid to think he could get away with it."

"Man, that guy spread himself mighty thin. Damn—who would've figured he was running interference for the krauts on the take? No wonder he wanted to stay in Germany for another rotation. He was making too much money. Still, I don't think he was stupid. He just bit off more than he could chew. Arrogance." Melcher repeated the word, spitting it out around his cigarette. "Arrogance. That's what I think."

"Same for Fulbright. Neither of those bastards ever thought they'd get caught. They got sloppy. Palls will rot in prison, and Fulbright? Well, he could wind up swinging for this."

"Nothing like working for a couple of corrupt bastards, huh?"

"Try being with a port city police department some time." They laughed, and then Bodowski added, "I almost feel guilty for trying to lump Kross in with these morons."

"No need to feel bad for Herr Leutnant. He didn't seem the worse for wear this morning when he surrendered Nowak to the MPs. Hell, I don't think he feels much of anything."

"You didn't see him out in the forest with his Lugar drawn

and that asshole gypsy on his knees. He was a second away from plugging the guy. Something got to him, believe me."

"Maybe the person I should be thinking about is that poor kid we rescued. All that's happened to her…it's a goddamned shame."

Bodowski hesitated. "Best to not to think about it."

The door swung open and the two MP guards came to parade rest, hands overlapping at the back of their waists.

"Here we go," Melcher said.

A major wearing an MP armband on his sleeve stepped out, followed by Colonel Fulbright, hatless, dressed in his dark green Class A uniform. Cuffed in front, he kept his head lowered as the officer guided him by the shoulder toward the waiting vehicles. Another officer, a full colonel also dressed in a Class A uniform, appeared in the doorway and fitted a cap on his head. He nodded to the MPs and the entire group stepped into the vehicles. The detectives watched gravel fly as the convoy took off and rounded the building.

"That's it?" Melcher dropped the cigarette onto the wet ground. "Not even a 'thank you' or a 'fuck you very much'? Hell, I feel cheated."

"I don't know. Maybe it's best we stay small and keep our own heads down. We just set off an explosion that's going to produce a lot of brass shrapnel."

The detectives entered the building and trudged up the stairs. "Hey, Mel? I'm probably going to need to stay at your place again tonight." It came out as a foregone conclusion.

"Okay, okay. Take it easy, man. You can camp on that lumpy couch for as long as you need." Although assigned a private room at the MP barracks, Bodowski had not slept there since he and Nancy had moved in together. In the detective's absence, the Battalion Sergeant Major had turned it into a storage room.

"Sorry, that came out a little strong." Bodowski shoved his friend in the chest.

"Again with striking a superior officer. I'm going to fill out an arrest warrant for your Polish ass."

"Well, then I'm safe." They stopped on the stairwell landing. "Before we get to that, we have to finish the zillion forms we generated while on this case. That ought to take until the turn of the century."

"Oh, Christ. Don't remind me. I'll see you in there in a minute. I got to go hit the head."

Entering the CID office, Bodowski looked toward Nancy's empty desk.

Mavis noticed and said, "She's taken the rest of the day off. I'm sorry."

He tried to appear nonchalant. "No big deal."

"Oh." Mavis sounded tentative. "I have some other news."

"What?"

"Sergeant LeMarc's been released on order of the commanding general."

"Christ sake. Don't they have any idea how dangerous that man is?"

"They couldn't keep him. Not with the CG telling them to release him. Also, you didn't file a complaint, not that it would have made much difference."

"I've been just a little busy."

"Hey, you don't have to bite me."

"Sorry, Mavis." Bodowski rummaged through the top drawer of his desk. "I'll get that going right now. At least it will help the next time that idiot tries something."

"Steve, what's the difference?" She stood up and approached him. "You can make out the complaint, but who's going to enforce it?" Standing next to him, she said, "Nancy will come around, you'll see."

"Where'd that come from?"

"She hasn't talked to you?"

"Just the one phone call telling me to find some other place to sleep. She just said it and hung up. I tried calling back, but no answer."

"You should've seen the state she was in when she heard about you almost dying in the forest. She was beside herself—

said she couldn't take it anymore."

Bodowski sighed and shook his head.

"Time heals all wounds, Steve. Give her a little," Mavis suggested.

Bodowski clacked his teeth and threw the blank complaint form back into the drawer. "Black tape. Never fool with the brass' pet monkey. Hell, that should be inscribed in stone outside the front gate. LeMarc's a time bomb. They don't realize what this guy is capable of."

Mavis patted his arm and returned to her desk.

# Chapter Forty-Two

## Jackpot

The loud, tinny ring of Melcher's telephone woke Bodowski. He swung his feet to the floor and rubbed his eyes. Waking up without Nancy at his side left him feeling hollow. From down the hall, he heard his friend answer the telephone but couldn't make out what he said. He got up and walked into the tiny kitchenette to inspect the humming refrigerator for something to drink.

"Jesus. You got anything besides beer?" He shut the door and grabbed a jelly glass decorated with cartoon characters from the cupboard. "Cheapskate," he muttered.

Melcher rushed into the kitchen as his friend reached for the faucet.

"What was that about, Mel? What time is it, anyway?"

"Bad news." He looked grim.

"What? Spill it."

"It's LeMarc. He's holed up in his apartment. And they've heard gunfire."

"Jesus! We have to get over there."

The detectives dressed, ran down the steps of the Bachelor Officers' Quarters and tore out in Melcher's assigned radio car.

"Is that right?" Bodowski asked about the time on the dash clock while checking the magazine of his automatic. "It says two. It's two in the morning? I don't have my watch."

Not taking his eyes off the road as they sped through the Kaserne, his partner answered, "Yeah, I think so."

"Why did they let this asshole go? What the hell's wrong with these people?"

"Later, man." Melcher swerved to pass a slower vehicle. "I'm a little busy."

Minutes later, the detectives drove past the unguarded gate of the housing area and reached a roadblock established two hundred meters up the street from LeMarc's apartment building. An MP dressed in full combat gear bent over to speak into the open driver-side window.

"I can't let you pass, sir. You got to turn around and leave the area. We got us a dangerous situation here."

Melcher produced his badge.

The MP nodded and pointed to the parking lot of the nearest apartment building. "Pull in over there, sir. You're going to have to hoof it down to the scene. Stay close to the buildings on this side."

"We know where we're going, soldier."

"Okay, but—" The MP flinched as a shot rang out in the distance. "Some fucker's taking pot shots at our guys. You got to stay close to the buildings on this side to keep out of the line of sight."

"All right. I got it, thanks."

After parking the car in the nearest lot, they hurried down the wide sidewalk. The rain had stopped hours earlier but clung to every surface in the cold, humid air. The ever-present cloud cover insured that nothing was visible beyond the reach of the streetlights and the incandescent headlamps of the military vehicles.

Within minutes, they reached LeMarc's apartment building. Several dozen MPs waited behind cover. The detectives, moving in a crouch, located the commanding officer on the scene. Before they could speak, LeMarc appeared behind the jagged remains of his second-story living room window and fired a round from an M1 rifle. The bullet ricocheted off the wet pavement of the building's parking lot and caromed into a mailbox with a loud bong.

"Fuck you, you motherfucking slopes. Come and get it!" He disappeared into the darkened apartment.

"Jesus, listen to that asshole." Squatting behind his jeep, the MP commander hit the fender with his fist. Then he noticed the detectives. "Who the hell are you?"

Melcher, sitting on his heels against the rear wheel of the jeep, opened his badge. "Melcher, CID. This is Bodowski."

"I'm Captain Phelps. What are you doing here? You're a little early to investigate this, aren't you?"

"Bodowski here knows the guy, sir. Maybe we can help."

"I don't know. This idiot's crazy—yelling shit like he's in combat."

"He is," Bodowski said. "This man's a Korean vet. He saw a hell of a lot of action. I know him." They heard the sound of breaking glass followed by a dull thump.

Phelps peered over the fender of his vehicle "What the hell? He just threw a chair out of a window." Sitting with his back to the jeep, the officer took a moment to size up the detectives. "Okay, maybe you two can help. Last thing I want to do is shoot this guy. What do you have in mind?"

"Is his family in there?" Bodowski asked, fighting with his anxiety.

"No clue."

"How'd this start?"

"We got a complaint about noise. Two of my men showed up and knocked on the door, and he answered them with a rifle blast right through the goddamned keyhole. He barely missed them."

"Mel, it's the middle of the night. His family has to be in there." Looking at Phelps, Bodowski asked, "You haven't heard any other voices?"

"Hey, I just said I had no idea. I haven't heard a damn thing coming out of that apartment other than this sonofabitch shooting and ranting."

"I could talk to him."

"I don't know how you're going to do that."

"We'll go up the stairwell. I'll talk to him through the door."

"Shit, why not? Nothing else seems to be working. Myron!" He snapped his fingers at an MP hiding behind a large oak tree several meters away. "Sergeant Myron, get over here."

Holding onto his helmet, the MP ran toward the jeep and squatted next to his commander.

"Yes, sir?"

Pointing at the agents, Phelps said, "Melcher and Bozaski from CID."

Bodowski opened his mouth to correct the officer, but thought better of it.

"Take these men up to the landing and tell Cuthbert to let Bozaski here talk to that fucking loon. But he's got to do it from the stairwell."

"Roger, Captain."

"Bozaski? You and your pal here do what the hell the XO tells you once you get up there. Listen to him and don't try anything stupid. If you screw up, I'll have you standing before the man. Understand?"

"Eat this, you fucking zipperheads!"

A dresser drawer flew through the broken bedroom window. Dozens of pairs of white socks and underwear spilled out as it crashed on the soft ground.

"Okay, follow me."

Myron waved at the detectives and they fell in behind him as he ran toward the building. Rain began to pour. Hugging the wall, the three men sidled along until they reached the stairwell door and entered the building with their weapons drawn. They climbed past the first floor landing before encountering a half-dozen MPs lining the flight of stairs that led to LeMarc's apartment. Pressing their backs to the wall so they stood parallel to the door, the soldiers all held automatic pistols except for the corporal at the top of the stairs, who readied a twelve-gauge riot gun. Sergeant Myron led the detectives to the second man in line, Lieutenant Cuthbert.

"Captain says to let these guys talk to him, sir."

"Are you fucking kidding me? Who are you people?"

Bodowski, standing ahead of his partner on the stairs, answered, "We're CID. I know this man. I'll try to talk to him through the door."

"I already tried. He wouldn't answer."

"Give me a chance. I'm telling you I know the guy."

"You'll do it from right here. Yell if you have to. I'm not letting you go near the door." Sergeant Myron backed down the stairs to give the detectives room to maneuver.

Bodowski remained on the step but moved to his right to lean against the broad metal railing. From his position, he could just make out where LeMarc had splintered the keyhole with a rifle shot. He noted that the bullet had left a clean hole in the apartment door on the opposite side of the landing.

"LeMarc, can you hear me? It's Bodowski." Getting no response, he added, "Bodowski. The guy you gave a big headache to? C'mon, LeMarc, let's talk."

"Bodowski?" came from behind the door.

"Yeah. Let's talk." His heart beat as though it was trying to burst out of his chest.

The metallic click of the deadbolt lock resounded through the stairwell. The men on the stairs tensed. The door swung inward. Cuthbert reached out and grabbed the detective by the arm as the corporal knelt on the top step and leveled his weapon.

"You bring some friends with you, asshole?" LeMarc stood just inside, but given the severe angle, no one could see him.

"Just a few."

"Good, I'm glad you did."

"You are?" The detective, still in Cuthbert's grip, could not hide his surprise.

"Yeah, I was getting real tired of waiting. Now I can get a little rest."

LeMarc jumped out onto the landing and aimed his rifle at the first man he saw. The explosion from the corporal's riot gun deafened the men on the stairs and produced a shower of blood and flesh as the buckshot carved away half of LeMarc's neck. His head flopped to his chest and he crumpled to the landing. His rifle slid off the concrete floor and into the well between the stairs, smashing against the metal railings as it fell to the basement. The odor of spent gunpowder filled the stairwell.

Lieutenant Cuthbert loosed his hold on the detective and commanded, "Get in there!" The corporal pumped the slide of his gun and rushed into the apartment. The lieutenant went next, followed by the detectives and the other MPs.

In his rampage, LeMarc had turned the place upside down. Not a piece of furniture stood upright, and the floor was buried beneath a sea of paper and garbage.

"Oh, my God. Over here, Lieutenant. My God."

Bodowski barely heard it through the whistling in his ears. He and Melcher joined the two soldiers standing in the middle of the room.

Lying amid the trash, Monica LeMarc held both boys close to her, a placid look on her face. He noticed the ligature marks on their necks and knelt to look at them from a low angle. The cold, hard detective in him pulled a pencil from his coat pocket and used it to lift her left hand—the one draped over Tony's shoulder in a cold embrace. A voice inside of him said the teenager was the first one killed. The men standing around him talked, but he could not make out what they said. He heard a man vomit. Still on his haunches, he swiveled to see the corporal retching away from the bodies. Turning back, he took the pencil and lifted Monica's housecoat just below the neckline.

*Where's the dollar bill?* he thought.

He smelled whiskey.

Moments later, he stood on the front lawn of the apartment building doubled over with his hands on his knees. Melcher held onto his shoulder. The rain came down like hail.

"It's not your fault, man. It's not your fault."

Bodowski stood up, shaking off his friend's hand. The drops spattered against his face as he stared up into the darkness.

# Chapter Forty-Three

## It's a Dirty Job
**Sunday**

Bodowski gazed through his windshield at the unbroken layer of gray clouds. A car tore past him along the narrow street, sending up a spray from the wet pavement. He looked out the rear window in time to see a second vehicle fly past. Both cars disappeared down a long line of tiny row houses. All painted white. All with the same iron railings climbing identical steps. He sighed. Old habits made him reach for the glove compartment, but he caught himself. The only smokes would be those left behind by Melcher. The unfiltered stuff was not for him no matter how desperate his need. Hoping the craving would pass, he occupied his hands by beating on the steering wheel as if it were a snare drum. At last he stopped hammering and leaned forward on the wheel, pressing his forehead against his hands. His headache throbbed, a bitter reminder. Despite the pain, exhaustion overtook him and he was out in seconds, surrendering to a kaleidoscope of shapeless dreams.

He started from sleep with a gasp. Frau Mueller, Monica LeMarc's maid and friend, walked past his vehicle singing a German hiking song. Trailing behind, a small girl wearing a black woolen coat called out in English for her to wait. He recognized the face and the pigtails from the photograph.

There were people for this. People paid to deliver the bad news, to deal with children under these circumstances. But he was going to do it.

He got out of the car and walked behind them, unnoticed. A

moment later, they entered one of the little houses. He climbed the steps and stood on the landing. Taking a deep breath, he knocked.

# ABOUT THE AUTHOR

Bruce Rehburg

A freelance writer living in Austin, Texas, Bruce Rehburg has lived a colorful life. Whether soldier or actor, software designer or theatrical producer, he has maintained a lifelong interest in crime fiction. His early experiences, first as a U.S Army dependent and later as a young veteran, serve him well as an author of fiction with a military connection.

Set in Germany during 1963, NOVEMBER'S SHADOW is the initial offering in a planned series of detective stories that will feature Rehburg's melancholy but resolute protagonist, Steve Bodowski of the Army's Criminal Investigation Division (CID). Rehburg's writing is a heady mix of darkness and optimism that owes much to his early experiences in the shadow of the Iron Curtain.